DIRTY LITTLE MIDLIFE SECRET

HEART'S COVE HOTTIES: BOOK SIX

LILIAN MONROE

Cover design: Qamber Designs
Editing: Shavonne Clarke
Proofreading: Jane Beyer

Published by Method and Madness Publishing PTY LTD
PO Box 168 Subiaco, WA, Australia 6008

Print ISBN: 978-1-922986-46-7

ONE

LILY

THERE ARE TWO SECRETS, really. One is a blessing, and the other is a curse.

I'm still coming to grips with them both—and trying to figure out how to tell my family. My mother, Lottie, won't know how to react. She'll be ecstatic and dismayed and overwhelmed. She'll tell her best friend Dorothy, which means the whole town will know what's happening within minutes.

My two sisters, Candice and Katrina, will burst into mother-hen mode.

Telling them what's been going on will be a good thing. They'll be supportive. They'll have my back. I'll be able to grieve all the things that have gone wrong, and maybe even celebrate the things that might go right. I'll be able to move on.

So why haven't I told anyone yet?

The past six weeks have felt like I'm driving through a snowstorm in the dead of night. I can see four or five feet ahead of me, a small cone of light that quickly falls away to complete darkness. Snowflakes swirl and dart above the blacktop in front of me as my windshield wipers flick over and back at full speed, and I'm just gripping the steering wheel praying there isn't a patch of black ice beneath my tires. Ask me what bends are coming up in the road, and I'll just laugh. How the hell would I know? I'm barely able to keep the car between the lines, let alone see what kind of hairpin turns are coming up next.

Running my finger along the edge of one of the ten thousand brochures I've been given over the past four weeks since I've been back in Heart's Cove, I try to focus on what my doctor is saying.

My obstetrician, Dr. Alder, leans against the edge of his desk, crossing his legs at the ankle. He's a handsome man in his late fifties. He has an easy confidence about him that put me at ease the first time I met him. Now, the familiar nerves that have been plaguing me for just under two months are bubbling up again. "We've reviewed your file from the hospital in Milan and are happy to monitor your condition for the next three to five weeks. As you know, we won't be able to start any further treatment until you enter your second trimester."

I nod. I do know this. I probably have three or four or ten brochures shoved in one of my kitchen drawers that say something to that effect.

I found out I was pregnant six weeks ago. The first day of my last menstrual period was three weeks before that, which means I'm nine weeks along. I found out about the second big bombshell in my life four and a half weeks ago and ran back to Heart's Cove a few days later.

So, here I am. Surrounded by loving family, feeling isolated in my own personal midnight snowstorm.

"Now, with geriatric pregnancies there are a host of added risks." Dr. Alder looks at me with his warm brown eyes, his voice soft and understanding. "Not to mention the treatment plan we've put together for your—"

Before he can finish his sentence—and before he can jump into the even longer laundry list of things that might go wrong with me—I sit up. "Can we call it something else?"

Dr. Alder frowns. "Pardon?"

"'Geriatric pregnancy,'" I explain. "I'm turning forty next week. That's hardly geriatric, and I feel old enough as it is." I spread my hands. "Maybe, 'mature?' Or, um... 'sunset?' 'Grown-up pregnancy?'"

Dr. Alder gives me a patient, kind smile that makes me want to throttle him. "It's just the term used for pregnancies in women over the age of thirty-five. Some doctors use it for women over thirty. It doesn't mean you're geriatric."

"No, only my womb." I suck in a breath and shake my head. "Sorry. I guess 'sunset pregnancy' sounds ridiculous."

Dr. Alder studies me for a moment, then stands up as he inhales sharply. "I'm going to give you a referral to Dr. Melissa Gardner. She's a psychiatrist who specializes in fertility, pregnancy, miscarriage, and postpartum depression and anxiety."

"You think I need a shrink?" My voice comes out shriller than I'd intended. I haven't even told my mother about this, and he wants me to spill my guts to a stranger.

Dr. Alder flicks through dozens of business cards until he finds the right one, then hands it to me. "I think a woman going through as much as you should take advantage of all the support she can get." His face grows serious, and he leans forward to rest his elbows on his knees. "Iliana, this will only get more difficult. You'll need help."

I take the card and read it. Another piece of paperwork for my ever-growing collection. Gulping, I nod and wave the card in a small circle. "Thanks."

"Mention my name and Dr. Gardner will slot you in as soon as she can."

"Name-drop you. Got it. Does that work for other things? Exclusive clubs? Discounts at local restaurants? Do I get a senior discount card now that I'm officially geriatric?"

Dr. Alder starts typing on his computer and completely ignores my irreverence. "Make the call, Iliana."

Knowing when I'm dismissed, I gather my purse and bid him goodbye. After a quick stop at the reception desk to make my next appointment, I step outside into the mid-July sunshine. Northern California has never been my home, but I think I might have liked it here if my life wasn't a complete mess.

How can it feel like a snowstorm in the middle of summer? How can the sun soak into my skin, yet all I feel is cold?

The edges of the business card cut into my palm, and in some dark corner of my mind, I know Dr. Alder is right. I need to talk to someone. A *professional* someone.

My phone dings, pulling me away from my thoughts. I fish it out of my purse and look at the screen, heart jumping.

It's Rudy, the thirty-four-year-old who has been adding to my growing to-be-read list for the past couple of weeks. He works part-time at his grandmother's bookstore, and he's just about the hottest guy I've ever seen in my life.

Then again, I'm a hormonal, emotional wreck, and he happens to have a nice smile. I might be overstating his attractiveness.

I've gone to the bookstore twice since I arrived in Heart's Cove last month, and both times left me hot and bothered as I trundled back to my car with an armload of new books. I'm *fairly* sure he's been flirting, but...you know. Hormonal, emotional, et cetera. He could just be friendly.

How did he get my number?

I swipe to unlock my phone and read his message.

Rudy*: Hey Lily. Rudy here. Got your number from Candice. We just got the newest Lee Child book in stock and I set one aside for you. I'll be here until the end of the day if you wanted to grab it.*

I've got my phone in one hand, and Dr. Gardner's card in the other. I glance at both hands, eyes shifting from one to the other. It would be easy to dial the number on the card and make an appointment. Maybe it would be easier to talk to a stranger about everything that's going on.

Or I could ignore the shrink and answer Rudy.

Is it a good idea to continue this less-than-innocent flirtation with Agnes's grandson that will probably end with me heartbroken and embarrassed? No.

Is it a good idea to get involved with *anyone* considering what I'm about to go through? *Definitely* no.

Am I someone who usually makes good decisions?

I stuff the card in my purse and answer Rudy's text.

Me: *Be over this afternoon!*

BEFORE I CAN INDULGE in a little Rudy-shaped distraction, I have a date with my sister. A few minutes after my OB appointment, Trina meets me outside the local nail salon and gives me a big hug.

"I'm so glad you could make it." She beams at me, opening the door to let me in. "Things have been hectic, but the kids are with Mac, and Mom is busy at Candice's new house, so I figured we could use some alone time."

Tension still grips my chest, but I hide it behind a smile. "You always say a pedicure solves ninety-nine percent of problems."

"And it's true, too!" Trina laughs and waves at the nail tech who appears from behind a door at the back of the salon.

We're led to big, black massage chairs and told to sit down. I kick off my shoes and rest them on the foot pad, sinking into the seat. The chair starts vibrating and rolling along my back and instead of soothing me, it makes me feel like vomiting. I've been doing that a lot lately.

I turn the chair off and catch my sister's watchful eye. She arches a brow.

"So, tell me how you and Mac met." I give my sister my best casual grin. "You promised me the story when I first arrived in town, but all you've done is deflect."

Trina laughs. Since I last saw her, her whole demeanor has changed. Then again, last time I saw her was a couple of years ago, when she was still married to her jerk of an ex-husband. She looks younger and more vibrant than ever, and she tells me all about the whirlwind romance that happened between her and Mac. How he let her ride on his motorcycle and she just about died from how raw and sexual it was. Then they got— ahem—*messy* doing pottery together, and she thought she *had* died and gone to heaven. She laughs as she tells me how she thought everything went wrong, but now that all's said and done, she knows he's so perfect for her his kisses make her teeth ache from the sweetness of it all.

"You deserve someone to treat you like a queen," I tell her as I finally make my nail polish selection from the thousands of available shades. The nail tech smiles as if I've just made the most important decision of my life. She nods solemnly at the little plastic sample of nail polish and moves to the wall of bottles to grab my selection. It makes some of the tension in my shoulders seep out, and I wonder if Trina is right about the whole pedicures-solve-all-problems thing.

"Enough about me," Trina says. "You still haven't told anyone why you're back. Mom is asking me about it every day."

"Funny, she's not asking *me* about it," I deadpan.

"She's too scared you'll take off on an international trip and not come back for another three years." Trina laughs, but I hear the truth in her words.

I've spent the last fifteen—nearly twenty—years of my life traveling the world. Six months in one place, two years in another. Wherever I could get a visa, I'd lay some shallow roots and explore. I built my business to be entirely remote, and as long as I had my laptop and an internet connection, I was all set. It was perfect for me...until it wasn't. Until the freight train of life came down the tracks and flattened me.

The woman doing my feet squirts some lotion on my legs and starts massaging my calves, and a tiny bit more stress ekes out of me. Maybe I could tell Trina about the baby and about... everything else.

Stress seizes every muscle in my body at the thought of spilling my guts to my sister.

I grip the edge of the chair as my nail tech glances up, frowning. She can feel the tension in my legs as I do my best to let the thoughts pass through me and let my muscles relax.

How can I possibly say the words out loud when *thinking* them sends me into a panic?

I definitely need professional help.

"Okay, if you won't tell me why you're back, why don't you tell me why Rudy was asking Candice for your number?" Trina's eyes glitter, and I groan.

"No secrets in Heart's Cove, huh."

"Girl, get used to it." My sister laughs. "I went through hell trying to keep this thing between me and Mac under wraps. It's only fair that I get to have some fun too."

I roll my eyes. "Nothing's going on. He just got the new Lee Child book in stock and wanted to let me know."

Trina purses her lips and inspects her fingernails before flicking her eyes to me. "Funny, he didn't text *me* about any new books."

I wave a hand. "It's nothing."

"Don't bullshit a bullshitter, Lily." Trina grins. "From Jen and Fallon to you and Rudy, this summer is shaping up to be a lot of fun."

"There's nothing going on between me and Rudy. I'll prove it to you. Look." I pull out my phone from my purse. The movement sends part of my brochure collection spilling out of my bag, but I hold them back with a hand while I unlock and hand over my phone. "See? Books."

Trina reads the texts with an arched brow as I try stuffing my crumpled brochures back into my purse. When Trina passes my phone back, she catches a little square of cardboard as it slips off the arm of my chair.

Before I can snatch it back, Trina pulls the business card toward her. "Dr. Melissa Gardner," she reads. "Perinatal psychiatry." Her eyes widen as her head whips around toward me. "Lily…"

I extend a hand. "Give it back."

"Is this why you came back? Are you…?" Trina lets the word hang. Her eyes drift down to my stomach, but I know I'm not showing yet.

I clench my hands into fists to stop myself gripping my middle. The last thing I need is the game of Heart's Cove Gossip Telephone to start about me. "Give it back, Trina." My words tremble, and I stare into my sister's eyes when she meets my gaze again.

She says nothing as she hands the business card back to me.

I stuff it back into the depths of my purse and shake my head. "It's nothing."

Trina stays quiet for a few long minutes. We finish our pedicure in silence and when I stand up to leave, I jerk my thumb over my shoulder. "I'm going to go to the bookstore. I'll see you around."

Trina opens her mouth to say something, but reconsiders. Finally, she just nods. "Okay. And Lily?"

"Yeah?"

"You know you can come over whenever you want, right? I can ask Mac to watch the kids or get a sitter or whatever. We can grab dinner or just go for a walk. I'm always here. I won't tell anyone about the business card."

My throat is tight and I manage to nod. "Okay. Thanks."

It's not until I'm down the street and out of sight that I manage to take a full breath.

TWO
LILY

WHEN I ENTER THE BOOKSTORE, Agnes, the silver-haired owner, has her hands on her hips, her face screwed up into a frown. For the life of me, I can't figure out why—until I look at the back of the store.

She's staring at a dozen children aged three to seven sitting in a semi-circle around a soft leather chair.

And in the chair is Rudy, holding a picture book out to face the children so they can see the illustrations. He puts on a scratchy voice and pretends to be an evil witch, and a little girl squeals and claps her hands over her face in fear. From the far side of the chair, Rudy pulls out a toy sword and brandishes it out as the knight in the story comes riding to the rescue. The same little girl thrusts her arm in the air, mirroring his motion with a triumphant giggle.

It's the cutest thing I've ever seen.

Then my gaze turns to Rudy.

I only just manage to stay standing as my knees turn wobbly.

This has got to be pregnancy-related, right? Seeing an attractive man in charge of a room full of children must send some instinctive signal to the cavewoman in me. Things went horribly wrong with the father of my unborn child, and now my hindbrain is looking for someone to fill his shoes.

Someone who might be sitting in a leather chair, captivating a dozen children with nothing more than his beautifully deep voice and a plastic prop.

I squeeze my eyes shut and suck in a deep breath. I need to get a grip. I'm here for a book—nothing more.

"Oh, not you too," Agnes says with a huff. I open my eyes to see her scowling at me. "I've got enough women falling over themselves to come watch my grandson read picture books."

I blink, then notice the crowd of mothers standing along the edges of the bookstore. Oh dear.

"I'm here for a book," I explain. "Rudy texted me earlier."

Agnes's eyes narrow. "You're Lottie's daughter."

"That's right."

"Are you staying at that bedraggled excuse for a hotel?" Her voice takes on a sharp edge.

I gulp, then shake my head. "I've rented an apartment in town."

The old woman lets out a grunt that might be approval, and I remember that she and Dorothy, who owns the hotel with her twin, have had a long-standing feud. Apparently not staying at the hotel means I'm allowed to buy books here.

I'm saved from this minefield of a conversation by clapping

coming from the depths of the bookstore. Rudy's done with story time. I watch with a touch of amusement as he's mobbed by children and mothers alike, then stand to the side as the mob moves to buy every single copy of the book Rudy just read.

Agnes rings them up one by one, looking none too happy even if she does give her grandson a satisfied nod. Rudy meets my gaze from the far end of the narrow, long bookstore and gives me a look that I think means, *Wait for me. I'm almost done.* I watch him skillfully direct a particularly handsy mother toward the cashier's counter, where he slides behind it to give himself some space.

"Well, you have my number," the woman says, completely unbothered by Agnes's derisive snort. "Don't be a stranger." She turns to the little girl who was so captivated by Rudy's story and takes her hand before leaving the bookstore.

Rudy meets my eyes, and I think I see a little bit of embarrassment flushing over his cheeks.

"That was quite the performance," I say.

A rueful smile curls his lips, and my knees do that wobbly thing again. He didn't grin like that when that handsy mother begged him to call her, my brain helpfully points out.

"Children's books are popular," he answers noncommittally. "I do a few readings a month. Everyone loves a fairy tale, especially little kids."

I snort. "I don't."

"I like her more and more every minute," Agnes says, scowling at her next customer, who looks suitably terrified.

Rudy ignores his grandmother and arches a brow at me. "No?"

"Too...unrealistic," I answer. "Not every damsel in distress gets saved by a knight in shining armor."

Agnes agrees with one of her expressive grunts. "*Hmph.* Maybe you have a brain in that head of yours, after all."

"I... Thank you?" I answer, frowning.

Rudy covers his laugh with a cough.

"Fairy tales are for children," Agnes says as the last customer leaves the shop. "But story time sales cover most of our bills. Silly mothers think I don't see them drooling over my grandson, but their money spends just like everyone else's."

Rudy gives me a wry grin over his grandmother's head. Before I can ask him about the new Lee Child thriller—or maybe talk to him without his slightly terrifying grandmother hovering between us—Agnes pulls out a box of lightbulbs and thrusts it at Rudy's chest. "Help me with that."

We both look where Agnes points to see a dark bulb in the ceiling at the back of the store. Rudy gives me one more apologetic glance, then moves to get a stepladder.

I pretend to browse the books while mostly staring at Rudy. Somehow, over the next few minutes, I find myself drifting to the back of the store where Rudy and his grandmother are trying to fix the light. When he's at the top of the stepladder, he reaches up to unscrew the bulb and his shirt rides up the tiniest bit. He has a trail of burnished golden hair running from his navel to his belt buckle. It's darker than the hair on his head—a fact that I notice for no significant reason whatsoever.

"It's the wrong wattage, Grandma." Rudy's voice is patient, and my eyes snap up from his stomach. His face is calm as he meets his grandmother's eyes. In profile, Rudy looks almost aristocratic. Strong jaw, straight nose, barely tamed hair come together to give him a handsome, effortless appearance.

I don't blame those mothers. Not one bit. Who knows? In a couple of years, I might be one of them. I turn to the stack of books and realize I'm looking at biographies. I grab one at random and pretend to read.

"Those are the same bulbs I've bought for thirty years," Agnes grumbles. As Rudy starts coming down from the stepladder, she turns her ire to me. "What do you want, anyway? Why are you still here?"

I jump and nearly drop the biography. "Um...I want a book?" I answer, eyes flicking to meet Rudy's.

His lips curl into a smile, and he gives me a small, self-deprecating roll of the eyes. "Grandma, I held one of the new Lee Child books for Lily. She's been waiting for me to help her for fifteen minutes, so I'd better go ahead and do that. I'll buy the right bulbs this afternoon and put it in before you open tomorrow."

"I told you not to hold books for people. Especially not new releases. Lee Child is a big seller around here."

"We have a hundred of them, Grandma." Rudy makes it to the bottom of the ladder and wipes his hands on his pants, jerking his head to the front of the bookstore for me to follow.

I'm not scared of Agnes, I swear. She's four foot nine, has to be nearly ninety years old, and I could definitely take her in a fight. Well, I'm fairly sure I could take her in a fight. Probably.

Still, as I step around her and join Rudy, my shoulders soften.

The store is deeper than it is wide, with three rows of bookshelves arranged lengthwise from the front of the store to the back. The thousands of books are mostly arranged like a normal bookstore. I say mostly, because there are signs denoting various genres, but the political thrillers are next to the cookbooks, and the spy novels are on the other side of the shop next to the steamy romance section. The children's books, for some reason, are arranged by color instead of by author name, which almost looks like it was done at some point in the past and no one ever bothered to change it back. One whole shelf is empty, and I'm guessing it's as a result of Rudy's performance today.

In the depths of the bookstore, two large, soft, leather-clad wingback chairs are arranged around a small table, which Rudy moved back into place after story time. It would be an inviting place to sit and read a book, if Agnes didn't make a habit of sitting behind the cashier's desk like a dragon guarding her gold.

I follow Rudy through the stacks to the front of the store. We definitely could have grabbed a copy from the massive display set up with the newest thriller from Lee Child, but I stand in front of the counter as he reaches into a cubby below. He pulls out a copy of the book.

"You really did set one aside for me," I say, then give a pointed glance to the table laden with hundreds of copies of the same book behind me.

Rudy grins. "You never know when a stampede of readers will come through and pick us clean." His long, masculine fingers brush the front of the book, smoothing over a yellow sticky note with my name on it. For some reason, the thought of him writing *Iliana Viceroy* on a sticky note, asking my sister for my phone number, and making sure to set this book aside makes my insides melt. I watch him peel the sticky note off the glossy cover before pushing the book across the counter to me. "Here. Take it."

I reach for my purse, careful not to disturb my pamphlets, and pull out my wallet.

Rudy shakes his head. "I already paid for it. It's my gift for all the business you've given us over the past couple of weeks."

"Oh," I answer, too shocked to answer properly. I don't remember the last time someone bought me a gift without an occasion. "Thank you."

His hand moves back over the book, and a gleam enters his eyes. "There is a condition, though."

"Here we go," I say, arching a brow. "Didn't anyone ever tell you that a gift with conditions isn't a gift at all?"

"She's right!" Agnes's voice calls out from the front of the bookstore.

Rudy laughs. It's a warm sound that sends a thrill rushing through my middle. His eyes grow serious as he leans his strong, narrow hips against the counter. Even with Agnes apparently able to hear everything, his closeness still makes me forget we're not alone. "Have dinner with me tonight."

His voice is low, intimate—and having dinner with him is a bad, bad idea.

What I should do is reach into my purse, open my wallet, and pay for the book myself. I should thank Rudy for the offer, but tell him I'm not interested in dating anyone right now.

I just came from my obstetrician's office, for crying out loud. I'm going to be having a baby in thirty-one weeks or less. Not only that, but there's my second secret sitting like a hot coal in my chest.

I haven't even told my family about any of it! Not the baby, not the other stuff.

Getting involved with a man would be such a bad idea, it's not even funny. Dating is so far off the table, it's not even in the same neighborhood. Pretty soon, I'm going to be a forty-year-old single mother...if I'm lucky.

Rudy leans forward, his palms resting against the counter in a way that makes the muscles on his arms pop. His eyes are brilliant blue, and laughter dances in them as his lips curl into a smile. "Come on, Lily. One meal. No strings attached. If you don't enjoy yourself, you never have to speak to me again."

"That's the problem," I hear myself saying. "I think I might enjoy myself too much."

Rudy's smile widens and damn him, but he looks too good to resist right now. "Doesn't sound like a problem to me."

"Do you have a thing for older women?" I blurt.

Rudy tilts his head.

"First Fiona, then my sister Candice, and now me? Are you just trying to work your way through the Four Cups Café ladies in record time or something?"

Rudy grins, raking his fingers through his hair. "Fiona and I never did anything. As I recall, all I ever did was ask her if she wanted a tour of Heart's Cove when she first arrived." He moves around the counter and drops his voice. "Candice and I went on one date, we had a chaste after-dinner kiss, and we went our separate ways. Amicably. I'm quite sure she's moved on, as have I." He takes one more half-step toward me, his toes brushing mine, chest only inches from my own. "Does any of that bother you?"

Ugh. Of course it doesn't bother me. How am I supposed to resist him when he's so damn irresistible?

When Rudy reaches over to grasp my hand and give it a squeeze, I can feel my resolve crumbling. So, rising from the ruins of my defenses, I make a decision.

One meal won't hurt. Maybe this is a good thing! Maybe Rudy can be my one final hurrah, one last tryst before my life changes forever.

He said it himself: no strings attached.

What if I just indulged, for once? What if I go out to dinner with him, maybe enjoy a chaste kiss of my own, and lock that memory away somewhere precious? Why do I feel like I have to deny myself things that please me?

Because I have a child on the way? Because that child's father left me when he found out? Because things are about to get a whole lot more complicated, and I'm too terrified to even think about the reality of it all?

One dinner. One meal. One date. One night that involves a whole lot more than a chaste kiss, hopefully.

Tonight, I can feel like a human—like a woman. I'll enjoy Rudy's company and *indulge*. Then, in the morning, I'll call Dr. Melissa Gardner and I'll get my life in order. I'll tell my sisters and my mother about the baby—and everything else. Both secrets will be out in the open, and I'll be able to deal with the consequences. Rudy and I can have the same post-date amicable split he had with Candice, and everything will work out all right.

Easy. Freaking. Peasy.

"Fine," I hear myself say, a smile tugging at the corners of my lips. "But only as a thank you for the book." I hug the thriller to my chest as Rudy rewards me with a dazzling smile.

"Works for me." He squeezes my hand again, then brushes past me as he calls out for his grandmother. "I'm leaving!"

I hear a harrumph from the depths of the stacks and hide a smile behind my fingers. Rudy reappears at my elbow and gestures to the door. "Let's go. It's nearly five. We can have an early dinner."

"Right now?" I make sound that is embarrassingly close to a squawk. "Don't I get a chance to go home and change?"

"Nope. I'm afraid you'll reconsider, and you look perfect anyway. Got to strike while the iron is hot." He says the words near my ear, and I inhale the delicious, manly scent of his cologne.

His words catch up to me then, and...he thinks I look perfect?

When I turn my head to look at Rudy, his lips are only an inch from mine. Something passes between us—a flash of tension. A moment. My body grows taut, and I know in the depths of my heart that going out with him tonight is a very, very bad idea.

THREE
RUDY

LILY PULLS at her hand and I spin around on the sidewalk without letting go, tugging her closer. She catches herself against my chest, dark tendrils of hair bouncing around her face. Gorgeous woman, all curves and angles.

"If we're going on a date right now," she says, "I have conditions."

"Are you a lawyer, Ms. Viceroy?" My voice drops as I say the words, and I'm rewarded with a flush on her cheeks.

"No. But I have to be honest with you."

Nodding, I put an inch of space between us. "Sure." My hand finds the curve of her hip and I notice it fits perfectly there. Like her body was made for me to touch. To hold.

"This is casual," she says in no uncertain terms. "There's a lot of stuff going on in my life right now, and I absolutely do not have time for a relationship. The only way I'll go to dinner with you is if we agree that this is going nowhere."

I arch a brow. "Nowhere?"

"Nowhere serious," she amends.

"Are you planning on taking off on another international trip soon?" I'm surprised to realize I don't like that thought. I don't like it at all. Having her this close to me is making my cock harden shockingly fast—and she's thinking of leaving already?

Lily's lips bunch. "Something like that."

Shaking off the weird feeling I just got, I give her a shrug. "Baby, I'm the King of Casual. If you don't want anything serious, that works for me."

Her eyes narrow. "And no pet names."

I can't help it. I grin. Somewhere in the back of my mind, I realize it'll be much harder to keep things casual with Lily than it has been with other women...but why would I think that? I haven't had a relationship in five years. Not since my ex took everything from me—including the family I thought we were building together—and I vowed to never put myself in that position again. I'm not lying when I say I'm the King of Casual. I don't *do* serious relationships.

I should be jumping for joy right now. Lily Viceroy is basically offering me a fun, no-strings-attached sex fest on a silver platter. Her requirement that we keep things casual is a *good* thing.

But I feel...odd. A bit bereft.

She's still scowling at me over the "baby" comment, so I relent with a deep nod. "No pet names. We keep things casual." I put a hand on my heart. "I solemnly swear to not talk about the future or the past, and to tamp down my irresistible charm to give you a chance to walk away from me when this is over."

Lily rolls her eyes, but her twitching lips betray her. "Fine. Let's go."

My cock pulses again, telling me he's very happy with the way this conversation is going. I give her a broad smile. "You won't regret it."

In the next town over from Heart's Cove, a town called Edgeville, there's a famous fish-and-chips restaurant that sits on a boardwalk overlooking the Pacific Ocean. As I open my car door and help Lily inside, I already know I'm going to take her there. We should make it right in time for sunset.

Not a bad place for a first date—even if it is casual.

Lily settles into the passenger seat, setting her purse on her lap as I slide behind the wheel. She's wearing a loose summer dress and white sneakers, her dark hair tied back in a messy bun. The strap of her sundress slides off her shoulder, revealing the top curve of her breast. I stare at it for a beat too long, wishing I could reach over and push it down all the way. Would she make a soft, sweet noise if I took her breast in my mouth? Would her nipples turn to hard little points against my tongue?

I turn the key in the ignition and give her a smile, hoping she's not regretting her decision to accept my invitation. The Lee Child book sits on her lap next to her purse, a reminder that I'm not above bribery to get a date.

A few weeks ago, Lily walked into the bookstore looking beautifully undone. Her cheeks were rosy, her lips full, and her eyes raked over me like a physical touch. She walked in like a woman who knows what she wants, all confidence and quiet swagger.

I wanted her right then and there. We were alone in the

bookstore and my brain served up images of me bending her over the counter and making her come with my mouth, fingers, then my cock. I think I've been hard ever since.

"Where are we going?" Lily asks, tucking the book into her purse.

"You like fish and chips?" I glance over in time to see her smile.

"I lived in London for three years. I have a very discerning fish-and-chips palate, so I hope you know what you're getting into."

I grin. "I'm ready for anything."

A strange look crosses her eyes, and she turns to stare out her window. I frown, reaching to flick on the radio. Did I say something wrong?

"How long have you worked for Agnes?" Lily asks, sounding almost desperate to change the subject.

"Since I was thirteen," I answer with a laugh. "My grandmother raised me. Knowing the value of money was a priority in our home."

"I can only imagine what a slave driver she must have been." Lily grins.

I shrug. "Sometimes, but I'm grateful for everything my grandmother did for me. She's only tough on the outside." I put my turn signal on and merge onto the freeway with signs pointing to Edgeville.

Lily shifts in her seat and hums. "I always liked Agnes."

That makes me laugh. No one likes my grandmother, except her long-time partner Hank Cheswick and, I suspect, Dorothy, the local hotel owner—although she does her best to pretend otherwise.

"I'm serious!" Lily laughs. "She strikes me as a realist, and I like that in people. I've been around a lot of people from a lot of different cultures, and I can spot someone who's genuine."

Her words make something still inside me. I've grown up with my grandmother being the butt of jokes and comments, but she's a special woman. Strong. Hearing Iliana say good things about her makes me want to reach over, grab her hand, and press my lips to her fingers.

Someone in a casual relationship doesn't do that, though. Especially not on a first date.

Instead, I rest my hand on the gearshift and settle back in my seat. We drive in silence until I take the exit to Edgeville and make my way down the coast. We have to park a little way away from the boardwalk, but Lily tells me she doesn't mind walking.

"Good thing you're not wearing heels," I say, nodding to her sneakers as I turn the car off.

Lily scoffs. "Wouldn't catch me dead in them. Heels are nothing more than instruments of torture."

I grin and shrug. "They look good, though."

Lily cups her ear. "You hear that?"

"Hear what?"

"That's the sound of me not caring." She arches her brow, then opens the car door and steps out.

I laugh, surprised, loving her snark. I'd kiss the attitude right off her mouth if she let me. When I make my way around the vehicle, I extend an arm and watch Lily hesitate for a moment.

Then, with a sigh that seems to say, *Oh, what the hell*, she links her elbow in mine and lets me lead her down the gently sloping street toward the boardwalk.

She smells sweet and floral, and I want to wrap that scent around me like a blanket. Her fingers tighten on my bicep, sliding up an inch, as if she can't help feeling the shape of my muscles. I like her touching me, I decide. I like it a lot.

The sound of seagulls and crashing waves grows louder, and Lily inhales the scent of seaweed and salt. Her smile makes my heart stutter, and I wonder if what I said earlier is true.

No strings attached? One meal? Would I really be satisfied with so little?

Of course I will be. I wasn't lying when I said I only do casual. Lily is no different.

We make it to the restaurant and get a seat on the patio. A gentle breeze sweeps over us as I pull out Iliana's chair, admiring the curve of her neck and the grace with which she moves to sit. She smooths her dress over her stomach and sides, then gives me a shy smile as I move to sit across from her. That damn strap slides off her shoulder again, and she scoops it back into place.

When she refuses wine and asks for water instead, I follow her lead. The sun is starting to set and the sky is slowly transforming into a tapestry of colors. We both look out over the waves in comfortable silence until Lily turns back to me.

"So what do you do when you're not in the store?"

"How do you know I ever leave?" I grin. "Maybe this is the first time I've been out in weeks."

"Just a bookstore goblin, huh?" Her eyes twinkle.

"Someone has to change the lightbulbs."

Lily laughs and leans back in her chair. "Seriously. You told me you're only there a couple of times a week. What do you do with the rest of your time?"

"I run a real estate brokerage. Got my realtor license right out of high school because I felt like I needed time to figure out what I wanted to do before committing to college. I was good at it, so I eventually got my brokerage license and started hiring other realtors to work for me. Sixteen years later, and I'm still wondering what I should major in," I say, happy when Lily laughs. I hold up my hand. "I know, I know. Hold onto your seat. I live a dangerous life."

Another laugh slips through Lily's lips and she tries to tamp it down, as if she feels like she's not supposed to be enjoying herself. "Well, I'm an accountant, so I think I've got you beat in the living-life-on-the-edge department."

My eyebrows arch. "An accountant?"

"So surprised?"

I shrug, glancing down at my menu after studying Lily's face for a moment. The fine-boned features, full lips, bright eyes. "You don't look like an accountant, is all."

Lily snorts, her own eyes dropping to her menu. "I'm not sure what that means, exactly, but it's not the first time I've heard it."

"I meant it as a good thing," I amend, scrambling to think of something better to say. I just meant that she's beautiful and funny and charismatic. Not someone I'd imagine sitting in front of spreadsheets and tax forms all day.

"For someone who works in sales, you're doing a good job of

sticking your foot in your mouth." Lily's eyes glimmer as she meets my gaze.

The waiter interrupts us to take our order. Conversation moves on to more neutral topics—the best coffee in Heart's Cove (from her sister's café, naturally), Jen and Fallon's recent television appearance (hilarious and heartwarming), Katrina's scandalous love affair. I love making Lily laugh, and she teases me about the fact that I've flirted with half her friends. It doesn't seem to bother her, which is more of a relief than I like to admit.

When our food arrives, I wait for Lily to take a bite of her fish, and smile when she nods appreciatively.

"Passed the test?" I ask.

She grins, dunking a chunk of battered and fried cod in tartar sauce. "It's decent."

"It's delicious, is what it is."

Lily laughs and crunches on another bite, and I realize I'm enjoying this. I've been on a lot of dates—a lot of first dates, mostly—and none of them have felt this easy. I've rarely wanted to know more, but with Lily, I find myself asking question after question. I want to know what's the best fish and chips she's ever tasted. I want to know her favorite memory, her favorite trip, her favorite country. I want to know why she took off and decided to travel the world while both her sisters seem to have chosen a different path. I want to know why she came back.

But when I ask that question, Lily's spine stiffens. She keeps her eyes on the last few French fries sitting on her plate. The easy laugher and conversation from a moment ago is trickling away like sand through my fingers.

As the sun touches the horizon, Lily glances at the glittering ocean—

And a man walks up to our table.

"Well, if it isn't Rudy Dorset," Jared Spark says with a cocky smile. My cousin has his arm around a younger woman's shoulders, her own arm slung around his waist. "Another first date, huh?"

Lily arches a brow at him, then at me.

I give my cousin a flat stare. "Nice to see you, Jared."

"I'd say the same, but I only like to speak the truth." His laugh sounds like a donkey's bray, and his girlfriend giggles beside him.

He gives me that cocky, punchable grin, and jerks his chin at Lily. "How much did Rudy bribe you to accept this date? I know you're only here out of pity."

Lily just blinks at him without answering.

Jared doesn't let up. "Is Rudy bringing you to the charity auction next week? He's been trying to find a date to the event for ages. I keep telling him to just give it up and accept that he'll end up alone. No sense beating a dead horse."

Lily bristles. "As scintillating as this conversation is, you're blocking my view of the sunset." Her voice is ice-cold, and a surprised chuckle falls from my lips. Then, for added emphasis, she waves her hand for him to clear out of the way.

Jared gapes at her, mumbles something under his breath that sounds a lot like an insult, and sneers at me. "You seem to have found your match, Rudy. Congratulations."

The two of them walk away, and Lily stares at their

retreating backs before flicking her gaze to meet mine. "They were pleasant," she deadpans.

"I'm sorry about that," I say. "He's my cousin. Well, my great-aunt's grandson. So...second cousin? Removed? I don't know, I just call him my cousin. He's always had this weird competitive streak with me."

"He's kind of a jerk."

I laugh. "And a sunset-view-blocker."

"One and the same." Lily's eyes crinkle at the corners. The sun has almost slipped below the horizon, and the last few rays of golden light are glowing across her face.

"I have to say, the way you dispatched him was pretty hot."

She sips her water and gives me a casual shrug. "I aim to please."

I bite back a growl. I like this woman. I like her fire, her attitude. I like that she's no wilting flower and that she's not afraid of standing up for herself. I wonder if she'd have that kind of fire in bed, if she'd rake her nails down my back and tell me exactly what she wants.

"So," she says, setting her glass down and flicking her eyes up to mine, "what's that charity thing about?"

I wave a hand. "A family thing. Jared's parents are throwing a silent auction to fight against elephant poaching in Kenya." I give her a grim smile. "Sounds great in theory, but is actually an evening of elitist drivel, full of people who peacock about the fact that they're doing a good thing. I'm dreading it and I was planning on going alone. It happens every year, and every year it's torture."

"I'll go with you if you want. If you think it'll annoy Jared."

A mischievous gleam flashes across her eyes. "I'll even wear heels."

A strange kind of excitement curls in my stomach, but I school my features into a casual expression. "You don't have to do that."

Lily laughs. "I know that, Rudy. What if I *want* to?"

FOUR

LILY

STUPID, stupid, stupid.

What was I thinking?

Rudy pulls up outside the Four Cups Café, where I asked him to drop me. I can see the lights on in the private library space above, and I know my sisters are up there. Being around a band of chattering women so I can unwind some of this tension in my gut is far, far preferable to going to my lonely apartment and thinking of Rudy.

The car's engine turns off, and my fingers smooth over the strap of my purse. Rudy's hand moves to the back of my seat, and I gather my courage to look at him.

Night has fallen around us, and he looks harsher in the shadow from the streetlights. His hand is inches from my face, his thumb moving to brush the very top of my shoulder.

"I had a good time," he tells me, his voice a low growl.

I nod. "Me too."

This is where we kiss, I realize. I made that whole speech about keeping things casual, and if I want to have some hot roll in the hay with him, things are going to get physical.

I *want* things to get physical.

As if he can read my thoughts, Rudy moves his hand to my cheek and shifts closer. He stares into my eyes for a beat, then closes the distance between us. His lips brush mine, barely even touching, his hand gripping my jaw and neck so tenderly it's like he thinks I'm made of glass.

Then he pulls away.

I blink.

His moves his hand back to the gearshift between us, and my brows draw together.

"That's it?" I blurt.

His eyes cut to mine again, amusement dancing in their blue depths. "Were you expecting more?"

"Um, yes." My body is tense, nipples tight, core pounding. He barely even touched me, and I feel horribly off-balance.

This is bad. I should just run away. Forget the charity auction, this was a terrible idea. Why would I think going on a date was a good idea? I can't start something with a man. My life is in shambles!

I reach for my door and start mumbling a goodnight when Rudy's hand reaches out to curl around the back of my neck again. Just as I part my lips to ask him what the hell he's doing, he takes my mouth in a hard kiss. I gasp, my hands flying to his chest as my fingers curl into his shirt.

He deepens the kiss, sliding his tongue into my mouth and groaning at the taste of me. My hand moves to slide through his thick, blond hair, and Rudy tilts my head to kiss me harder. My body is on fire. My breasts are heavy, aching, and the space between my legs feels painfully empty.

I want to climb onto his lap, shove his pants open, and sink down on top of him. I pull his hair and kiss him back, tangling my tongue with his as he lets out another sexy, masculine growl.

I think I've lost control of my body. My panties are drenched, my blood is molten lava, and I might die if I don't feel him inside me.

"Fuck, you taste good," he growls, leaning his forehead against mine.

I pant, closing my eyes as I try to figure out what the hell just happened. I want to invite him to my apartment. Screw the library. Screw my sisters and their friends. I need Rudy inside me *now*.

Then my phone buzzes. I ignore it, still panting with one hand curled in Rudy's hair and the other gripping his shoulder. It buzzes again.

Groaning, I pull away and hunt through my purse until I see the screen. "It's my sister," I say when I see Candice's name. Suspicious, I angle my head to look at the second-story windows. Sure enough, there are three or four faces pressed against the glass. "I'd better go."

Rudy lets out a low chuckle, but it sounds kind of pained. He shifts in his seat, pressing the heel of his palm against his crotch. Then he nods. "I'll talk to you tomorrow."

"I'd like that," I whisper, surprised to realize it's the truth. In a distant part of my brain, a little Iliana screams that it's a bad, bad sign how much I want to see Rudy again.

But I ignore her because what's happening between my thighs is much more potent. Smiling at Rudy, I climb out of his car and make my way to the red door beside the Four Cups Café. When I close the door and lean against it, I take a deep breath. The soft thud of my head hitting the door fills the space, and I groan.

That was supposed to be a one-time thing. A pleasant evening and maybe—hopefully—sex. One last hurrah before my life changes forever...and then I go ahead and invite myself on a second date with him? One where I'll meet his entire extended family? What the hell is wrong with me? Tonight was supposed to end in sweaty, hot sex that scratched an itch for me one last time.

But that kiss...

One night of sweaty sex with Rudy won't be enough. Not with that kind of chemistry between us.

Now I'm standing in the dark, heart pounding, cheeks flushed, knowing I'm entering dangerous territory. Maybe I should have taken him home and screwed his brains out all night. That way, I could point to my actions and say to myself, *See? It's only physical.*

But this? This is turning complicated.

I can't enter a relationship with him—with anyone! Not just because of the baby, but because of everything else. How am I supposed to date someone when there's a guillotine hanging over my head? I'm leading Rudy on, because I know this rela-tionship can't go anywhere.

But I *told* him that, didn't I? We agreed. Maybe things can be casual, even if we do go on another date.

But then my phone dings, and I pull it out to see his name on my screen.

Rudy: *I had a good time tonight. And I might regret this, but I'm looking forward to the charity auction for the first time in my life.*

I clutch the phone to my chest and close my eyes, only opening them when I hear the door at the top of the stairs open.

Simone's red head pokes out of the opening as she flicks on the lights in the stairwell. She glances at me, then turns back to the room behind her. "It's Lily. She's just standing at the bottom of the stairs like a total weirdo."

Then she turns the light off, closes the door behind her, and I'm alone again.

Huffing out a laugh, I make the trek up the creaky stairs and enter the library. Wes—Simone's husband—renovated this space for her, and it's become like a second home for the ladies of Four Cups. There are bookcases lining an entire wall, filled with floor-to-ceiling steamy romance. There's an entire section of regency romance. Must be hundreds of books.

I remember tiptoeing into my mother's bedroom as a child to take furtive glances at the books she kept on her nightstand. The stepback covers—the images inside the front covers with the models in scandalous poses—were pretty much burned into my mind. I remember the exciting thrill of flipping open the book and seeing those covers, then sneaking minutes to read the books on my own. I even dove into my mother's closet and hid there with a book a few times.

Blinking away the memory, I greet the ladies in the room. They all answer with hellos and good evenings, then stare at me expectantly.

Simone and Fiona are sharing a sofa on the far wall. Fiona is blowing over a mug of tea while Simone swirls red wine in a glass. Beside them, in an armchair, my sister Candice has a mischievous look in her eyes as she leans over the arm of the chair toward me.

My other sister, Trina, chews her lip and tries to burn a hole through my face with her eyes.

"So," Simone starts, rolling her wrist in a *go on* motion, "why were you in Rudy's car at this hour?"

"*Lingering* in Rudy's car, no less," Candice adds.

"I'm sorry, Lottie?" I ask Simone, ignoring my sister entirely. "You look a lot younger and more redheaded than you did a few hours ago. Didn't know my mother was here to give me the third degree."

Simone just cackles. "You're not getting out of this that easily, Iliana. Go on. Spill."

I shrug. "There's nothing to spill. We had dinner."

Candice squeals. "Excellent. Wonderful. Where? How was it? Did you kiss?" She turns to the group. "Rudy is a good kisser. I could tell even if I wasn't into it."

You have no idea. Somehow, I know down to my marrow that the kiss I just shared with Rudy was very, very different than what happened between him and Candice.

The other women nod sagely, even though Trina still steals

furtive glances my way. I really wish she hadn't seen that business card this morning.

Flopping onto the only remaining armchair, I slouch down and end up with a hand over my stomach. Trina's brows arch, and I quickly move my hand away.

I should just tell them. I could tell them everything—the baby and the other thing. But when I open my mouth, nothing comes out.

Candice takes over and gives us all a rundown of her failed date with Rudy, peppered with Fiona's recollection of the few times he flirted with her. The consensus is that he's a stud, and they're glad we seem to be hitting it off. Personally, I think they're crazy and possibly delusional since they've all paired off with hot men, one after the other. I happen to live in the real world, where that doesn't happen to people like me.

But my sister's friends are good people, and for the first time in a long time, I find myself relaxing into my seat—and I realize why I came back here. I've been traveling the world for years. I've been the wild child, the free spirit. I haven't had a home since I left my mother's house—college dorms felt like more of a prison than a home to me—but I knew that coming back here would feel safe.

And that's why I can't tell them what's going on. Not yet.

If I open my mouth and spill my guts, everything will change. I'll be on the outside again. I'll have to endure their sympathy, their questions, their pity. I won't be Lily, the one who travels. I won't be the one who's had countless trips and adventures.

I'll be the one who made a mistake. The one who's going

through a hard time. The one who might not make it to next year.

I *like* being the person who laughs, who has no roots, who isn't tied down by the normal rhythms of life. All that will change, of course, but maybe I can cling onto it for a little while longer.

"So?" Fiona leans forward. "You haven't said a word. Where did you eat?"

"He took me to Edgeville. We had fish and chips." I shrug. "It was cute. Casual."

Candice whistles. "Sunset on the boardwalk. Romantic. Did you go for a walk along the beach afterward?"

"What am I, a walking cliché?" I throw my hands out to the sides and when none of them react, I relent. "Yes, we went for a walk on the beach."

The ladies squeal, and I tamp down the smile threatening to curl my lips.

"Is he a good kisser?" Simone leans forward. "I don't trust Candice's opinion on the matter."

"Hey!" Candice sits up, outraged.

"We need a second opinion," Fiona says, nodding to Simone. She turns to me. "So? The kiss?"

I straighten my dress and cross my feet at the ankles, shrugging. "It was okay."

Liar, liar, panties on fire.

Silence descends on the room for a few moments and I take a peek at the women around me. Trina has been unusually silent. She's still studying me with that assessing stare, but it's not judgmental. I wonder what she's thinking.

"Just okay?" Simone cries, breaking the tension. "What a disappointment! What a waste!"

I laugh. "I didn't know you all were counting on me making out with him to get your thrill for the evening."

"Well, now you know, honey," Fiona says, standing up to put her mug in the kitchenette sink. "At least think of us a little next time," she adds with a grin.

"There will be a next time, right?" Candice arches her brows at me.

I clear my throat. "Yeah. I'm going to some charity event with him next weekend."

Simone blows out a breath. "That boy moves fast."

I laugh. "Except I kind of invited myself to it." I tell the group what happened with Rudy's cousin, and they all nod in approval when I tell them how I reacted, and hoot when I say Rudy texted me that he was happy I'd be his date to the event.

Trina finally clears her throat to speak. My chest seizes as she meets my eyes, and for a horrible, interminable moment, I think she's going to ask about the pregnancy. But she just gulps and jerks her chin at me. "What are you going to wear?"

Tension melts away from me as I shrug. "I was hoping you might help with that."

Trina gives me a soft smile. "Of course."

"Speaking of help," Fiona cuts in, "is everyone helping out with Dorothy's community garden project tomorrow? She's been pestering me about it all week." Dorothy and her twin Margaret recently got approval from the town to create a community garden on the lot where Candice's old café used to be before it got condemned and demolished.

"Jen's coming out of her love nest with Fallon to help with the planting," Candice says. "She said to be there at eight o'clock tomorrow morning with work clothes on."

I hum. "I have a few clients waiting on work from me, but I can be there in the afternoon."

"Jen is out of her mind," Simone says as she drains the last of her wine. "I'm not going to be there before eleven, and she better not complain about it."

"She'll complain about it," Candice replies with a laugh. "But you'll both live."

When we break up for the evening, I feel lighter than I did when Rudy dropped me off. I've spent so long on the road that I'd forgotten how good it felt to have a home—a real home. Somewhere where people are so comfortable around each other that they know each other's moods and reactions. Where it's a given that there will be an army of helpers for a new town project. Where I'm automatically included.

So, with a smile on my face, I head back to my new house and wonder if it's already a home. Even when things end with Rudy, it doesn't mean I have to give it all up and leave again.

FIVE

RUDY

THE DAY after my date with Lily, it's hard for me to focus on work. One of my employees is sick, so I end up having to show a new client around a few potential homes. It's been a while since I did this type of work, but at least I don't have to be in the office on a Saturday.

I drive up to a stately house that sits on two acres a few minutes before a sleek Mercedes pulls up behind my car. The woman who gets out of the vehicle is beautiful. Tall, lithe, built like a supermodel. She's a bit older than me, but that never bothered me before. I've never been picky. Her hair is shiny and curled to perfection, and every inch of her looks like money and class.

She's looking at a four-million-dollar home, so it's not surprising.

What *is* surprising, however, is the fact that I don't feel an ounce of attraction to her, even when she rakes her eyes over my body in an overtly suggestive way.

"You must be Mr. Dorset," she says, extending a hand toward me. Her nails are long—really long. Lily kept hers shorter.

"Call me Rudy. Mrs. Neves?" I paint a professional smile on my face and shake her hand.

"If we're doing first names, you should call me Georgia." Her smile is flirty.

In response, I angle my body toward the property. "Gorgeous, isn't it?"

"You can say that again," the woman says, still looking at me.

She's laying it on thick. Tamping down my frustration, I jingle the keys in my hand and start rattling off statistics about the property. Number of bedrooms, bathrooms, square footage, the smattering of outbuildings, including a workshop.

Georgia follows me, her heels clacking on the wide paving stones that lead us to the front door. "Is there a view?" she asks.

In response, I take her through the home to the huge windows overlooking the ocean. Forgetting her flirtation, Georgia Neves's jaw drops. She floats through the room, ignoring the expensive finishes, and stares out at the lawn that falls into the ocean beyond.

We live in a beautiful part of the world. There are old-growth forests all around, with national and state parks protecting the beautiful landscape. Heart's Cove is nestled on the coast and has recently gained notoriety for being a haven for artists.

Since Candice started dating Hollywood star Blake Harding, I've noticed the luxury properties around here have been snapped up too.

Ms. Neves turns shining eyes to me. "This is gorgeous." Her flirtation is forgotten, and I wonder if she was doing it out of habit more than anything. Maybe she's as desperate for distraction as the rest of us.

"It is." I nod.

"I divorced my husband a few months ago, and this is exactly the type of place I've been looking for. Somewhere private but not secluded. A cute town, a beautiful landscape, and maybe the possibility of a new life." For a moment, her face is part sad, part wistful. Then, like a mask dropping, she turns a flirty smile to me, and I know with odd certainty that she isn't flirting because she necessarily wants me—or any other man. She just wants to forget whatever happened before. "A new life sounds fun, don't you think?"

"Lucky for you, this place is available." I smile my best salesman's smile. I'm a bit rusty because Georgia just tilts her head.

"And you?"

Clearing my throat, I frown. "Me?"

"Are you available?"

Her question shocks me. It shouldn't, because she's been giving me the eye since she got out of her car, because I know her interest in me is some kind of fleeting habit designed to distract her. But what surprises me most is the answer I give. "No, I'm not."

"Shame," she says, almost to herself. "I'm going to take a look around the rest of this place."

"I'll meet you in the kitchen once you're done."

She waves a hand and her heels echo down the hallway. Sighing, I make my way to the vast kitchen and pull out my files. If she wants to place an offer on this house, I can get the ball rolling now. I'm still sorting through paperwork when she comes back to the kitchen.

I look up just as she turns the corner, the light from the windows almost giving her a halo. She really is very beautiful. Exactly the type of woman I'd be interested in on a regular day. Fit, unattached, uninterested in commitment. She would be more than willing to have casual sex with a younger man, then let things fizzle out naturally.

So why do I feel nothing toward her?

Every time I look at her, all I can think of is Lily. The way Lily's dark hair reflects more reddish shades than Georgia's. How her effortless sundress-and-sneakers outfit turned me on far more than this pseudo-corporate tailored dress complete with stiletto heels. Objectively, Georgia's outfit should be sexier. But my cock was hard as rock all evening yesterday, and it hasn't so much as twitched today.

"I know I said I wanted this place, but the layout is all wrong. Do you have any other properties that are similar to this, maybe with an extra bedroom? I'd like a pool, too."

I incline my head. "Of course. I can have one of my team members call you on Monday with some options."

"I'd rather deal with you," she replies, smoothing her manicured hands over her thin body. Too thin, maybe? Lily has more curves.

I shove the thought aside. I'm here to sell a house—not

compare two women and dissect why I might be more attracted to one over the other.

Biting back a word of protest—I don't do much realtor work anymore, choosing instead to manage the agents who work for me—I nod. If she wants a modern, move-in-ready six-bedroom home, plus pool, plus ocean view with this size lot? That's pushing five million, maybe even more. I can't afford to lose that sale.

If she wants to deal with me, I can manage a bit of flirtation.

"No problem." I flash her my best smile. "I'll be in touch."

"I hope so." She winks at me, and I lead her back outside. "You know," Georgia says, "I think moving here might be the best thing that ever happened to me."

I smile as politely as I can manage, ignoring the hunger in her gaze. "You wouldn't be the first person to feel that way."

We make a plan to talk soon, and I head for my car. Sighing as soon as I'm behind the wheel, I close my eyes and let her drive off before me. The smile that's been plastered to my lips melts off, and all I feel is exhaustion. Not wanting to go to the office, I head home to start on her file. I have a few properties that might work for her, and I'd like to compile a list of them before Monday. I'll have to call a few local agents to see if they have any properties that aren't on the market yet.

But when I get home, all I can think of is Lily.

That woman today—Georgia—wanted to sleep with me. Under any other circumstances, I would've wanted her too. So what changed? One date with Lily? The promise of another one? What the hell happened to casual? She never said we had to be exclusive, but the thought of another woman turns me off completely.

Unsettled, I walk to my home office and slump down in my desk chair. I stare at the blank screen of my laptop for a while, then scrub my hands over my face and stretch my neck.

I haven't enjoyed myself that much on a date in a long, long time. Not since I fell head over heels with my ex-girlfriend nearly six years ago, and it ended in disaster. As I lean back in my office chair, overlooking the backyard I've carefully tended for the past three years, I think of last night.

That kiss will be burned in my mind for the rest of my life. Even thinking about it now makes my shaft stir in my pants, and I rub my palm over my jeans in an absent motion. I smelled her on my skin all evening. I dreamed of her. I woke up harder than I ever have, and I made myself come to the thought of her lush, pink lips wrapped around my cock. Her hair would look good wrapped around my hands, I decide, and even better splayed across my pillow. Her skin was buttery-soft under my fingertips. I can still feel a whisper of it across my skin. If I woke up to her curled around my side, I think I could die happy.

But I held back from taking her home and screwing her senseless. In the light of day, I'm not even sure why. We had a good time. We're planning a second date. She's funny, snarky, intelligent, and drop-dead gorgeous.

I should have just gone for it—but it felt wrong. For some reason, I want to take my time with Lily. Of course, I would have loved to bury my hands in her hair and hear her moan against my lips. I would have loved to strip that dress on her body and make love to her all night...but then what?

I've slept with women after a first date before. Hell, I've been doing that since Tracey and I broke up. My ex-girlfriend was supposed to be my wife. I was supposed to adopt her daughter, and I planned on being the best stepfather that kid would ever need.

When we split, it broke something inside me and I'm not sure I've ever tried to fix it. I've been dating women casually since then, and nothing has ever stopped me from getting them in bed after a successful first date.

The thought of waking up next to Lily and having that awkward morning-after conversation makes my stomach turn. I want our mornings after to include pancakes and bacon and sex and coffee and endless hours together. That's not how this morning would have been if I'd taken her home with me last night.

The doorbell rings.

My chair creaks as I stand up and I take a moment to arch my back, feeling the satisfying crack and pop of my too-stiff spine. Barefoot, I pad along my knotty pine floorboards to the front of the house, seeing a large, dark shape in the frosted glass of the front door.

Lee Blair is standing on my stoop wearing jeans and a black tee. He arches a brow at me. "You don't call. You don't text. I thought we had something, Rudy. I thought it was special."

Grinning, I step aside to let him in. His motorcycle boots echo in the hallway as we make our way to the kitchen at the back of the house. Lee flops down onto the sofa in the open-plan room as I start making myself a sandwich for lunch. He nods when I offer to make him one, then stands up to grab himself a soda out of the fridge.

The tab on the can pops as the drink fizzes and Lee takes a long drink. Then he sets the can down on my counter and crosses his arms. "How was your date with Lily Viceroy last night?"

I choke on air and clear my throat, then glance at him. "How did you know I was out with Lily?"

Lee grins. "Lily told Trina. Trina told Mac. Mac told me." Mac—Lee's brother—and Trina are together. Apparently all three of them are worse gossips than the hotel ladies are with my grandmother.

When I tell Lee that, he just laughs. "Come on, Rudy. We all know she's been going to the bookstore. Took you long enough to ask her out."

"She's only been in town for a few weeks," I protest.

"My point exactly."

"This is ridiculous. So I went on a date—so what?"

"You didn't take her home, though. Was she not into it?"

"I'm not talking about this." I slam the top piece of bread on his sandwich and toss the whole thing onto a plate. "Eat that and be quiet."

Lee laughs again, and I'm sure he's doing it because he knows it's getting under my skin. I take a huge bite out of my own lunch and chew angrily, then go on the offensive. "What about you? You spend all your nights at your father's bar just to avoid meeting anyone. You've been wallowing since Drea left you."

Lee rolls his eyes, red tinging his ears. "Yeah, right. I don't wallow, asshole."

We eat in silence for a while and the food settles my stomach. Thoughts of Lily pop up uninvited, like the way her eyes looked in the front seat of my car last night, or how her laugh made something stir in my chest—and my pants.

I want to see her again—but maybe it's a bad idea. We both agreed to be casual, and I have no desire to make things any more serious than she does. Maybe it's better for me to just back off.

"You coming to help out with the community garden?" Lee says, brushing a few crumbs off his fingers onto the plate.

I glance at the time and swear softly. "I forgot about that. I told Dorothy I'd be there two hours ago."

Lee arches a brow. "We'd better get going, then."

"Let me change."

I live in a three-bed, one-bath house that I bought when I was thirty-one, intending to fix it up. I haven't gotten very far. In the three years I've owned it, I've managed to rip the tiles off the kitchen backsplash and fix up the office. My mattress in the bedroom is still on the floor.

In those three years, however, I've managed to sell countless properties and grow my real estate business to the point that I have a comfortable lifestyle, look after my grandmother without making it obvious that I've been looking after her, and work part-time at the bookstore. I'm not lazy; I just haven't quite cared about my house enough to finish fixing it up.

When I make my way upstairs and enter my bedroom, my stomach clenches. I can't bring Lily here. A woman like her? A woman who knows what she wants, who's seen more of the world than most flight attendants? She'd take one look at my place and think I'm a permanent bachelor.

She wouldn't be wrong.

Throwing on some work clothes, I bound back down the steps and find Lee leaning against the wall next to the front door. He jerks his head at me. "I rode my bike here, so I'll meet you in town."

I grunt in agreement and listen for the roar of his motorcycle as I slip on some old steel-toed work boots I've had since the days I worked as a construction laborer in my teens. They're stiff, with gray concrete stains splattered over the tan material, but they still fit.

Locking the door behind me, I exit my old house and make my way into town.

Maybe this is exactly what I need. A bit of physical labor to get me away from my computer screen—and away from thoughts of Lily.

SIX

LILY

SNEAKERS on my feet and sun hat firmly stuffed over my head, I make my way down Cove Boulevard, the main street that runs through the center of Heart's Cove. It's lined with quaint shops and full-grown trees, the leaves bright green and rustling in the warm summer breeze.

I walk past the hardware store and take a quick peek at the bookstore, quickening my steps as I reach the Four Cups Café. I wave at Allie, Candice's daughter, who's busy behind the till. It's only another block and a half to the hotel, and just beyond it is the new community garden.

Wes's pickup truck is parked on the street along with a large trailer full of supplies. The whole area is abuzz with activity and people and that pleasant, energetic feeling of people who are doing a good thing.

Margaret is the first one to spot me. Dorothy's twin is the more refined, elegant of the two, with her favorite hairstyle being a French twist and her neck almost always adorned with pearls. Today, she's managed to look dignified in dirt-stained gardening clothes.

She gives me a broad smile and a tight hug. "Thank you for coming, Iliana."

"Of course." I reach into my bag and pull out a pair of stiff, brand-new gardening gloves of my own. "I came prepared."

"Good, good." She ushers me onto the lot, which has been flattened and cleared of the building that used to stand here. On the back of the lot, Grant—Fiona's husband—and Wes are halfway through building a row of raised planters. The leftmost wall is already done, with an army of people filling up the timber boxes with rich, dark earth. Jen, the resident baker, is standing with a clipboard, barking orders at people along the line. Fallon, the chef who stole Jen's heart, has a little grin on his face as he walks by with a bag of potting mix slung over his shoulder. He pauses beside Jen and leans down to bite the space between her shoulder and her neck. Jen immediately stops talking and her face takes on a dreamy look. She closes her eyes and leans into him, turning her head to accept a gentle kiss.

I glance away, feeling like I'm intruding on a private moment. My attention snags on the right side of the long, narrowish lot. Rudy is here, and he's not wearing a shirt. He has his back to me, and I can't quite tear my eyes away from the bronzed, glistening skin. Even from a distance, I can see the sweat dappling his shoulder blades, the writhing of his muscles as he moves.

Can I blame pregnancy hormones for the rush of lust that

nearly knocks me over? My stomach tightens as I watch his beautiful, strong body move in the sunlight.

He's using this large tool that looks like a combination of scissors and a scoop to create a post hole in the ground. I stand entranced as he lifts his arms above his head and brings the post hole digger down into the hard earth, only to lift it out again and dump earth onto a small mound at his side. There's a row of posts already secured into their holes, where more helpers are pouring quick-set concrete into the bases.

Rudy pauses, wiping his forehead on his arm.

Movement snaps me out of my stupor as Simone appears at my side, dabbing at my face with a tissue. "You've got a bit of drool there, Lily," she says. "Let me get it for you."

I give her a flat stare and bat her hand away, and Simone just cackles.

The noise draws Rudy's attention. He turns to look over his shoulder and pauses when he sees me, then turns the whole way around. I freeze, caught in his stare—and in the tractor beam created by the honed masculine perfection of his chest.

He's lean and muscular, with a sprinkling of golden hair over his chest. He has abs—real, visible abs. Eight of them that lead my eyes down to the carved Adonis belt that disappears into his low-slung khakis. I get a good, long look at that trail of hair I noticed yesterday.

Oh dear.

Suddenly, my lips are tingling, as if my body wants to remind me what it felt like to kiss him. I fell asleep thinking of the growls and the rough timbre of his voice when he pulled away from me. Would his voice go gravelly and harsh if I used my tongue to follow that happy trail all the way to its destination?

Somehow, I manage to drag my eyes up to Rudy's face when he comes to a stop in front of me, leaning on his shovel-thingy.

"Hey, Lily," he says, and those two words send heat rushing through my core.

"Hey," I manage. "Nice...shovel. It's really...big."

What the hell did I just say?

Rudy's eyes twinkle as he shrugs. "Thanks. I get that a lot."

Now heat is rushing up my neck and over my cheeks too.

Simone, still standing beside me, snorts as her shoulders start shaking. "I'm going to leave you two kids to it," she finally says. "Jen is giving me a death glare."

I glance over at the baker who, sure enough, is looking our way with an expectant arch of her eyebrows. Simone calls out and glides across the lot toward her, and I'm left with Rudy and half a brain in my head.

Say something. Say anything.

"You're building a fence?" I give him a smile and hope I don't look stupid.

Rudy glances over his shoulder at the row of posts, and I steal a glance at his chest and stomach. He has muscles I didn't even know existed. His body could be an anatomy textbook. Where's that tissue Simone was holding?

"Lattice," Rudy explains. "We're going to grow a vine over it."

Before I can answer, Dorothy calls my name. She's wearing a matching cheetah-print shorts-and-tee combo, with a straw hat that has a decorative band of the same material. "Lily, get your butt over here! You can help us paint." She glances at Rudy. "And you get back to work, young man. Those post holes aren't going to dig themselves."

"Who knew Dorothy was a slave driver?" I say with a smile.

Rudy winks at me, then gives me a fantastic view of the muscles on his back as he makes his way back to his half-dug hole. When I make it to Dorothy's side, she gives me a long look, then thrusts a paintbrush in my hand and commands me to start working.

We have a fence to paint around the whole garden, pavers to lay between the raised beds, and shade cloth to install over some of the shade-loving plants. Most of the planting won't happen until the cooler months, but Jen has a list of plants and timing for the garden. Of course she does. Her notes are color-coded and marked up with her usual precision.

Time flies, and I only steal a few glances at Rudy. Okay, more than a few.

Once he finishes the post holes, he helps with the concrete bases, then starts hammering the lattice to the newly installed posts.

"Nothing better than a man with a hammer," Fiona says with a secret grin on her face.

My cheeks heat as I look away, dipping my paintbrush into the pot, then freeze. Is it even safe to be doing this? I stare at the white paint dripping off my brush as my heart starts pounding. I've been standing here for two hours inhaling these fumes. Is that going to hurt the baby? I didn't even *think* about that!

I'm so incredibly unprepared for this. I can't be a mother! I know I'll be forty next week, but honestly, I feel no different than I did when I was twenty-two. Fine, okay, I'm a little sorer after a workout and hangovers seem to last four days instead of four hours, but I'm still *me*. I'm not fit to be a parent!

What else have I done to put the baby in danger? I've tried to stay away from coffee and soft cheese and processed meat and sushi and, and, and...

My chest is heaving as I drop my paintbrush. Fiona calls out my name and I wave her away, stumbling over an uneven paver as I try to get away from the paint smell. I'm going to throw up. I used to love the smell of paint, but now it makes me feel like I'm endangering my unborn child.

Trina is the one who follows me onto the sidewalk and around the corner. I'm sucking in a breath of fresh air when I feel her hand on my forearm. "What's wrong? Do you need me to take you to your doctor? Are you in pain?"

"I've been inhaling paint fumes for two hours," I hiss, glancing over my shoulder to make sure no one can hear me. "I didn't even *think* about it, Trina. I can't do this. I have no idea what I'm doing and I'm going to screw up."

Instead of answering, Trina just wraps her arms around me and squeezes. Her voice is low, gentle. "We're outdoors, Lily. You're fine. I had the same worry when we did Toby's nursery. My doctor told me that sanding and scraping is a no-go, especially if it's older, lead-based paint, but most modern paints are fine. You didn't hurt your baby. If you're worried, just ask your obstetrician about it next time." When she pulls away, her eyes are kind. "And we all screw up. It's just part of being a parent."

I close my eyes. Trina rubs my back until I take a deep breath and nod. "I'm fine. I just freaked out a bit."

My sister studies me for a moment. She opens her mouth, then closes it again. After taking a breath, she finally speaks. "Are you going to tell anyone?"

"Yeah," I say. "Eventually. I mean, it'll be obvious in a few months anyway."

"And Rudy?"

Her voice is neutral. Non-judgmental. Still, I wince.

What am I supposed to say? I could tell her that I just wanted to sleep with him last night in order to have one last night of fun before my whole life changes. But if I told her that, I'd probably have to tell her everything I've been hiding besides the baby. And if I do *that*, then it becomes real. It becomes everyone else's problem too. All this happy, buzzing energy? All the laughter and lightness? I can pretty much kiss all of it goodbye.

But it wasn't just one night of fun with Rudy, was it? Because today, the sight of him made me stop in my tracks. And I'm going to that charity auction with him. And it might make me an irresponsible, bad person, but I *want* to go on another date with him.

"It's casual," I finally say.

Trina just nods. "Well, come on. I was on my way to the café to get drinks and treats for everyone. You can help me with that."

Heaving a sigh of relief, I nod to my sister and follow her to my car. It's only when we approach that I see Rudy on the sidewalk. I don't think he heard anything Trina and I said, because he just meets my eyes with a concerned expression on his face.

"You okay?" he asks, catching my hand in his and squeezing.

"You rushed out like something was wrong." His other hand slides over my hip and damn it, but it feels good to be wrapped up in his arms.

"Just got a little nauseous from the smell of paint," I tell him. It's the truth—sort of. I point my thumb over my shoulder to my sister and her car. "I'm going to Four Cups to grab drinks and snacks for everyone. You want anything?"

"One of Jen's salted caramel brownies," he says. His hand drifts lower, fingertips touching the cleft of my ass. "Those things are like crack. I think I'm addicted."

My eyebrow arches as I let my eyes roam down to his chest and back up again. I even work up the nerve to slide my hand over his sweaty bicep and squeeze. There's not an ounce of excess flesh on him. "Somehow I doubt you're eating too many of them."

Rudy gives me a grin that makes my knees weak, that hand on my lower back pressing ever so slightly.

Then I realize he's hard. I can feel it up against my stomach, and I'd be lying if it didn't send my body into a lust-induced tizzy. If I keep hanging out with him, I'm going to need to start carrying spare panties in my purse.

Just then, Trina honks her horn, and I jump. He gives it one last squeeze and lets me go. I feel his eyes on my back until I'm safely in the passenger seat of Trina's car.

She gives me a completely unimpressed stare. "Casual, huh?"

I just click my seatbelt and nod. "Yeah. Casual. We agreed."

SEVEN

TRINA

I NEVER KNEW how good I was at biting my tongue until I found out my little sister was pregnant and couldn't tell anyone. As we load up boxes with pastries and sandwiches from the Four Cups Café, I steal surreptitious glances at Lily.

She looks...fine. Maybe there's a little tension in her shoulders, and her smiles are a touch forced. But if I hadn't seen that business card, I doubt I would have even known there was anything wrong. I would have assumed she was just a bit awkward being in Heart's Cove instead of some multi-month, multi-country trip.

She's never been good at staying in one place. Did she come back here because of the baby? Because this is the only place she has any family?

"Allie," my sister asks the curly-haired blond girl behind the counter, "would you mind wrapping up a salted caramel brownie separately for me?"

Candice's daughter nods, a rogue curl bouncing with the movement. "No problem."

As Allie works, I lean against the counter. "Are you excited about leaving for college?"

My niece glances at me and gives me a brilliant smile. "Can't wait. Six weeks seems so far away and I just want to go now."

"It'll fly by, don't worry," Lily says. "Time seems to speed up these days—or maybe I'm just getting older."

I throw her a sharp glance, which she ignores. Her words had a distinct flavor of...dread.

Behind us, the café door opens, and I hear Nora Richter's voice. "This is the best café in town," she proclaims.

"I thought you said it was the only café in town," a wry voice answers.

I turn to see a beautiful woman who could be anywhere from her mid-fifties to mid-seventies standing beside an equally beautiful Nora. The older woman is short—shorter than Nora, who can't be more than five foot five. The woman's back is straight as a rod, her silver hair streaked with black, tied back in a thick braid that falls over her shoulder and down to her ribs. Her skin is deeper than Nora's, a rich bronze color, and her eyes are as black as Fallon's. She casts an assessing eye over the eclectic mix of tables and chairs, the local artwork, and the handmade cups and saucers that give Four Cups its unique vibe.

She must be Nora and Fallon's mother.

When the woman's gaze falls on me, she tilts her head.

I wave. "Hi. You must be Mrs. Richter. I'm Trina and this is my sister, Lily."

"Call me Prisha," she says with a kind smile. "So this is where my son worked for so long?"

Nora gives her a gentle nudge closer to the counter as Allie finishes loading up our boxes of goodies. "Ma insisted on helping me set up my new place in town," she explains. "But I think it was just an excuse to finally meet Jen."

Prisha grins, her dark eyes twinkling. "Any woman who gets my son to knock on my door after so many years must be special."

"Jen is special, all right," Lily answers. "She's a force to be reckoned with."

"She's down at the community garden," I say. "You two would be welcome to come join, but be prepared for someone to hand you a spade or a paintbrush and put you to work."

"Oh—is that today?" Nora asks, eyes wide. "I told Dorothy I'd help. I completely forgot."

"She'll forgive you if you show up with food," Lily says, thrusting a box of goodies toward Nora with a smile. "Just pretend that was your plan all along."

Nora gives her a grateful smile. We say goodbye to Allie and head back outside. The four of us pile into my car, and I drive back down the few blocks to the worksite. Lily's eyes immediately stick to Rudy like glue, and I bite back a snarky comment.

She's got it bad...and that's not a good thing. Lily has other things to worry about right now, like the tiny human growing in her womb.

But I know it's not my place to say anything, so all I do is turn off the car and help the other ladies get the boxes of food out of the car. Fallon appears beside us, one of his muscular arms curling around his mother's shoulders as he gives her a tender kiss on the temple.

"Food's here!" I call out.

The army of helpers looks up at me, and then the stampede starts. Rudy makes a beeline for Lily, who presents a paper-wrapped brownie to him like it's precious. His smile is warm and secretive, and he says something near her ear that I don't catch.

Mac, my man, manages to elbow his way closer to the boxes of sandwiches and treats, but he doesn't stop there. He reaches me and wraps his arms around me, dipping me down and kissing me square on the lips. When he straightens me up again, I'm flushed. "What was that for?"

"You looked like you were in need of a kiss."

"Gross, mommy!" Katie says, a smear of white paint across her jeans. She's been helping with the fence, apparently.

"We got here while you were at the café," Mac explains. "Toby's not bad with a hammer."

My son blushes, grabbing a sandwich from the box and scampering away. I smile, tilting my head as Mac lays another kiss on my jaw.

I look at the assembled crowd and see a real community. Everyone is laughing and eating and working together. Dorothy and Eli are having a heated debate, waving their arms as they gesture at a wrought-iron arch that will serve as an entrance to the garden.

Margaret has her head bent near Hamish, Mac's father.

Hamish, being the old biker he is, is wearing a leather vest and an old Harley-Davidson tee, and somehow beside Margaret's classy, put-together outfit, it works.

Wes, Grant, and Blake are all topless and attacking sandwiches, while their respective women look on, smitten. I don't blame them. There's a lot of male flesh on display, and all of it is drool-worthy.

I lean my head against Mac's shoulder and glance up at him. My kids are eating and laughing, my sisters are here, and even if Lily's secret is weighing on me, I can't deny that I'm happy.

Then my mother appears beside me and slips her hand into the crook of my elbow. I glance at her, brows arched in question. "Everything okay?"

She pinches her lips and glances at Lily. "Your sister still hasn't opened up about what's going on. She's not herself, and I think something's wrong. She tell you anything?"

I gulp. "No," I answer. It's not *exactly* untrue. Lily never actually *said* anything—I just happened to find a business card and Lily never denied it.

My mother hums, eagle eyes still narrowed on Lily.

Feeling protective of my little sister, I blurt out, "She's going to some charity event with Rudy next weekend."

Mom's eyes light up as she turns to look at me. "She is?"

Uh-oh. Maybe knowing about the pregnancy would be better than my mother thinking she can play matchmaker. But I just nod and run with it. "Yeah. They went out on a date last night. She said it was fun."

My mother lets out a squeal that is decidedly un-Lottie-like.

"Fantastic. Great! I'm going to go tell Dorothy. She likes Rudy, even though he's related to Agnes. I'm sure she'll tell me all there is to know about him."

As my mother rushes toward her friend, Mac lets out a chuckle. "You sure that was a good idea?"

"Nope," I answer, and that, at least, is the truth.

EIGHT

LILY

SOMEHOW, I manage to convince my family that I don't want
to do—or get—anything for my birthday. It's a relief when they
mostly agree. On Wednesday, I turn forty with little fanfare and
only a quiet family dinner at Trina's house. I watch Allie with
her cousins, Toby and Katie, and it takes all my self-control not
to run my hand over my stomach.

I'm going to have a child. The three of them will have a new
cousin in a matter of months.

The thought of it is enough to make me want to run down
the street in a panic—but that would *definitely* raise a few
eyebrows...and questions.

So instead, I shift my eyes away from the kids and refuse, for
the thousandth time, Candice's offer of wine.

"You used to love wine," she says, eyeing me suspiciously.

"I'm not drinking this month," I say, hoping that's the end of it. Maybe I can keep using that excuse for the next six months or so.

Candice nods and moves to the next half-full glass that needs a top-up.

"So, Lily, tell us about this second date you have with Agnes's grandson," my mother says. She's already asked me about it half a dozen times since she found out about it at the community garden, but obviously I haven't satisfied her curiosity.

"It's not a date," I lie. "I'm just helping him stick it to his arrogant cousin."

"Okay," Candice hums, "and what are you going to wear to your non-date? It's a black-tie event, right?"

"Trina's in charge of that," I answer with a grin. "I'm hoping she has a plan."

At my words, Trina launches into a detailed explanation of what she's thinking for my outfit, hair, and makeup. She expertly navigates the conversation to clothing, then to her own business ventures as a new stylist, and I use the opportunity to slip out the back door for a breath of fresh air.

After a few moments, the patio doors open and Trina joins me. She gives me a small smile and jerks her head to the door she just closed behind her. "They're talking about Candice's new house, so it's probably safe to go back inside now."

I grin. "Thanks for helping me deflect."

Trina laughs, then clears her throat. "Listen, I know you said you didn't want anything for your birthday..."

"I don't. I'd rather just forget that I'm forty altogether."

She laughs. "Hey, now. Careful. You make it sound like a

bad thing. My forties have been the best decade so far." She jerks her head to the side. "Come here. I want to show you something."

Our footsteps echo on the timber patio until we take the three steps down to the gravel pathway leading to the side of the house. Trina walks ahead of me in the gathering dusk, a motion-activated light illuminating our way. She stops at the side door that opens into the garage, and steps inside.

Flicking on the lights, Trina walks to a corner of the room where a half-dozen unopened boxes are neatly stacked. A tarp covers a knobby-shaped piece of furniture beside the boxes, which Trina removes with a flick of the wrist.

Beneath the blue plastic, a crib and stroller appear. They're wrapped in protective plastic and look a little worn, but still in good shape.

I take a step backward.

"I don't even know why I kept all this stuff," Trina says, opening up one of the boxes and peering inside. "But I did." She points to the boxes. "There's clothing, swaddles, blankets, toys, books. I'll go through the stuff this week and keep some of the more sentimental items, but the rest is yours if you want it. I'm sure in the past six years, there have been a thousand new baby items on the market that are bigger and better than all this, but at least it'll get you started. I have a car seat somewhere, too, and a gliding rocking chair that was a lifesaver for feeding and soothing. I got rid of the changing table because it was a bit rickety, but I'm sure you can get one that isn't too expensive."

My heart is pounding. My breath is coming in short gasps,

and I can't quite find the words to say anything. I don't even know what I would say.

Trina glances at me and frowns. "Lily?"

"I... Thanks. It's just..." I turn my back on all the baby things and suck in a shaking breath. I square my shoulders and manage to get my breathing under control before turning back around. I look at my sister and nod. "Thank you," I croak. "It just seems a little...real."

"Like if you start thinking of logistics, you'll have a panic attack?" Trina asks as the corner of her lips tug.

I nod.

"Well, don't worry. I felt the same way, and I was married and settled when I had Toby. I think that might be normal." She glances at the door across the garage that leads to the house and jerks her head. "Come on, let's go back. We can tell everyone I was showing you outfit ideas for this weekend."

We walk to the door and I catch my sister's arm. Before she can pull away, I wrap her in a hug. "Thanks, Trina."

She just smiles at me. "You'll be fine. Trust me."

Instead of comforting me, her words send a chill skittering down my spine. If it were just the baby I was facing, I'd believe her. I know I'll love and protect my baby...it's everything else that scares me.

SATURDAY COMES AROUND FASTER than I can blink, and I find myself in my apartment with my sisters and their friends. Every horizontal surface is covered in various bits of makeup, skincare, hair tools, and wine glasses. Simone is trying one of the dresses I vetoed, smoothing it over her curves as she takes a sip of wine. It's a red dress with a keyhole neckline that shows a hint of scandalous cleavage, a form-fitting bodice, and a skirt that hits right above the knees. Way too sexy for a black-tie charity event, but it looks like dynamite on her.

Candice is doing dishes I hadn't gotten around to this afternoon, and Fiona is lounging on my couch watching everything happen with Jen at her side.

Trina taps my shoulder to make me turn toward the vanity mirror again as she sections another piece of hair to curl. The dress I chose is hanging on the top of the door, the black velvet fabric looking luxurious even from a distance.

"There," Trina says as she gives my hair a last spritz of hairspray. "We'll let the curls cool, then we'll brush them out. You'll look like a goddess."

"Question," Candice says, evidently done with the dishes as she runs her hands over a sequined yellow gown lying on the sofa. "Why do you have so many formal dresses? What kind of events were you attending before you came here?"

Trina grins. "Not many, but I like pretty things. They come in handy in times like these." She taps my shoulder and gestures to the dress. "Put it on. You got a strapless bra?"

I nod and make my way to the bathroom to change. The only strapless bra I own is a lacy black La Perla thing that cost an ex-boyfriend of mine far too much money—but it fits me like a second skin and makes my boobs look incredible. The pregnancy helps in that department too.

As soon as I put it on and look in the mirror, that same sick feeling of dread twists in my gut. I run my fingers over my chest and blink away a wave of emotion that threatens to make me cry. Can I blame that on the pregnancy hormones or on the terrifying issues that loom behind me like the grim reaper? I touch the lace edge of the bra, where the soft skin of my breast meets the fabric, and I close my eyes. I won't be able to do that soon.

Shaking my head, I turn to the velvet dress. I will *not* ruin the makeup Trina just spent an hour putting on my face. I'm ten weeks pregnant, but thankfully not showing yet. When I slip the dress on, it feels like a second skin. The floor-length gown is inky black, the fabric thick and well-tailored. The straps are spaghetti-thin, but the dress is so well made that I'm pretty sure it'd stay up without them.

Looking at myself in the mirror, I gulp. I look...*good*.

For someone who's spent a large part of her life living out of a suitcase, glamorous evenings like this don't happen very often. I'm used to either being sweaty from plane or bus rides, or tired from walking around a new city for a day. When I work, I usually wear sweats and tees. A glamorous woman, I am not. And ever since I found out about the pregnancy and everything else going on, I've made even less of an effort.

The man who was supposed to be by my side walked away when he found out about the baby, and I've been hanging on by my fingernails ever since.

But this... Even if my date with Rudy turns out to be a total disaster, at least I can look at my forty-year-old self in the mirror and know that I look good.

When I open the door and walk out of the bathroom, the

thigh-high slit at the side of the dress makes the fabric kiss my just-shaved legs.

A chorus of wolf whistles sounds in the room, which makes me blush and roll my eyes. Trina snaps her fingers and waves me over. "Let me finish your hair." She brushes out the curls, puts a few pins in my hair, sprays it one last time with the bottle of hairspray that has to be nearly empty by now, then spins me toward the mirrored closet doors next to the entrance to my apartment.

"There," she proclaims.

"Damn, Lily," Simone says. "Rudy isn't going to make it all the way to the event without ripping that dress off of you. I hope you have time to stop off for a quickie before dinner starts."

I roll my eyes, but my cheeks flush. Ducking to my bedroom, I reach into the top drawer of my dresser and pull out one of the only pieces of jewelry I own. It's a simple tear-shaped pendant with tiny diamonds studded all along the border. In the center is a larger pear-shaped sapphire of the darkest blue. The chain is white gold, which Trina helps clasp behind my neck as I hold up my dark hair.

"You carried Grandma's necklace around the world with you, huh?" Candice asks, suspicious moisture gathering in the corners of her eyes.

I look at her in the reflection of the mirror and shrug. "What else would I do with it?"

Trina stands behind me, looking over my other shoulder, and the three of us stand in silence for a moment. Our father passed away nearly twenty-three years ago. Before he died, he gave each of us girls something from his side of the family. Candice got his mother's engagement ring, Trina got beautiful dangly earrings, and I got this necklace. I've worn it a grand total of six times, and the chain rests against my neck feeling a lot heavier than it should.

I might not get many more chances to wear it, so I might as well have it on tonight. Who knows if I'll ever attend a black-tie event again?

Fiona gives me an approving nod. "You look amazing. I approve."

Then the apartment buzzer sounds, and butterflies explode in my stomach.

Rudy's here.

NINE

LILY

BY SOME DIVINE MIRACLE, I convince the girls to stay in my apartment while I go meet Rudy outside. The door is always locked from the outside, so all they have to do is pull it closed when they leave. The last thing I want is for a whole stampede of women to follow me down the stairs to wave me off like proud parents sending their eldest kid to prom.

Still, when I step outside, I feel their eyes on my back. I'd bet if I looked up, there would be faces pressed against the front windows.

My attention isn't on the windows, though. It's on Rudy.

There's something uniquely powerful about a good-looking man in a well-tailored tux. Fabric of the deepest black is cut close to every hard line of his body, with a crisp white shirt clinging to his chest. I watch him straighten up from where he'd been leaning against the black car behind him, a different one than he had on our date—this one a sleek Audi that looks like money. Tugging at his cuffs, Rudy straightens his jacket while his eyes run from the black strappy heels on my feet all the way up my body.

His gaze lingers on the pendant necklace that rests just above the straight-cut neckline of my black dress. Then he meets my eyes, and there's something in his expression that I can't read. He extends a hand toward me, and I've slipped my palm against his before I even realize I've lifted my arm.

"You look incredible." His voice is half an octave lower than usual, sending a hot thrill to pierce my stomach.

"Jared will eat his words," I reply.

Rudy shakes his head. "I'm finding myself not caring about my cousin at all right now."

I blush as Rudy tugs me closer, his other hand moving to the small of my back. The touch is intimate, possessive, and I can almost hear the squeals coming from the upstairs window. Somehow, I resist the urge to look.

Rudy opens the door for me and waits until all the velvet fabric has been tucked inside the car, then he moves to the other side of the Audi. He gets behind the wheel as I strap on my seatbelt, his eyes lingering once more on my dress, my shoulders, my face.

Then, shaking his head as if to clear his thoughts, he puts the car in gear.

"Are we picking up Agnes?" I ask as he turns the car around to head down Cove Boulevard on our way to the freeway.

He makes a noise at the back of his throat. "She's driving over with Cheswick. My grandmother doesn't like to rely on anyone else for a ride. She'll probably stay long enough to sneer at her sister, then walk out."

I grin, turning my face to the window so Rudy won't see. I can't deny it: I like Agnes.

"I like my grandmother," Rudy says, as if he could read my thoughts. "I mean, I love her, obviously, but I like her too. Once you get past the bulldog exterior—"

"She's just soft and gooey inside?"

Rudy laughs. "Don't know that I'd go that far." He chuckles again. "And I certainly wouldn't say that to her face, but she's loyal and tough and she taught me how to take care of myself."

"She raised you?" I remember him telling me that on our last date—and then my muscles seize, because I'm going on a second date with a man and I'm ten weeks pregnant. What the hell am I doing?

This time, Rudy doesn't read my thoughts and doesn't seem to notice the tension hardening every muscle in my body. He just drives the vehicle past the town limits and merges onto the freeway, every movement confident and in control. "She did," he finally says. "My mother had me young—really young—and I never knew my father. Grandma adopted me when I was born."

"And your mom?"

His hands clench for a moment. "She died in childbirth." Then, as if it takes a great effort, he relaxes.

"I'm sorry," I say.

He shrugs. "Your father died when you were young too, right?"

"Seventeen years old," I say. "But I'm grateful I had those years. Must be hard to not have any memories."

"I had a good childhood. My grandmother was everything I needed."

I nod, even though he's staring at the road in front of us. The night is as velvety as my dress, and even with the streetlights illuminating the freeway, it feels like a cocoon shrouding our car. I find myself running my finger over the pendant necklace, over and back along the tear-shaped diamond border.

It was only six months after my father died that I went on my first trip. I went to Peru by myself, visited Machu Picchu, and felt a bit of my grief eke out through my pores at the sight of the ancient Incan citadel. I felt awe—real awe—and it was the first good feeling I'd had since cancer had ripped my father away from me.

Sometimes I wonder if I've been running ever since, hunting for that feeling of calm.

"Does Mr. Cheswick live with Agnes?" I find myself asking, just to pull myself out of my own memories.

To my surprise, Rudy laughs. "No. They've been dating for as long as I can remember, but Grandma says she's too set in her ways to share her space with anyone else. She says the key to their relationship is healthy boundaries."

I grin. "She's not wrong."

Rudy laughs, and we lapse into comfortable silence for a while.

"So who is going to be at this gala?" I ask, trying to keep my voice light. "Am I meeting all your extended family under false pretenses?"

Rudy throws me a rueful grin. "What false pretenses are those?"

"That we're dating."

"Are we not?"

I grin as another thrill spears through me. "You know what I mean."

I'm not sure *I* know what I mean, but Rudy inclines his head in acknowledgement. "You'll meet most of them, but don't worry. If it all goes wrong, I'll just get my grandmother to play guard dog."

I laugh, relaxing into my seat. It's easy with Rudy. From the first moment I walked into the bookstore a few weeks ago, it's been easy to talk to him, easy to forget about all the problems plaguing my future.

The car slows as he takes an exit, and within minutes we arrive at the venue. It's a yacht club in Edgeville, lit up by a thousand fairy lights strung up on the building, with a valet booth and a parking lot full of luxury cars. Considering the hostels, cramped airplane seats, and stinky busses I've spent the last decades of my life in, this is definitely out of my comfort zone.

Still, when my heel touches the ground outside the car that costs as much as I make in a year or two, Rudy's hand is there to help me. His lips are tipped in a secret smile, and he tucks me close to his side as he tosses the keys to the valet.

Rudy places my hand in the crook of his elbow and leans toward my ear. "Let's have some fun."

With those four words, Rudy manages, once again, to make me forget about all my worries. I forget about the upcoming challenges I face, about the baby, about everything that may or may not come after. I forget that my body will soon change in more ways than one, and I just let Rudy lead me through a vine-covered arch and into a courtyard of twinkling lights.

The air is warm in the middle of summer, but there's still a chill. The shawl Trina persuaded me to bring slips off my shoulder and Rudy's fingers brush my skin as he brings it back up again. The touch is soft, but it speaks volumes. His blue eyes meet mine for a moment, then turn to the entrance door which has already been opened for us.

If we were in a foreign country where no one spoke English, I'd feel more at home than in this place. I'm accustomed to feeling uncomfortable. I thrive on it. I enjoy walking out of an airport I've never been to before and being mobbed by taxi drivers clamoring for my attention—and my money. I like feeling the sticky heat of the tropics or the chill of a Siberian wind. I like treading on streets I'll only ever see once.

What I'm saying is, I *like* the discomfort of the unknown.

But a yacht club in Edgeville full of rich people wanting to save elephants is a whole other beast.

Rudy is a warm presence at my side, strength and grace and confidence. He leads me into a large reception room that over-looks the water and all the million-dollar yachts docked in the bay. Delicate music floats through the air from a string quartet as waiters drift through the crowd carrying trays full of food and champagne.

"You want a drink?" Rudy says quietly, his voice pitched so only I can hear it.

I shake my head. "Not drinking for the month." Or the next, or the next, or the next...

"Might take the edge off."

I shrug. "I like a challenge."

"Rudy!" a booming voice calls out. A man with pure white hair spreads his arms, the shoulders of his tux pulling against the movement. "Get over here, kid!"

"Hey, Uncle Mike." Rudy paints on that charming grin he deploys when he needs it and moves to give the older man a hug. Then his hand moves to the small of my back and he tugs me closer. "This is Lily. Lily, this is my uncle Mike and my aunt Nancy."

"Lily," Nancy cuts in, extending both arms toward me. "You're even more gorgeous than Jared said. Lovely to meet you."

Somehow, I doubt Jared was extolling my virtues and beauty, but I manage to smile and make small talk long enough that Mike and Nancy are called away.

Rudy searches my face with a gleam in his eyes, his hand still lingering on my hip. "That wasn't so bad, was it?"

"Champagne, sir? Ma'am?" A waiter presents us with a tray of bubbly. Rudy grabs one and raises his brows at me, but I shake my head.

When the waiter walks away, I let out a sigh. "That's the beginning of the end."

Rudy arches a brow. "What is?"

"He called me ma'am. I might as well get my senior discount card now."

I love the way Rudy laughs. It takes him from attractive to out-of-this-world. A few heads turn at the sound, and this time I find myself putting a possessive hand on his arm.

I quickly pull it away, but the damage is done. Rudy's eyes

lower as he tugs me closer and jerks his head to the open space in the middle of the floor. "Dance with me."

Nights like these are dangerous. Not because I'm uncomfortable being around people whose net worth probably rivals that of small countries, but because it makes me forget about all the things that are bearing down on me. All the problems knocking on my door that I'll only be able to ignore for a few more months.

And I'm not talking about the baby. That's not so much a problem as a...change. It's everything else that worries me.

Nights like these make me forget that Rudy and I have an expiration date, and that we're not supposed to actually like each other beyond something frivolous and casual.

But Rudy puts his untouched champagne on a waiter's empty tray. He takes my hand and places it on his shoulder, then grips my other hand in his. "Just follow my lead," he says, and then we dance.

We glide, twirl, and dip, and it's true—I forget about everything except the music and Rudy. The scent of his cologne that seems to embed itself into my skin every time he tugs me close, the feel of his hard body against mine, the way my dress whispers and flows over my legs.

By the time the music ends, the dance floor has filled with a few other couples. We clap for the musicians and I feel flushed and happy.

"May I cut in?" a familiar voice says behind us.

I turn to see Jared standing there in a tux, a funny kind of smirk tugging at his lips. I want to refuse, but Jared extends a hand toward me. Rudy has a question in his eyes, and I know I could say no if I wanted to, but in the interest of not causing a scene, I incline my head. "Sure."

Rudy backs away from us and is immediately accosted by a few elderly ladies who paw and fawn over him like it's their job.

"So, you and Rudy, huh?" Jared puts his hand on my waist and pulls me closer than I'd like.

I put a few inches of space between us again. "Me and Rudy," I repeat noncommittally. The music starts, and Jared starts leading me through the steps of a dance with practiced ease. Maybe they had to take classes at rich-boy school.

"I hadn't realized he was seeing anyone." He spins me, and I have to admit he's competent, but he doesn't have the same grace as Rudy.

When he tugs me back against his body, I pop a brow. "I hadn't realized it was your job to know."

A flash crosses the man's eyes, then his lips curl into a dangerous smirk. "You could do better, you know." The music swells, and we glide through other couples.

"Let me guess. With you?"

"Your words, not mine," he answers with a laugh. Then he spins me again and pulls me hard against his chest. I pull away again, but it makes me stumble in the dance. I bump into an old couple and have to apologize.

"When I saw you at the restaurant, I had no idea you'd clean up this well," he says, his lips near my ear. "But why would a beautiful, classy woman like you want a guy like Rudy? You must have heard that he never lasts more than a few weeks with a woman? How many other chicks does he have on the side? He's just using you, Lily."

His words needle at a worry that shouldn't even exist. Rudy and I are not exclusive; it doesn't matter if he's going on dates with other women.

But...it *does* matter. It bothers me a lot.

I jerk away from him and narrowly miss banging into another couple. "I'm not doing this." I spin around and clomp off the dance floor, searching the room for Rudy.

I find him chatting with Agnes and feel a wave of relief when she turns her scowling face to look at me. "How the hell did you get stuck dancing with Jared the Dolt? There's something wrong with that boy. I keep telling Nancy about it but she won't listen."

I grin, tension melting away. "Hi, Agnes."

Hank Cheswick has his half-dozen gray hairs combed over the liver-spotted skin on top of his head, and his old body is clad in a sharp tux. His twinkling eyes meet mine. "We haven't met." He extends a gnarled hand toward me and we shake just as a waiter appears with a tray full of delicate little bites of fancy-looking somethings. Hank plucks one from the tray as the waiter explains that it's some sort of Greek shrimp canapé.

"Perfect," Hank says. "I'm on a seafood diet."

Agnes snorts. "Here we go."

Cheswick winks at me. "I see food, I eat it."

Rudy throws his head back and laughs, as if it isn't the oldest dad joke in the book. Somehow, his laugh clears the last of the discomfort from my body and I find myself giggling along with him.

Rudy's arm curls around my shoulders, and I find that I like having it there. Surely he's not dating other women right now?

Where would he find the time? And why do I care? His breath ruffles my neck as he leans in to say, "Was everything okay with Jared?"

"Fine," I lie. "I just found I was sick of dancing."

He pulls away and stares at me for a moment, then nods. There's a strange look in his eyes that he clears as soon as Agnes says something to catch his attention.

If someone had told me that Agnes and Mr. Cheswick would look at home at some fancy charity gala, I wouldn't have believed it. But both of them expertly navigate the conversations of people that drift in and out of our little circle, and I find myself relaxing and even enjoying myself.

When Mr. Cheswick convinces Agnes to dance—after many protests from her that I think might be exaggerated, based on the grace she displays on the dance floor—Rudy smiles and takes my hand. He tugs me through the crowd of tuxedo- and gown-clad people glittering with jewels and expensive accessories, out through a glass door that leads onto the wooden pier.

"I'm wearing heels," I warn him. "So either walk slow or risk me getting stuck between these slats."

Instead of answering, Rudy just bends over and picks me up like a groom carrying his bride. I yelp, arms hooking around his neck, and he brings me down to the end of the pier. By the time he sets me down again—carefully, making sure my feet are solidly on the wide planks of wood—I'm laughing so hard my cheeks hurt.

Rudy's hands linger on my waist, his thumbs sweeping soft arcs that brush the bottom of my ribs. "I like this," he says softly, eyeing my dress. "Soft."

"Velvet," I explain as I let my hands rest on his arms. His tuxedo jacket is unbuttoned and I can see the strong body beneath it. "It's my sister's," I add. "She's a lot more glamorous than I am."

"Could have fooled me." His eyes are on mine now, and soft pressure from his hands makes me take a step closer to him. My hands slide up to his shoulders and I distract myself from the pounding in my chest by straightening his bowtie.

Waves lap at the timber pier as yachts bob up and down in the water beyond. The bay arcs around us, with lights from houses dotted on the dark landscape. It feels like we're the only people in the world.

"Thank you for coming," Rudy says in the soft silence. "This is the most fun I've had at one of these things in a long time."

When his eyes drop to my lips, my breath hitches. The fabric of my dress doesn't shield me from the heat of his hands as they wrap around to the small of my back. My body grows taut, the soft fabric of my gown suddenly feeling rough. The lace cups of my bra abrade my skin as Rudy tugs me closer and presses his chest to mine.

Every time I'm with Rudy, I forget myself. I forget the promises I made to myself ten—nearly eleven weeks ago. I forget what it felt like to see the father of my child walk away. I forget that the grim reaper might tap my shoulder any minute and rip all this away from me.

I forget about the secrets that made me run home to my family, because all that matters is the feel of his fingers digging into my hips and the way his eyes darken at the sight of me.

I swore off men when my last partner walked—ran—away. And look at me now. Arms around another man's neck, feeling ten years younger and a lot healthier than I truly am.

Rudy's arms are a warm cage that I don't want to escape. When his hands move lower to rest on the swell of my ass, I don't pull away. I crave it. Crave him.

His head dips, and I know he's going to kiss me.

If we'd only had the one date, I think I would've been able to walk away. We could have slept together, and it would have been casual. But as Rudy's tongue darts out to moisten his lips and my heart beats a rapid drum inside my chest, I know this kiss will ruin me.

Thankfully, when his lips are a fraction of an inch from mine, close enough to feel his breath ghosting across my cheek, a voice calls out his name.

"We're about to do the champagne pour, Rudy!" Agnes's voice carries to us, sharp and unyielding. I wouldn't be surprised if people in the houses on either side of the bay can hear her too.

Rudy closes his eyes for a moment and rests his forehead against mine. Then he pulls away to answer, "We're coming!"

Agnes grumbles something, but it's too quiet to hear the words. I have a feeling she knew what she was interrupting, though. Part of me wants to throttle her—and the other part wants to thank her.

"To be continued," Rudy says grimly, clamping his hand around mine.

"That sounds like a threat more than a promise," I quip, arching a brow at him to hide how much the moment rocked me. If I'm snarky, at least it hides the tremble in my voice.

"Maybe it is," he answers in a soft growl, that roguish grin returning to his lips. "I guess you'll find out."

With the heat of his words lingering, I turn to walk back to the party. By some miracle, I manage to make it all the way back without losing a heel to the pier's wooden slats.

TEN

LILY

THE CHAMPAGNE POUR IS A TRADITION, I'm told, that marks the start of the silent auction. What looks like hundreds of champagne coupes are arranged in a crystal tower on one side of the room. The hundred or so guests are arranged in a loose semi-circle around the tower as a crisply uniformed waitress stands on a step stool holding the largest bottle of champagne I've ever seen. Another worker, a young man, stands on another step stool supporting the bottom of the massive bottle.

"That's called a Nebuchadnezzar bottle," Rudy says in my ear, his body pressed up against the back of mine from where he guided me through the throng of guests. "It holds the equivalent of twenty standard bottles of champagne."

"Seems excessive," I answer in a low voice.

I feel Rudy's smile against my cheek more than I see it. "It is."

We shuffle a bit closer as more people crowd in. Rudy leads me to the left of the tower of glasses. The light plays on the crystal as the two workers shift their grip on the huge bottle of champagne.

Rudy's aunt steps in front of the delicate tower of crystal, and a hush falls over the audience. Nancy seems perfectly comfortable in front of the crowd, her hands clasped gently in front of her stomach as her multitude of diamonds glitter at her neck, wrist, fingers, and ears. Suddenly, my delicate pendant doesn't seem so over the top.

"Thank you all for coming," Nancy says in a voice that feels quiet but carries to the far reaches of the room. "Your generosity tonight will go to help not one but three elephant sanctuaries in Kenya and will help fight the scourge of poachers in the region."

She pauses for polite applause, and I know she's made many of these speeches before.

"We will open the silent auction after the champagne pour. I encourage you to be generous, and don't be afraid to outbid your best friend or your own mother."

I smile as a laugher sounds in one corner of the crowd. There must be some inside joke there, but I'm more focused on the feel of Rudy's hands on my arms. When his aunt started talking, he moved to grip my biceps, and now his hands are stroking my arms slowly, torturously, and I wonder if he craves the feel of my skin as much as I seem to crave his.

Leaning against the hard wall of his body, I let myself relax. Nancy's voice lulls me as she stands in front of the audience of rich yacht owners, delivering a speech with practiced ease. I don't belong here—I know that. Not only is my net worth probably small enough to get me turned away at the door on a regular occasion, but my life itself has been the opposite of what this represents. I've been a nomad. I've lived out of a suitcase for most of my adult years; none of the things I've wanted have been silent auctions with people dripping in jewels.

But for now, it feels good. Maybe it's the fact that Rudy radiates safety. That with him—if nowhere else—I feel at peace. I don't have to think of yesterday or tomorrow, unless it's to imagine what it'll feel like when we finally kiss again. His hands sweep up and down my arms, moving up over my shoulders and sending shivers coursing down my body. His fingers brush my collarbones, a spot on my body I hadn't realized was erogenous until this very moment. My skin tingles from my chest down to my navel, my nipples tightening at the featherlight touch of his hands.

Eyes half-closed, I listen to another successful joke land with the audience, followed by Nancy's direction for the two waiters to start pouring champagne. With the audience gasping, champagne starts pouring out of the massive bottle and down the tower of glasses, spilling over and down in a cascade of bubbles and excess. I watch the bottle tip higher, more golden liquid filling another glass, and another, and another, until the entire tower of glasses is spilling with the golden drink. All the while, Rudy's fingers dance over my shoulders, my collarbones, my arms. When his thumb traces the strap of my dress, I can't help the way I soften against him. He's turning my body to jelly in a room full of people, and I can't quite remember why that should bother me.

That's the reason I'm not braced for the collision.

Between one breath and the next, I go from relaxed and a little turned on to off-balance and stumbling. The hem of my dress gets caught in my stupid spike heel, and I can't take a step. Rudy grabs my waist, but he's as off-balance as me. When his hands wrap around my middle, the momentum of his body sends us both crashing into the tower of crystal and champagne, just as the last drops are poured from the huge Nebuchadnezzar bottle.

I fall on the floor, crushing the table that held the tower of glasses, and the sound of shattering crystal echoes along with gasps from the guests. Rudy, through some sort of masculine-strength-induced voodoo, manages to yank me at the last moment and shield most of my fall. He lands mostly underneath me with only the sharp bite of broken glass eating against my arm. Champagne sloshes and falls to cover us both in sticky shards of glass.

For a few heartbeats, I lie still.

Rudy is beneath me, his arm clamped around my waist. I'm gripping his tuxedo as a drip of champagne runs down the side of my neck. Rudy's cheek is bleeding and when I use my hand to turn his chin in order to check the wound, I notice my arm and hand is sliced too.

Blinking rapidly, I stare at the blood, the glass, then at Rudy's face.

"You okay?" Concern is written all over his features, his arm still banding tight across my back, his other hand cupped over my cheek.

I do a quick inventory of my body. A sharp stab of worry

pierces through me when I think of the baby, but when I feel nothing more than the ache of the cuts on my arm, I nod. "Yeah. I think so. For someone with such a hard body, you make an okay cushion."

Tension leaves him in a whoosh, and his lips tilt into that smile that makes my knees go weak.

Then, as if a spell has been broken, I hear Nancy calling out orders as dozens of hands reach over to help the two of us up. Two unfamiliar male hands lift me right off Rudy and when I'm standing, I totter on my heels again. Stupid things. The strange hands on my arms linger until Rudy glances over my shoulder with a hard expression on his face.

"What the fuck was that about? I felt you push me."

Jared's hands drop from my arms as I turn, and he throws up both his palms. "Someone nudged me, man. It was an accident."

Rudy's jaw clenches as a bead of blood trickles down his cheek. I've never seen him like this—angry. Fearsome. He has one arm curled protectively around my shoulders as he takes half a step to put the bulk of his body between me and his cousin.

His cousin's girlfriend curls her hand around Jared's arm, her eyes flicking between the two men. Jared ignores her. My gaze snaps to Rudy, who swears quietly and viciously. Jared bristles but says nothing.

I find myself turned on by the fury written on Rudy's face, and then I wonder what the hell is wrong with me.

The easygoing Rudy is the one I was first attracted to. The man behind the bookstore desk with laughing eyes and a mischievous smile. That's the man I laughed with as the sun went down while we ate fish and chips. That's the man who asked me for salted caramel brownies as he worked on the community garden.

This Rudy is entirely different. I find myself noticing just how much taller and stronger he is than me. How much I like the way his arm is still wrapped around my shoulders and how he seems angrier that I could have been hurt than the fact that he's clearly bleeding from multiple injuries.

"Wait until Dorothy hears about this," Agnes grumbles as she elbows her way to the eye of the storm. At four feet, nine inches, Agnes should not take up as much room as she does. The woman is made of iron and acid, and her mere presence seems to make everyone give us a wide berth. She manages to look down her nose at Jared for a long moment, until he drops his eyes and takes a step back.

"I'm sorry, Aunt Agnes. It was an accident. Someone bumped me and I bumped into Rudy."

Agnes says nothing. She stares him down for another long moment, then snorts. Just like that, Jared is dismissed. Agnes turns to Rudy and me, arches a brow at the lines of red carved into his cheek, his neck, his hands. She grips Rudy's chin and turns his head, making a low, harsh noise at the sight of his blood. Then she turns to me and takes my hand, turning it this way and that to assess the damage.

Without Rudy's presence beside me, I feel suddenly bare. I'm sticky with champagne, my arm is bloody, I know my face and hair are a mess, and it's possible I've ruined Trina's dress.

Even worse, the eyes of all the guests are on me, and I can almost hear their whispers.

I close my eyes against the humiliation of it all.

Rudy must notice, because he disengages my hand from Agnes's and leads me to the edge of the room and down a hallway. Within moments, he's pushing open the door to a unisex bathroom. Unsurprisingly, it's gorgeous. The vanity is long and looks like real stone, white interspersed with pink and grey veins. The taps are a trendy matte black, the soaps look expensive, and there are soft-looking towels rolled and stacked in a basket beside the sink.

Rudy turns the lock on the door and points to the vanity. "Sit."

When I don't move, he just grabs my waist and lifts me onto the counter himself. Then he leans over and produces a first aid kit from underneath the vanity, placing it on the other side of the sink.

"We should check you first," I say, even though Rudy is already opening the first-aid kit and sorting through its contents until he finds a pair of tweezers in a sterilized packet. He opens it up without even deigning to answer. Then he begins a thorough, methodical examination of my injuries. First, he checks the half-dozen cuts on my forearm and hand for shards of glass. He plucks two tiny pieces out of the largest cut and places them on the counter, his face set in absolute concentration.

This is new to me—having someone look after me. I've been on my own a long time, but even the last few boyfriends I had wouldn't have reacted like this. For all I call myself a strong, independent woman, I find myself enjoying this moment with Rudy.

The last time I was vulnerable with a man was when I told my ex-boyfriend about the baby. We'd been dating for only ten months, but it felt like so much longer. We'd talked about him coming here, meeting my family. We'd talked about the future. I'd been living in Milan for twice that length of time and had fallen into a whirlwind romance with a man who was in Italy on a work assignment. Phil was a fabric supplier for all the major fashion houses, so he was always flitting between Paris and Milan and London and New York and any other fashion mecca, seeing me every few weeks and promising me the world.

I thought I was in love with him, which was not my brightest moment. It was only after I told him about the baby that he admitted he had a wife and three kids back home in Paris. I didn't even know he had a home other than his apartment in Milan. That's how blind I was. We'd dated for *ten months*, and I had no idea I was the other woman.

When I told him I was keeping the baby, he walked out and hasn't spoken to me since.

I suppose it would have been devastating, if not for the news I got a week later. The news that I haven't even been able to face, even though the reality of it looms like a black cloud. Since then, I haven't been able to catch my breath.

Until now.

Rudy runs clean water over my forearm and hand, patting it dry with a white towel that's soon streaked with pink. He places bandages over every cut, smoothing them down over my skin with more care than I'd have for myself. Then, when it's over, he lifts my palm up and places a kiss in the center of it.

"I'm sorry," he says quietly.

"Don't be ridiculous," I answer. "Is there another pair of sterilized tweezers in there?" I jerk my head to the first-aid kit. "Seems to me it's your turn."

Rudy holds my gaze for a moment, then rustles through the kit for another pair of tweezers. Still sitting on the counter, my knees having spread open at some point to let him inspect my body, I nod to his jacket. Without a word, Rudy removes it and stretches to hang it on a hook behind the door. He keeps his hips firmly planted between my thighs.

Blood has soaked into the collar and cuffs of his shirt. Gently, I undo his bowtie and unbutton the top three buttons of his shirt. I try to stop myself from inhaling sharply as a triangle of bronzed male skin is exposed at his throat. My hands, thankfully, manage to stay steady as I start my own methodical examination of his injuries.

Rudy took the brunt of the damage. Besides the champagne drying in his hair and making his skin sticky, both his hands, his neck, and his cheek have been cut. He leans his palms against the counter as I start with his face, using a clean towel to wipe the dried blood away once I've checked for shards of glass.

Thankfully, the cuts on his face and neck are shallow nicks, and there are no pieces of glass. Once they're cleaned and bandaged, I ignore the movement of his chest with every hitched breath and I try not to think about the scent of his cologne embedded in my nose.

This feels intimate. I'm not sure the way I'm tending to his injuries is exactly medical, either. My fingers might have drifted over his cheek a little more softly than I intended. I might have stared at the shape of his lips for a moment too long.

When I take his left hand, Rudy winces. I give him a sharp look, then pinch my lips at the sight of the bloody piece of glass in the largest cut.

All thoughts of intimacy and lips leave my mind as I use the second pair of sterilized tweezers to rid his wounds of glass, then clean and bandage his hands. He stands between my spread knees, stoic, still. Neither of us says anything.

It's better that way. I'm not sure I'd be able to speak, anyway.

The last of the bandages feels rough under my fingertips as I smooth it over the back of his palm. His cuffs have been rolled up to reveal strong forearms, his shirt open at the neck in a way that feels more undressed than if he weren't wearing a shirt at all.

When I finally find the courage to lift my eyes to meet Rudy's, I know I've already lost the battle against my own self-control. His bandaged hand cups my jaw as he tilts his head up to mine, his other hand resting so high on my thigh his thumb might be brushing against the edge of my panties through the black velvet of my dress.

Without saying a word, Rudy kisses me. There's no hesitation in the way his lips claim mine, in how his hand tightens over my neck and jaw, in the way he crowds me against the mirror. I find myself clinging to his shoulders and pulling him closer, deepening the kiss until I lose myself in his touch.

This is better than the first time.

A growl rides out through his lips, a very masculine noise that comes from the back of his throat. The hand on my thigh moves to my hip, then my waist, then my ribs. When he moves to kiss my jaw, I tilt my head and close my eyes, gulping down breaths as my hands scramble to unbutton his shirt and push it off his shoulders.

Rudy's lips find mine as he rips his shirt out of his pants, helping me with the last of the buttons. The shirt falls away and his hands are on me again, as hungry as his mouth.

He cups my breasts, and a dart of panic makes me freeze.

Rudy immediately lifts his head. "What's wrong?" His eyes search mine, a little wild.

I shake my head and swallow a breath. "Nothing." It's a lie, but the truth is worse.

The frantic need that had gripped us a moment ago seems to ease out of both of us. I put my hands on his chest and trace the hard muscles of his body, closing my eyes as he kisses me again more tenderly. When he touches my breast again, I manage to keep my body from seizing, but Rudy must still feel something in the energy between us, because he drops his palms to the counter on either side of my hips. He leans his forehead against mine and lets out a shuddering breath.

"I'm not doing this here," he tells me quietly. "Not with my entire extended family in the other room. Not when you feel like a scared rabbit every time I touch you."

I pull away and arch a brow. "A scared rabbit? I'm a forty-year-old woman, Rudy."

"A forty-year-old scared rabbit," he amends, then chuckles at the look on my face.

I open my mouth to explain why I reacted that way to his hand on my breast—but nothing comes out. The words are there, on the tip of my tongue, but I just can't make them come. Relenting, I straighten up and nod to the crumple of white fabric on the ground. "You think your shirt survived the evening?"

Still standing between my spread knees, he glances at the bloodstained shirt on the floor. His hands move to my thighs as he gives me a gentle squeeze, then he leans over to pick it up. After he flicks his wrists to straighten the shirt with a snap, turning it this way and that to inspect it, he gives me a rueful glance. "Barely."

After sliding his arms into the shirt, he leaves it open and turns to me. Strong hands wrap around my waist as he lifts me off the counter and deposits me gently on the floor, his bare chest brushing against the soft fabric of my dress. His finger tilts my chin up, and he kisses me gently.

Even in the soft brush of his lips against mine, I feel a fire burning low in my gut. It's like my body is fully attuned to his, and any touch can make me melt.

Then, we're both busying ourselves cleaning up first-aid detritus and straightening our clothes. The reflection that stares back at me in the mirror is one of a flushed woman with bright eyes. I brush my fingers through my hair and do my best to tame the hairspray-and-champagne-soaked mess, then tug my dress to straighten it over my chest.

I don't know what the hell I'm going to tell Trina about her dress. The truth, I guess. Knowing her and her cackling coven of girlfriends, they'll probably think it's funny.

When my hands brush the curves of my breasts, my throat tightens. But I shake the thought away and turn to face Rudy, who's straightening the cuffs of his shirt to let them poke out of the black tuxedo jacket.

His gaze meets mine. "Ready?"

Suddenly nervous about facing a room full of people after falling into a tower of champagne glasses and making out with a man six years my junior, I nod and manage to keep my voice neutral. "Let's do it."

ELEVEN
NORA

THE LAST OF my boxes is finally unpacked. It took me nearly a month to get my new apartment set up, but it feels good to be here. I've made a few trips over and back from Reno, transitioning to a full-time work-from-home arrangement. Well, mostly full-time. There seem to be more mandatory meetings in the office than I remember ever having before.

My mother straightens up from putting a mug in the dishwasher and glances at me from the kitchen, arching a brow at the box at my feet. "Is that the last of them?"

"I'm officially a resident of Heart's Cove," I say with a smile. I can smell Ma's famous carrot cake baking in the oven, and my mouth waters. She knows it's my favorite, and she said she made it to celebrate me moving in—which I understood to mean that I needed to unpack every last box if I expected to eat any.

She tilts her head, studying my face. "You like it here."

"If you stick around more than a week, you might start liking it too."

My mother waves a hand, but there's a grin on her face. I'm driving her back to Tahoe in a few days' time, and now that I'm settled into my new place, I'm sure she feels more comfortable going back. My mother might let Fallon and me live our own lives, but she's got a protective streak a mile wide.

I know part of the reason she's staying here has to do with Fallon too, of course. The two of them have been spending time together for the first time in two decades. Her staying with me doesn't fool me—she just wanted to give Fallon enough space to retreat if he didn't want to see her.

What my mother doesn't understand is that Fallon pushed her away because he was ashamed of *himself*, not her. Since he met Jen, that's changed.

A knock on the door draws our attention. I cross the small, open-plan living room to unlock the door, only to see Dorothy and Margaret, the two ladies who own the Heart's Cove Hotel, on the other side. They're both wearing leather jackets.

"Someone let us in downstairs," Margaret says after nodding to me to explain how she and her sister bypassed the buzzer. She glances over my shoulder. "Hamish wanted to know if you wanted to go for a ride, Prisha."

My mother frowns. "A ride? Who's Hamish?"

"Hamish is my lover," Margaret says in that confident, nonplussed way that older people use the word *lover*. "And he rides motorcycles." She steps inside and closes the door behind her.

To my surprise, my mother's eyes spark with interest. "A motorcycle? I've never ridden a motorcycle before."

"You'll love it." Dorothy bustles past me and hooks her arm through my mother's to start tugging her to the door, then pauses. "You'll need closed-toed shoes. Actually, you'll need to change out of that dress and into jeans. You can borrow my jacket and helmet."

"You ride motorcycles as well?"

Dorothy straightens up. "I'm learning. Doing the test for my license next week."

My eyes bug. "Really?"

Dorothy turns on me with an arched brow. "Are you so surprised that an old woman like me could try something that's supposed to be reserved for younger men?"

I throw my palms up at the challenge in her tone. "Of course not. I think it's great."

Dorothy settles back and gives me an impish grin. "I'm planning a custom paint job for my new bike. Hamish, Mac, and Lee will help me pick one out, and their man at the body shop, Remy Something-or-Other, said he knows someone who can paint it the way I want."

"Dorothy's very proud that she'll have the only motorcycle in Heart's Cove with a leopard-print body," her sister cuts in, mirth dancing in her eyes.

I exchange a glance with my mother, and when I see the question in her gaze, I shrug. "It's up to you, Ma. You want to go for a ride with Hamish?"

There's a moment of silence, then a smile breaks over my mother's face that makes her look ten years younger than she is.

"I'll go get changed. Nora, if I'm not back in time, can you take the cake out of the oven when the timer goes off?"

"Sure, Ma. No problem."

When the door closes on the bedroom, Margaret gives me a nod. "I like her."

It shouldn't please me as much as it does that these women like my mother. Maybe I inherited a protective streak from my mother.

Re-emerging in jeans and sensible shoes, my mother and I follow the twins down the stairs to the ground floor. On my way past, I glance at the door across the hall from mine, but I haven't heard Lily come back from her date. Earlier, I was just hauling a few broken-down boxes to the recycling bin in the basement when her sisters and friends came spilling out of the door and told me all about her upcoming evening with Rudy. I hadn't even realized we'd be neighbors, but the thought pleases me. I'll have to pry details of her date out of her tomorrow morning. Maybe I can bribe her with fresh carrot cake.

The ladies and I spill out onto the sidewalk to see half a dozen motorcycles parked up against the curb. The men are huddled near my building, two of them leaning against the brick with one leg pulled up. A toothless man holds a cigarette and laughs at something one of the older men said.

I recognize Mac, Trina's partner. He's wearing a leather jacket, black jeans, and motorcycle boots, and he looks very, very sexy. When Trina told me he was a second-grade teacher, I thought she was pulling my leg. And when she told me he also did pottery and was almost famous because he was so good at it, I was sure she was making fun of me somehow. Then I found out it was all true and I just felt jealous of her—in the best possible way.

Beside him is the second of the younger men, and he looks similar enough to Mac that he could be related. A brother, maybe. Despite myself, I notice that he's tall, muscular, and he has very nice eyes that happen to be roaming over me from my feet up to my face.

I think I saw him at the community garden, but he certainly wasn't looking at me like *that*. Like I'm a special treat that he can't wait to devour.

I arch my brows at the pack of badass biker dudes waiting for the little old ladies from the hotel. "You all came here to see my mother?" Something warm slides through my chest at the thought that these women would come here with the sole intention of inviting my mother along for a motorcycle ride.

"I'm a slave to my woman's wishes," a salt-and-pepper (mostly salt) haired man says, making moon eyes at Margaret. That must be Hamish.

"You. Mac." Dorothy thrusts her finger at Trina's partner. "Give Prisha a helmet. She's riding with you. Nora, are you coming along? We're going to get ice cream."

For some reason, the thought of these six burly men riding with a contingent of elderly ladies at their backs going to get ice cream, of all things, makes me laugh. I start shaking my head— but before I can say anything, Dorothy's phone rings.

She makes a little "Oo!" sound and shuffles through her crossbody bag for her phone. Squinting at the screen, she turns it toward me. "I haven't got my glasses, dear. What does that say?"

"It says 'Lily,'" I read.

"Well, what could Lily possibly want?" Dorothy swipes her finger across the screen, and Lily's face appears. "Aren't you supposed to be rubbing elbows with rich, snotty people?" Dorothy asks instead of greeting Lily like a normal person.

Lily is laughing. "Dor, you've got to see this."

The camera flips to show total carnage. There's broken glass all over the ground that workers are hurriedly sweeping up, and in the middle of the mess is Agnes, Dorothy's sworn enemy. The small woman has her index finger in a younger man's face, and she's stringing together swear words and insults in a way that makes my eyebrows climb higher and higher with every word.

Lily's voice sounds, but the camera stays pointed at the scene. "They were doing the champagne pour—you know, like a tower of glasses and they pour champagne so it flows down and fills every one?"

Dorothy snorts as the rest of us—burly motorcycle men and all—crowd around. "Wasteful, but yes, I understand."

"Well, Rudy was standing behind me and someone bumped him, so he bumped me. Anyway, that happened." Her hand appears in the screen as she points to the smashed glasses. There are bandages all over her arm and hand. "Rudy and I went to clean up"—did her voice sound strange when she said that?—"and we came back to see Agnes ripping her grand-nephew a new one. Apparently, she got him to admit that he bumped into Rudy on purpose because I wouldn't dance with him."

"You should be ashamed of yourself, you, you, you

cockroach!" Agnes's voice rises another octave, and her grand-nephew cowers. "*We all put up with these silent auctions every year and being here is torture enough.*" She takes a step toward the man. "*You see those cuts you put on my grandson's skin? You see them?*" She thrusts a finger off-screen.

"*Agnes, I'm sorry. I didn't mean it.*"

"*And then you lie to me!*" The terrifying, tiny old woman stomps her foot, and it looks like she's about to charge like a bull.

"Oh," Dorothy says with a Cheshire-cat grin on her face. "This is fantastic."

"I know, right? I knew you'd enjoy it." Lily sounds like she's holding back a laugh.

"The Hag isn't so bad when you aim her at someone else," Dorothy replies sagely.

Margaret just rolls her eyes. I meet my mother's gaze and shrug.

"Anyway, as soon as Rudy can make sure his grandmother isn't going to murder Jared, we'll be on our way back." The camera flips around to reveal Lily's broad smile and dancing eyes. "Just thought you'd like that."

"I did, sweetheart," Dorothy replies. "And so did everyone else." She sweeps the camera at the assembled crowd of seniors and motorcycle riders, and we all wave.

Lily laughs. "I haven't had this much fun in months. Years, maybe. I'll see you tomorrow."

Dorothy hangs up with that wide smile still clinging to her lips. She meets my eyes and arches her brows. "See? Aren't you glad you moved here? Much more fun than stinky Reno."

"You've never been to Reno, Dorothy," Margaret cuts in. "How do you know it's stinky? I've heard it's lovely."

"You know what's lovely? Ice cream." Dorothy marches toward one of the bikes and pulls a helmet on. "Nora, are you coming?"

My eyes dart to the crowd, to my mother, who has already acquired a helmet and is pulling it on, and I shake my head. "There's a cake in the oven. Maybe some other time."

For some reason, my eyes drift to the man who looks related to Mac. His eyes meet mine and linger for a moment, until the roar of the first motorcycle snaps me out of my stupor. Clenching my fists to hide the trembling in my hands, I smile and nod at the departing motorcycles.

His is navy blue, I note, with subtle smoke swirling over the body in slightly lighter shades. A very pretty motorcycle. Masculine, yet unique.

Mac's probably-a-brother leaves last and I find myself tracing the blue swirls on his bike—until I snap my eyes up to his face and realize he caught me staring.

Giving him a dorky wave, I try to ignore the insistent thumping of my heart. He guns the engine, then takes off down the road after everyone else. I stand on the sidewalk until he's out of sight. Then I head back upstairs to wait for the cake to finish baking.

TWELVE
LILY

AFTER RUDY MADE sure his grandmother wasn't going to commit homicide with a room full of witnesses, we snuck away and drove to our now-favorite fish-and-chips spot, both agreeing that we didn't feel like sticking around the yacht club for dinner. The food was great, and the company was better. When I kicked my heels off under the table, Rudy picked one up to inspect it. "I guess I can admit they look uncomfortable," he told me. "But they're hot as hell."

"If they look so great, maybe you should wear them," I'd shot back, then immediately clamped my mouth shut. That was exactly the type of comment my ex would have sneered at. He always thought I was too classless to understand *fashun*, which irked me. I understand it just fine—I'm just not that interested.

But Rudy just laughed at my quip and told me I had a point.

Now, as we drive back to Heart's Cove with nothing but the soft sounds of the radio filling the car, I let out a happy sigh.

Tonight was fun—more fun than I expected. But when I think of what happened in the bathroom, dread curls in my gut.

Since Rudy gave me that last kiss right before he opened the bathroom door, he hasn't touched me. Even when we left the restaurant and he lingered at my car door, he didn't lean down and kiss me even though it was obvious we both wanted it to happen.

And I know why.

It's because of the way I reacted in the bathroom. He sensed my stress when he touched me, and he backed off. But the problem, I realize with a start, is that I don't want him to back off.

I should just let him walk away. This is supposed to be casual, and since we're obviously not going to have no-strings-attached sex—judging by how much we enjoy each other's company—it should end now.

"Open the glove compartment," Rudy says suddenly.

I frown, glancing at him.

His eyes are on the road, but I can tell his attention is on me. So, I press the button that has the glove compartment popping open. Inside, a book-shaped object is wrapped in gold paper.

"Happy belated birthday," he says. "I only heard about it afterward, otherwise I would've called on Wednesday."

"I was trying to pretend it wasn't happening," I explain, even if my pulse jumps. "I keep thinking that if I pretend I haven't hit forty, it won't be true."

Rudy's lips tilt as I turn the present over my hand. "What's wrong with being forty? Seems to me like it'd be the best decade of them all. Everyone's twenties are a mess. In your thirties you might find your footing and make some strides, but you might still wander and stumble. Your forties are when you know yourself and you know what you want. You should be happy that the messy years are behind you."

Ha! Right. If only he knew. I have a feeling my messy years are very much ahead.

"Now how could a thirty-four-year-old man possibly have any idea what it's like to be a forty-year-old woman?" I arch a brow, then drop my gaze to the present again. Something tightens in my chest. "You didn't have to get me anything."

"Open it."

"You shouldn't have done this," I chide, and I mean it. All week I've been telling myself that my dinner with Rudy was just a bit of fun, that this evening at the charity auction was a favor to stick it to his cousin. I've dismissed the memory of the community garden, and how it felt to have Rudy's hand squeezing mine. I've ignored the memory of our kiss, except when I'm alone in my bed at night with only my vibrator to keep me company.

I'm the one who said this was casual. No past, no future, no talk of relationships. Those were the rules.

People who are dating casually don't get each other birthday presents.

Still, I pull at the bow to remove it and tear open the wrapping paper. A beautifully embossed hardcover book appears, and my breath catches.

"You told me you didn't like fairy tales because they were unrealistic and fluffy," Rudy says. "I thought *Grimms' Fairy Tales* might be more your speed."

Despite myself, a smile curls my lips. "Are you saying I'm dark and twisted?"

"Hmm," Rudy says, his hand sliding from the steering wheel to the gearshift. I love his hands, broad and graceful with long fingers. He keeps his eyes on the road. "In the version by the Brothers Grimm, Cinderella's evil stepsisters cut off their toes and heels with a knife to fit the shoe. The blood soaking their stockings is what makes the prince notice he hasn't found his princess. In the end, the stepsisters get their eyes pecked out by pigeons and live the rest of their lives in blindness. Is that dark and twisted, or is it poetic justice?"

I can't help it, I laugh. "What about Rapunzel?" I ask. "She doesn't kill the witch by cutting off her hair and letting her fall to her death—the witch casts her out of the tower, then tricks the prince into coming up to the top of the tower so she can push him out the window. He ends up blind as well, as far as I remember, and nothing ever happens to the witch at all. All because Rapunzel's father wanted to feed his pregnant wife from the witch's garden. A cautionary tale about pregnancy cravings, maybe?"

Rudy's smile creases his cheeks. "But the prince finds Rapunzel, and when she cries on his face, he regains his sight." Rudy glances at me with a grin. "If that's not a happy ending, I don't know what is."

My lips twitch. "Sounds like the Grimm brothers had an obsession with blindness."

Rudy's laugh is warm and rich, and it feels like a blanket wrapped around my shoulders. He shrugs. "Maybe."

I open the book and let my fingers run over the thick pages, tracing the words. "This is beautiful. Thank you."

Rudy hums. "Grimms' fairy tales aren't so popular at story time, but I like them best of all. I found that edition a few years ago in a small bookshop in Boston when I was there on a vacation. Didn't know why I was so drawn to it, but when I learned it was your birthday this week, it felt..." He clamps his lips shut and shakes his head, snorting. "Never mind. Maybe I should stop reading so many fairy tales myself."

It felt what, I wonder? Like he'd bought that book years ago to give specifically to me?

My throat is suddenly tight. This is bad. This is very, very bad. It's been a bad idea from the moment I veered off course and entered the bookstore.

The car slows as Rudy takes an exit, and I fight to keep my breathing under control. When we roll into the Heart's Cove town limits, I know I can't push Rudy away without at least an explanation. He pulls up to my building and cuts the engine while my fingers are still tracing the swirls and floral patterns etched into the front cover of the book.

"Rudy," I start, then stop. The pause between us stretches.

"Walk with me." He arches his brows. "It's easier to walk and talk."

I huff, then nod. "Fine."

Like a true gentleman, Rudy opens my door for me and helps me out. My dress and skin are still sticky, but I hook my arm in his and let him lead me down Cove Boulevard. We walk in silence for a few moments until we turn into the new community garden. Doing a slow turn of the space, we pause near the new lattice. Rudy slides his hands over my hips and faces me.

"Look, Lily, you don't have to say anything. I'm sorry if I made you uncomfortable in the bathroom; that wasn't my intention. I won't push you to do anything you don't want to do, but I have to be honest and say that I want to see you again. We don't have to talk about the future and you don't have to tell me anything about why you want to keep it casual."

His words are soft, soothing. Something cracks inside me, some hard shell that had calcified around my heart sometime over the past months, years, decades. All the thoughts I had earlier melt away, and the last thing I want is for Rudy to walk away from me.

"You don't have to tell me what was going through your mind when I touched you, and I'm truly sorry if I made you uncomfortable. I don't—"

"I have cancer," I blurt, surprised the words came so easily when I've barely been able to even think them.

Rudy's hands tighten on my hips as I stare at his bowtie hanging undone on either side of his collar. I don't look at Rudy's face, but I hear the sharp intake of breath and feel the silence settle over us like a weight.

"You... Wait, what?"

I close my eyes. This time, it takes an effort to push the words past my lips. "Breast cancer. I found out about it nine weeks ago, give or take. Right after..." I stop myself. Right after I found out I was pregnant. But I can't say that, can I? I should. I know I should. I should be completely honest with Rudy, but one bombshell might be enough for the night.

Plus, we're not supposed to be talking about the future. People dating casually don't talk about future plans. Even though I'm breaking that rule by telling him about the cancer, I can pretend that's just to explain my reaction in the bathroom when he touched my chest.

That's what I tell myself, anyway.

I take a deep breath. "No one knows except my medical team. I came back here for treatment, but I've been too much of a coward to tell my family." I gulp, still letting my fingers run over his shoulders, avoiding his gaze. "I'm not saying this so you'll pity me, I'm saying it so you'll understand." I don't want to look at Rudy's face and see anything that might hurt my tender feelings, so I just stare at his chest and soldier on. "Ever since I got the diagnosis, it's been hard to look at my body—at my breasts—and see anything other than the cancer growing inside me. When you touched me, I remembered... I remembered everything. That's why I froze. It wasn't because of you."

There's a silence that seems to last forever, but it's probably only two or three seconds. Then Rudy's gentle voice says, "Lily, will you look at me?"

I shake my head.

"No? You won't look at me?"

"If I look at you and see pity, I'll break."

I hear him let out a huff of breath that kind of sounds like a laugh. "Okay." His hands slide up to my waist. "Well, everything I said is still true. I'll take things slow. I'll wait. I won't push you."

"Rudy, I'm going to *lose my breast*. They'll cut it off, because otherwise the cancer will spread and I will *die*. They can do a reconstruction, but at best I'll be scarred. I'll have to have chemo. It will be months—years, maybe—before I feel like myself again, and that's *if* I make it. What are you talking about, taking it slow? Not pushing me? You don't want to be with me at all! I have so much baggage, I should be running an airport. You should be running away from me." I snap my head up to look at him, and to my shock, there's no pity on his face.

He looks...patient. He blinks at me, and I blink at him.

"When's your surgery? My work schedule is flexible. I could drive you to the hospital."

"I..." I frown, then shake my head. "No. No, you won't drive me. This is not the time for me to be getting involved with a man. It's going to be hard enough on my family to deal with my treatment, I'm not going to ask you to take that on. If you want to have sex, fine. We can have sex tonight and be done with it. But I'm not going to date you and drag you into my shit. This is casual. I shouldn't even be telling you anything. I just...wanted to explain."

He arches a brow. "Lily," he says, "although I very much want to have sex with you, I'm not intending to 'be done with it' after we sleep together. I'm not sure tonight is the best time for it."

Great. Now he doesn't even want to sleep with me! What the hell happened to casual? We were supposed to hook up after fish and chips, then never speak to each other again.

"You won't have sex with me? Why the hell not?" I spit the words.

I don't even know where this anger is coming from. I'm not mad at Rudy. I'm being an ass, and I hate myself for it, but I can't help it. All the terror and stress and tension in my body suddenly wants *out*, and Rudy happens to be the person in front of me.

But maybe it's more than that.

Maybe it's the fact that I told him, and he didn't react with fear or pity and false sympathy. It didn't seem to change his opinion of me at all, which is crazy. Insane. He should be pulling away from me just like my ex did. He should be turning his back on me and walking away, because that's infinitely easier than dealing with someone who's ill.

He doesn't owe me anything, and the last thing I want to do is drag him down with me.

"Are you insane?" I ask him, totally serious.

Laughter lights his eyes for a moment, but his lips don't twitch. "Not that I'm aware, why?"

"Because it doesn't seem to bother you that I'm sick."

"You'll recover." He says it with such surety, such conviction, that I suck in a breath.

That's my greatest fear, isn't it? I haven't been able to think about the tumor growing in my breast because I'm scared to death that I *won't* recover. I saw my dad get eaten up by a cancer of his own. I saw the way it ripped my mother to shreds, and how it took her a decade to recover the same laughter that filled her up before. I saw my family adjust and fuss over my dying dad and take the world on our shoulders because that's what we had to do.

I don't want to make them do that for me. Not if I'm just going to die at the end of it all.

The worst part is if it weren't for the baby, I'm not sure I would even have come back here. I had international health insurance and I was eligible for treatment in Milan. I could have stayed. I could have hidden my suffering and spared everyone from the feelings of guilt and powerlessness that come with caring for someone you love.

But it was the thought of my baby that brought me back here, that made me make sure I had people around me who would take care of my child if the worst were to happen to me.

And now there's Rudy. It would be so much easier if I didn't have these budding feelings for him—if I could just convince myself to keep him at arm's length.

I close my eyes and grip his shoulders, taking stock of my situation. Rudy knows about the cancer, but he doesn't know about the baby. Trina knows about the baby, but she doesn't know about the cancer. My mother and Candice know nothing. I have ten weeks, give or take a few, until my bump starts showing. I have two weeks until I enter my second trimester and am eligible for my mastectomy surgery.

Time is ticking. The best course of action is just to be honest with everyone. I should deal with the pity, with the fussing, with the burden that everyone will carry because of me. I'm not doing anyone any favors by hiding these things. Rudy deserves to know that we have no future—not with a baby that isn't his growing in my womb. My family deserves time to deal with this news.

"Let me walk you home," Rudy says gently, and that's what he does.

As my thoughts whirl around me, Rudy is a steady presence at my side. We pause outside my door, and I almost manage to invite Rudy upstairs.

But if I invite him up, I'll have to tell him about the baby.

He must sense my hesitation, because he just tilts my chin up with the tip of his finger and presses his lips to mine so tenderly it makes my heart clench.

"I'll call you later this week," he tells me.

"We're not supposed to care about each other like this," I blurt.

His eyes crinkle at the corners, then his face grows serious. "I don't care about the cancer, Lily. I could help you with it."

I shake my head. "I don't want that."

He freezes for a moment, then relents. "I'll wait for you to call me, then."

Stomach in my throat, I nod. We hold each other's gaze for a few moments, then I make my way upstairs to my apartment.

Alone.

I STARE at the IRS audit letter in my hands, then lift my gaze to my grandmother. "This letter is dated April 15, Grandma. Why are you only showing me this now?"

It's been nearly a week since my great-aunt's charity auction, and Lily hasn't called. We've texted a few times, but she hasn't been to the bookstore and we haven't made plans to see each other. It shouldn't bother me though, right? She has a lot of shit going on; she told me she wanted to be casual. People who date casually don't see each other every day. This is normal.

The paper in my hand crinkles as I grip it tighter, trying to tamp down my frustration. I'm not mad at my grandmother, I just feel...unsettled.

"I forgot," she huffs.

"But you conveniently remembered only a few days before the IRS agent is scheduled to get here?"

"I remembered in time, didn't I?" My grandmother crosses her arms. "What's the big deal? I always pay my taxes. I have all my records saved in the storeroom."

An involuntary shiver courses through me. I've only opened the door to the storeroom a handful of times in all the years I've helped my grandmother. It's a dark, dank room with boxes stacked to the ceiling, old tools, and various bits of furniture stuffed in so tight it's almost impossible to open the door.

"This is a field audit," I say, waving the letter. "They're not just asking for a few documents, Grandma. They're going to go through your tax return from last year with a fine-tooth comb."

"And you're going to help them." My grandmother gives me a curt nod.

"I..." Pinching the bridge of my nose, I let out a long breath. "Grandma, I'm not an accountant. I have my own business to run—an important client wants to view half a dozen properties this week. I don't have time to do this."

Georgia Neves has been so demanding I've barely had time for anything else. We've already viewed a bunch of properties, and her list of wants and needs is getting longer every time.

"Well, make time." My grandmother's face is set in a hard glare, then her shoulders soften. "You know I can't see half as well as I used to, Rudy. I need your help."

I swallow past a lump in my throat, my stomach writhing with nerves. The IRS scares the hell out of me for no reason other than I know they could demand back taxes from my grandmother and ruin her, if their records show something different from ours.

But she's asking for help, and my grandmother is nothing if

not proud. The fact that she even admitted her eyesight is getting worse only hammers home the fact that she really, desperately needs me to help with this audit.

"I'm going to have to bring in a bookkeeper or an accountant to help, Grandma," I finally say. "But I'll pay for it. You don't have to worry about it at all."

My grandmother lets out a huff, then pats my cheek. "I knew I could count on you, Rudy."

The bell above the door dingles, and Dorothy comes through. She stands just inside and looks down her nose at the stack of books.

My grandmother freezes beside me and lets out a low growl. "What are *you* doing here?"

Dorothy flicks a piece of lint off her shoulder and shrugs. "Haven't seen you in over a week. As nice as it's been to have a respite from you, I've been meaning to tell you I enjoyed your little outburst after the champagne tower incident. A bit savage, but entertaining."

My grandmother studies Dorothy for a moment, then straightens. She lets out a little harrumph and shuffles to the front of the bookstore. She's pleased. She wouldn't admit it, obviously, but Dorothy just paid her the highest kind of compliment—wrapped up in an insult, of course.

"Did you hear about Victoria Cole?" Dorothy says in a sharp change of subject, thumbing through the nearest book.

"What, the messy divorce?" My grandmother makes her way behind the counter and sits up on the cushioned chair behind the till.

"She just took her ex-husband to court and got full custody

of the kids. I was going to send a gift basket." Dorothy's voice is casual. "I was thinking she might enjoy some books, too."

"She does love to read, and her little ones never miss Rudy's story time." My grandmother arches a brow, straightening a stack of papers next to the till.

Turning my head to hide my smile, I push the door marked "Staff Only" to make my way to the back room. My grandmother and Dorothy have an interesting relationship. Sometimes I think they enjoy taking out their pent-up aggression on each other, but they secretly enjoy each other's company.

Alone in the back room, I stare at the door across from me marked "Storeroom," and with a sigh, I march across the tight space and turn the knob.

The door moves about six inches before hitting the leg of an old chair. A wafting smell of must and mold billows out of the room and I groan, dropping my chin to my chest. I have all of six days to get these records organized. I need help.

The first call I make is to the accountant I use for my real estate business. There's no answer, until a message clicks on telling me that he's away for a month for vacation. I hang up the phone, knowing of one other tax professional who could help me.

But do I want to call her?

Lily and I left things open after the auction, but we haven't spoken. I want to see her again, obviously, but I just don't know…

Something tells me she's going to pull away if I push too hard. The thing is, though, I'm desperate to talk to her. I don't want to take things slowly. I want to be by her side, going to doctor's appointments, figuring out how to fight her cancer right there with her. This protectiveness is unfamiliar, but it blazes through me unabated. I want to be the man by her side. I want her to lean on *me*.

I haven't wanted a second date with a woman in years—but I want more than that with Lily. It makes no sense. Since I broke up with Tracey, I've made a point to avoid relationships. They're nothing but trouble and heartache. But now, the thought of going on without Lily by my side makes me want to put a fist through the wall.

But Lily was clear; she doesn't want anything serious with me.

Still, my grandmother needs my help.

Lily answers on the second ring. "Rudy," she says in my ear. "Weren't you supposed to wait for me to call?" There's a smile in her voice that makes me wonder if I should have picked up the phone days ago. Was she waiting for me to reach out to her?

"I'm calling you on behalf of my grandmother," I say, lips curling despite myself.

"Uh-oh," she says. "Do I need to skip town? Am I in danger?"

I chuckle. "No. She's being audited by the IRS, and she conveniently forgot to tell me about it for months. The agent is coming next week."

"A field audit," she says, then whistles.

"Yeah." I take a deep breath. "I called my accountant, but he's on vacation. What's your normal hourly rate for accounting work? I was wondering if maybe…"

"I'll help you. Of course I'll help you," she interrupts. "I can even give you a family-and-friends-and-scary-grandmother discount. You want to start tonight? We can go through her tax return and get all her records organized. Typically they'll only want to see the year they're auditing, but they can ask for up to six years' worth of records. As long as she's filed her taxes every year and kept the records, it shouldn't take too long."

I stare at the dark maw of the storeroom, breathing in the dank air, and let out a huff. "I wouldn't be so sure."

LILY ARRIVES at the bookstore after I've flipped the sign on the door to "closed." She's wearing loose, peach-colored pants and a fitted white blouse. Her dark hair is tied up in a loose ponytail with tendrils falling out to frame her face. In the fading summer sun, she looks like a goddess on the bookstore doorstep.

"Hey," I croak. Every second we spend together makes it harder to keep my distance.

"Hi." She smiles and gestures to the door. "May I?"

We walk through the stacks to the back of the store, through the door marked "Staff Only" into the tight space at the back of the shop. I turn to the storeroom door and arch an eyebrow at her. "Are you ready?"

"Why am I suddenly nervous?"

I grin and open the door, letting it jam against the chair leg. Reaching over the mass of old furniture, I pull the string to turn on the single lightbulb in the center of the room.

Lily rears back and covers her nose and mouth with a hand. "Smells...interesting," she says, her nose wrinkling under her fingers.

I laugh. "That's one word for it." I blow out a breath. "It's not too late for you to back out."

Lily drops her hand and shakes her head. "I'm here, aren't I? Let's get these things out. Did Agnes file her returns electronically?"

"Yeah, but that's the only electronic thing about her system," I say with a grin. I point to a few boxes lined near a wall behind me. "I've started removing some boxes of receipts, but I know she renovated this place three years ago. The storeroom became a dumping ground, and everything got shuffled around. Some of the boxes I've pulled out are receipts from 1983, and they were right beside the door. I have no idea where the more recent stuff is."

"Probably buried at the very back under a mountain of rat poop," Lily says with a wry grin. "No wonder you warned me it wouldn't be so easy."

I chuckle. "I was thinking we could haul this stuff to my house. I've got a spare bedroom that has no furniture in it, and we could use it to store the boxes. A staging area."

Her eyes dart to mine, a flush sweeping over her cheeks. Then Lily nods. "Sure."

It takes us the better part of an hour to load my car up with boxes. Then we load her car up until all that's left in the storeroom are dust bunnies and broken furniture. I pull the cord to turn the light off, then we head out.

When we get to my place, I'm slightly embarrassed. I'm supposed to be a real estate professional, but I live in a fixer-upper that hasn't ever been fixed up. Lily doesn't seem to notice, just helps me haul boxes inside. We joke around, laugh, banter, and get to work.

"There are receipts from the eighties in this box right beside receipts from last year." She waves a bright white receipt and a distinctly yellow one. "What's up with that?"

"I'd have to ask my grandmother," I say, lifting a water-damaged box to inspect the damage underneath. I huff. "She'd probably just growl and tell me to figure it out."

Lily grins. We work until the sunlight has disappeared and turn on some lights. When Lily's stomach growls loud enough for me to hear, I suggest we order pizza.

And that's how I end up leaning against the counter in my kitchen, eating pizza beside Iliana Viceroy.

I jerk my chin at her vegetarian pizza. "You don't like pepperoni?"

She swallows a bite. "I, um... I'm avoiding processed meat right now."

"No drinking, no processed meat...you on a health kick?"

Her eyes slide away from mine and she ducks her head as if to avoid my gaze. "Something like that," she says, wiping her hands on a paper napkin. "I need water. You want anything?"

I almost growl in pleasure when I watch her flick open a couple of cabinets until she finds the glasses. I like having Lily in my house, barefoot and helping herself to food and drinks like she lives here.

She leans against the counter and sips a glass of water while I crack open a beer from the fridge. I nod toward the hallway. "How long do you think the paperwork will take?"

Lily blows out a breath. "When's the auditor coming?"

"Wednesday."

She bunches her lips to the side. "We can probably sort through everything by then. We'll just separate them by year and work on reconciling last year's expenses in detail. I'll clear my schedule for the weekend."

I set my beer down and stalk toward her, placing my palms on the counter on either side of her. "You're too good to be true, you know that?"

"Most of my accounting clients say that, actually." Her grin is teasing, but there are shadows in her eyes.

"Lily," I say, my voice not much more than a growl, "I've been waiting for you to call for a week."

She shrugs. "I've been busy."

"I saw you working in the community garden nearly every day," I say.

Lily crosses her arms and gives me the sassiest look I've ever seen. "And what, that doesn't count as work?"

"That's not what I mean."

"No, *you* get to decide what counts as busy and what doesn't. I didn't call you—when, by the way, we decided this was a casual thing between us, so I have *no* obligation to shuffle my schedule for you—and now you get to decide how I spend my time—"

I silence her with a kiss, and immediately feel her soften. She curls her arms around my neck and pulls me close until I have her pinned against the counter. Nipping her bottom lip, I revel in the soft sighs she lets slip.

"Rudy," she whispers.

My hands move to her hips, sliding under her shirt to her

waist. "Yeah?" My lips find hers again, and I deepen the kiss until we have to come up for air.

"We should be working," she says, brushing her lips along my jaw.

"Shh," I mumble before kissing her neck.

She freezes and pulls away. "Did you just shush me?"

I grin against her skin, letting my hands curl around her back. "Quiet, Lily. I'm kissing you."

"And now he tells me to be quiet!"

Laughing, I tug her close and slide my hands down to her ass. When I squeeze her close, she lets out a whimper, her body soft and malleable in my hands.

"You have some nerve, Rudy," she says, but her voice is breathy and her hands cling to my shoulders.

The waistband of her pants is elastic, so I easily slide my hands down to her ass and groan at the feel of her bare skin against my palms. I knead her flesh and kiss her lips, loving the way she sighs and moans against my mouth. When I feel her hand tugging at my other arm, I let her guide it up her waist and over her breast.

Pulling away, I meet Lily's gaze. Her eyes are dark, hooded. She bites her lip and lets her eyelids drift shut as I wrap my hand around her breast. I have one hand on her breast, the other curled around her ass, my hips squarely pressed against hers, and I have no doubt she can feel that I'm hard as rock.

There's no scared rabbit here today. She arches her back into my touch, and I can hardly keep my hands from trembling as I undo the top few buttons of her blouse. Groaning at the sight of her bra, I pull the cup down and bring my lips to her breast.

When Lily's fingers tangle into my hair, I scrape my teeth over her nipple, then lave my tongue over the pebbled peak. Her moan travels right through me and my body winds tighter. Sliding my hand around her hip to the front, I slip my fingers underneath her panties and groan.

She's wet. Really, really fucking wet. Unable to resist, I push two fingers inside her and suck her nipple into my mouth, loving the way she gasps. Her hips roll against my touch as if she can't help herself from wanting more. I'm losing my mind at the wet, hot feel of her wrapped around my fingers, knowing that it'll feel like heaven when she's sheathing my cock.

And my fucking doorbell rings.

Lily freezes. "You want to get that?" Her voice is breathy and so damn sexy it makes all the blood in my body rush between my legs.

"Nope." I kiss her lips, palming her bare breast and groaning as she rocks her hips against my hand. Her body is perfect. She might lose her breast, but there are so many other parts of it to appreciate. That hollow in her waist. The way her ass swells past her hips. The graceful, long arms that wrap around me. Those lips and eyes.

The glorious, wet, hot space between her legs.

The doorbell rings again.

I groan.

Someone pounds on the door, and then I hear my grandmother's voice. "Rudy! I know you're in there!"

FOURTEEN
LILY

THERE'S no fear like the feeling of Agnes walking in on a topless me making out with her grandson. Or, horror of horrors, her walking in on me riding his fingers to orgasm. I shove away from him, scramble to button my blouse, and tamp down my hair, my heart hammering against my ribs.

For some reason, instead of staying in the kitchen and gathering myself, I follow Rudy down the hall to the front door. Don't ask me why. I have no idea. Maybe there's some tether attaching me to Rudy, and my tightly wound body just can't bear to be that far away from him. Rudy paints that charming smile on his face and opens the door once we're both decent. "Hey, Grandma."

"I found these ledgers at home. They have sales from when the computers go down." She hands him a stack of red-bound ledgers, then cuts her gaze to me. Her eyes travel down to my shirt, and I realize with horror that I misaligned my buttons.

There's a gaping hole in the front of my blouse right at boob level.

Wonderful. I wonder how long it'll take for the whole town to hear about this.

I clear my throat and duck into the spare bedroom to grab my purse. "I should go," I say, reappearing with my arms crossed to hide my chest. "I'll be back in the morning to keep working," I tell the room at large, looking at no one.

"Lily, wait," Rudy starts, but I just shake my head.

"Bye!" I make my escape, and don't take a full breath until I'm back outside my own apartment building. When my phone rings, I jump.

It's Trina. Somehow, I manage to keep my voice steady as she invites me over for dessert, since the girls somehow congregated there this evening and they were missing me. Not wanting to go up to my lonely apartment, I tell her I'll be there shortly. After a quick trip upstairs to get her freshly dry-cleaned velvet dress, I head across town to Trina's place.

The lights are ablaze when I get to Trina's house, and I enter just in time to say goodnight to Toby and Katie as Mac leads the kids upstairs. Trina, Candice, Fiona, Jen, Simone, and surprisingly, Nora, are sitting around the kitchen island sharing what looks like far too many bottles of wine.

They all cheer when I enter.

I drop my purse and the garment bag with Trina's dress on the kitchen counter and face them all. "Agnes just nearly walked in on me making out with Rudy."

If I thought their cheer was loud, it's nothing compared to

the squeals that follow my words. I bury my face in my hands until I'm pulled closer and told to explain.

The girls are in stitches by the end of my story.

"But why did you leave?" Simone says, outraged.

"Come on," I reply, giving her an incredulous look. "Would you have stayed?"

"With Rudy? Hell yes!" Trina giggles right after yelling the words.

More laughter sounds. Mac appears at the mouth of the kitchen with arched brows. "Do I want to know what you ladies are talking about?"

"That depends," Jen says just as Fiona interjects with, "Probably not."

Grinning, Mac just crosses to Trina and plants a wet one right on her lips. "I'm going to the studio. Be back in a couple of hours."

We all watch him walk away—it's a nice view—and then all attention returns to me. I jerk my chin to Trina's dress. "I think they got all the champagne out, but if not, I'll reimburse you for it."

Trina waves a hand. "If that dress died in service of getting you laid, it's a worthy sacrifice."

More cackles sound, and I just roll my eyes. I help myself to some sparkling water from the fridge and slide onto a barstool, then let the embers of embarrassment fade from my blood. I learn that Nora is an art director for a magazine in Reno, and has to drive back to Reno for what seems like the millionth time because her boss is demanding she attend a meeting.

"My boss said he was fine with me moving away as long as I

did the work, but there always seems to be some fire that needs to be put out in the office. It's costing me a fortune in gas," Nora says, sipping her wine.

"Clearly, he was lying," Simone says. "You should put out some feelers. I can ask around for you too."

"That would be good," she says. "I love my job, but the drive is getting old."

By the time a few hours have gone by, the remnants of my evening with Rudy have faded. I say goodbye to the girls and make my way home, sinking into my bed with a sigh.

Now I just need to face Rudy tomorrow, and the next day, and the next, until this audit is over...and somehow do it without falling for him or embarrassing myself.

A BROAD, bare chest greets me after I ring the doorbell. It glistens with sweat and heaves with deep breaths. Mute, I lift my gaze up to Rudy's face.

"You did that on purpose," I blurt.

His eyes crinkle, but his lips don't twitch. "Did what?"

"Answered the door without a shirt on." I wave in his general direction. "You're punishing me for running out last night."

Instead of letting me inside, Rudy leans a forearm against the doorjamb and arches a brow. "I didn't know the sight of me is so disgusting that you'd consider it punishment."

My eyes travel back down to the droplets of sweat diving down between the muscles in his stomach. I try to think of something to say, but my body feels like it'll spontaneously combust. Not so much punishment as torture.

Rudy takes a step back, his eyes glimmering. "You're early," he finally explains. "Caught me at the end of my workout."

I check the time on my phone and realize he's right. It's eleven, and I told him I'd be here around noon. "Oops," I say, even though I'm not exactly sorry.

"You want to get started while I get dressed?" He closes the door behind me, his body just inches from mine.

"Sure," I squeak, then make my way to the spare bedroom.

A few moments later I hear the shower start running, and the blush on my cheeks deepens. I don't know why, but the thought of Rudy upstairs...naked...with soapy water running all over him...

Blinking rapidly, I stare at the receipts clutched in my hands. I hadn't even realized I'd picked any up. Screwing my eyes up, I try to read the dates, then give up and grab one of the ledgers Agnes dropped off last night.

I'm still blankly flipping through one of them when Rudy reappears with two coffees in hand. His hair is wet, and he's wearing a T-shirt and jeans that sit low on his hips. He's barefoot.

The mug is warm, but what strikes me most is the feel of Rudy's fingers brushing mine when he hands it over. I nod my thanks, then turn to the boxes of paperwork. "We should start by sorting everything by year," I say, which is a completely useless comment because it's exactly what we were doing last night.

"Sure," Rudy replies, and we get to work.

We work late, and I leave before I do anything I'll regret, although I do indulge in a long, lingering kiss goodbye. Then I do the same the next day. Rudy sometimes has to take off for a couple of hours at a time to deal with things in his business, but I'm surprised to find I feel at home in his place. I resist the temptation to snoop, though. He usually gets back from viewings or meetings with clients looking tired and relieved to see me. Those smiles he gives me—like I'm a breath of fresh air—make something warm grow in my chest.

I try to ignore how good his presence makes me feel.

Pretty soon it's the weekend, and I realize I haven't worried about the baby or my illness for days. Since Rudy and I agreed to take Saturday off, I make my way to the Four Cups Café to meet my sisters for breakfast, feeling lighter than I have in months. We've almost finished all our work. I've reconciled everything from last year's tax, and there are just a few more boxes to sort through to make sure the past six years are in order.

It feels good, I realize, to accomplish something without worrying about what the future will bring.

FIFTEEN
RUDY

GEORGIA NEVES REACHES into her purse and pulls out a velvet case, from which she removes a weighty silver pen. Her eyes flick to mine as she gives me a seductive grin. "I'm about to sign my life away, Rudy."

"If I recall, you called it the property of your dreams." I give her a professional smile, my hands clasped on the table in my office conference room. After an eternity of viewings and two days of hard negotiation with the sellers—all while doing my best to keep my hands on Lily while simultaneously wanting to spend every waking moment going through old receipts with her—Georgia's offer on a coastal property ten minutes outside of Heart's Cove was finally accepted.

"So I did," she answers.

Pulling glasses out of a case, she props them on the end of her fine, aristocratic nose and starts reading the contract. She was one of those clients that demands time and attention way beyond the normal bounds of a job—but she bought a five-point-one-million-dollar property, so I can't complain too much. I haven't gotten a commission check as big as this one in many years. A few of my employees have shot me mock-dirty looks when Georgia insisted on dealing with me personally, but they know they'll all be rewarded for a good year once the time for annual bonuses comes around.

I sit patiently. Georgia really is an attractive woman. Beautiful, tall, with luscious dark hair and Mediterranean features. She's exactly the type of woman I would have brought to bed in the past—so why do I feel nothing for her? Ever since Lily walked into the bookstore over a month ago, I've lost all interest in other women.

With a swoop of her expensive pen, Georgia signs on the dotted line. "Done," she proclaims.

"I'll get this over to the seller right away," I tell her, tucking the signed contract back into its manila folder.

"I expect a phone call to tell me about the good news in a few minutes, and then we can celebrate." She extends a hand for me to shake. It's soft and feminine, and it makes me think of Lily. How it felt to have her skin under my palm, to feel her soft body wrapped up in my arms.

I need to get that woman into my bed, and soon.

Blinking the thought away, I force a smile onto my lips. "Of course." I gesture to the door and let out a heavy sigh once Georgia is gone.

The sun is shining outside, so I shrug off my suit jacket and decide to walk across town to the other agent's offices. After that, I'll stop by Four Cups for lunch.

Maybe, in the dark recesses of my mind, I'm hoping Lily will be at her sister's café. I've seen her every day for the past three days, and the thought of not seeing her until Monday seems hard to bear.

It doesn't take long for me to stroll down Cove Boulevard and enter the seller's agent's offices. We take care of the paperwork, and within an hour I'm heading back out into the August sunshine. I take a deep breath of sweet, ocean-scented air before my feet take me down the tree-lined street.

Inside the Four Cups Café, I see Lily laughing broadly, her head leaning against her sister's shoulder. My chest tightens and I make for the door, but my phone rings.

"Got your text," Georgia croons in my ear. "Gosh, you work quickly."

"Signed and finalized," I say, eyes still on the scene inside the café. "I just have to make a copy of the contract and I'll send you the original."

Georgia hums. "What about delivering it in person? You promised to celebrate with me."

My eyes pull away from the café and I stare at the pavement. "I..."

"No excuses. I just put nearly a hundred grand in your pocket, Rudy. The least you can do is share a bottle of champagne with me."

Holding back a sigh, I force my voice to stay light as I say, "Sure."

"Wonderful," Georgia says. "I'm heading to the Edgeville Yacht Club. I just paid for a membership, and they have a wonderful seafood pasta dish. Lunch is on me, and I'm not taking no for an answer."

"Sounds great," I lie, and throw one last glance to the women inside Four Cups. When I hang up, I release a breath and let my feet carry me back to the office.

One meal with Georgia to deliver the papers and discuss the logistics of payment and closing, and I'll be free of her. I do the required paperwork in the office until I really can't leave the woman waiting any longer, then hop in my car and head down the coast to Edgeville.

I'd much rather be taking Lily here—or better yet, skipping lunch altogether and dragging her to my bed—but I'm good at my job, and I'll see this sale through.

By the time I make it to the yacht club, I'm resigned.

Georgia has changed into a light, airy dress that nips at her slim waist. Her carefully styled hair falls in waves down her back, and she has oversized sunglasses on as she sits at the best patio table in the entire bay. She smiles at me when she spots me striding across the restaurant floor toward her, then presents a cheek for me to kiss when I make it to the table.

Her hand curls around my neck as she brushes her lips against my cheek, and it takes all my self-control not to jerk away from her.

"Congratulations, Mrs. Neves, you've got a new home." I put the folder with her contract on the table next to her, but she doesn't even look at it.

"You're the best realtor I've ever had the pleasure of working with, Rudy," she says, tipping her sunglasses down to rake her eyes over my body.

"Thank you, ma'am," I say.

She clicks her tongue. "Don't ma'am me." She pauses. "Unless that's what you're into." A flirty laugh, and I have to resist the urge to get up and bolt.

Just an hour with her, enduring this heavy-handed flirting, and then I can leave. I'll call Lily and ask her to coffee or dessert or dinner, or hell, I'll dig through my grandmother's boxes of old records and I'll enjoy it more than this.

But the waiter arrives and Georgia orders a bottle of their most expensive champagne, so I sit back and do my best to make it through the lunch.

SIXTEEN
TRINA

LILY LOOKS green in the face at the sight of the eggs being served at the table next to ours.

I arch my brows. Morning sickness, maybe? Lily hasn't mentioned the baby at all since I showed her the boxes of baby things in my garage. "You good? Not in the mood for brunch food?"

Lips clamped shut, she shakes her head. "No."

"Me neither," Candice announces. "I want...tacos."

"Let's go, then," I say. "We can go to Cantina." Cantina is a little hole-in-the-wall Mexican place that is delicious, fast, and cheap. It gets pretty busy, though, and early afternoon on a Saturday it will definitely be hard to get a table.

Lily's already standing up and striding for the door. "I'm in!"

Candice frowns and glances at me. "I'm still trying to figure out what is up with her. Have you been able to get anything out of her? She's not acting like she used to. I wonder what happened. She hasn't even mentioned her next trip."

"That's true," I answer noncommittally.

"When's the last time you remember Iliana being at home without plans to leave again?" Candice arches her brows at me. "Not since she was a teen."

"Let's go get tacos," I answer.

My two sister and I head down the street and with a few deep breaths, Lily's shoulders lower. She gives me a tight smile and shakes her head slightly, as if to indicate she doesn't want to talk about it.

"Blake wants tacos," Candice says, glancing up from her phone. "Should we get some for Mac too?"

"I'll ask him." I reach into my purse for my phone. "He's with the kids, so they might be ready for lunch too."

"What about Rudy?" Candice asks, a little glimmer in her eyes. "Lily?"

"Huh?" Lily stumbles on a crack in the pavement and my arm shoots out to steady her. She gives me a grateful look.

Candice presses on. "Maybe you should text Rudy and ask him if he wants tacos for lunch."

Lily rolls her eyes, and Candice laughs. I can't help but crack a smile. My sisters and I haven't lived in the same place for over twenty years. Being together feels...nice. Like Heart's Cove is becoming more and more of a home.

"You can't tell us you haven't been spending time with him," I tease. "We've seen you go to his house. Everyone's talking about it."

"Everyone as in who? Dorothy and Agnes?" Lily shoots

back, then snorts. "Those two gossip about the damn squirrels living in the trees on Cove Boulevard."

"Mm," Candice answers. "I just think it'd be nice to ask if he wants some hot, tasty lunch brought to him."

"You know what? Fine. I'll send him a message." Lily stops in her tracks and makes a big show of pulling out her phone. She mashes the screen until her message is sent, then glares at Candice. "Happy?"

Our eldest sister grins. "Very."

"Have you spoken to Nora?" I ask Lily, deciding she needs a reprieve from our teasing.

"You two have become close," Candice adds.

Lily shrugs. "We're the newbies in town, and we're neighbors across the hall from each other." She smiles at us. "And we're the only ones who are single."

"For now." Candice grins.

Sadness flashes in Lily's eyes, but she quickly hides it. "She's heading back to Heart's Cove tonight, I think. Her boss in Reno keeps calling her back even though he promised she'd be working remote."

"Again?" Candice arches her brows.

"I keep meaning to talk to Lee," I say, making a mental note to call Mac's brother tonight. "He might have a job for her or know someone who needs her services."

"Oh! We can introduce them at my housewarming party next weekend." Candice beams, whirling to smile at the two of us. "Mom is in party-planning mode, and if we give her a mission to pair the two of them up, it'll keep her out of trouble."

"Keep her out of your hair, you mean," Lily says with a grin.

I laugh. "Not a bad idea."

As expected, Cantina is jammed. There's a long line stretching down the block, and the three of us are thankfully standing in the shade. I pull out a bottle of water and offer it to my sisters before taking a sip. We chat about our week, about Candice's new house, about everything and nothing.

Then someone gets in line behind us, and Lily freezes.

I turn to see a man who must be in his early thirties, at most. He looks surprised to see Lily, then his lips curl into a smug smirk. "Lily," he says.

"Jared." She nods.

"Rudy not with you?" He tilts his head.

She grunts. "Not today."

"Oh, that's right. He's at the yacht club with..." Jared snaps his fingers. "I didn't catch her name. Just saw him there with another woman when I went to pay my tab from last night."

Lily's brows tug together, but she says nothing.

It's Candice who turns to Jared. "Rudy was on a date with another woman?"

"Candice," Lily says. "Please don't."

"No," my sister cuts in. "I want to know."

"I do too," I say, crossing my arms.

Lily just massages her forehead. "Forget it. This is Rudy's cousin—the asshole who bumped into us. He's probably just stirring shit up for no reason."

I stiffen at the same time Candice does—and Candice doesn't even know Lily's pregnant. She doesn't know this jerk could have hurt the baby by pushing her into that champagne tower.

Suddenly Jared doesn't seem so smug. He looks at his feet and shifts his weight, then lets his gaze crawl back up to Lily. "Listen, Lily…"

"Iliana," Candice cuts in. "You don't get to call her Lily."

Lily rolls her eyes, but there's a hint of a smile on her lips. I have a feeling she likes having us in her corner.

Jared lets out a sigh. "I didn't mean to bump into you."

"That's not what we heard," I say. The line shuffles forward, and we all step closer to the promise of tacos. Clearly, this conflict isn't stopping us from ordering food.

"It's true," Jared says, eyes turning to me. "My date was tugging on my arm wanting to dance when they were just about to do the champagne pour! I was just trying to get away from her and I stumbled into Rudy."

Candice snorts.

Lily lets out a sigh. "Fine. Thank you. It's okay, Jared. You're forgiven."

His shoulders drop. "Look—I was adopted, okay. And when Rudy and his ex broke up, and he never spoke to his step-daughter again, I just… It bothered me, okay? A lot. I can understand how he'd think I did it on purpose. We haven't exactly gotten along for the past few years. Everything comes so easy to him, and he just walked away from his ex and her kid, and there have been no repercussions. None. So I just…decided he was an asshole. He dates whoever he wants and then leaves them, and I hate watching him do it over and over." He finishes his little speech in a rush.

"What?" Lily asks, tilting her head. "What happened with his ex?"

Jared frowns, then shakes his head. "I shouldn't have said anything. I'm not a total asshole, okay? He just gets under my skin."

"What's that about a stepdaughter?" I ask, leaning toward him.

The line moves forward again, and we all shuffle a few feet. I can smell the fresh tacos and my stomach grumbles.

"Nothing." He glances at the entrance to the restaurant, then shakes his head and walks away.

"Wow." Candice whistles. "He was so uncomfortable he actually sacrificed the best tacos in town to get away from us. Must be serious."

Lily's frowning after him, and I take a moment to study her before we move just inside the door, nearly at the counter where we can put in our order.

"I wonder who Rudy was having lunch with," I say quietly. "Are you guys official?"

Lily just snorts. "Please. I made sure he knew we were casual. We never said anything about not dating other people."

Candice and I exchange a glance. She bunches her lips to the side. "Still."

Lily straightens her shoulders. She's younger than the two of us, but she's always been more independent. Ever since she took off on her first trip to Peru, she hasn't stayed home for longer than a few months. She built her business by herself, and flitted from country to country, relationship to relationship.

She always seemed to enjoy it more than any kind of stability.

Watching her chew her lip now, though, I wonder if she still feels the same way. Maybe she thought Rudy was different. Babies can change your outlook on life pretty radically—something I know from firsthand experience. Maybe Lily was hoping for something more with Rudy.

"He hurts you, and I'll chop his balls off," Candice announces, and then it's time for us to order.

SEVENTEEN

RUDY

I LEAVE my lunch appointment with three new contact numbers for friends of Georgia's that would just *love* to relocate, according to her. She somehow also manages to tell—no, demand—that we meet up again for the handover of the keys, and we might as well make a meal of it, shouldn't we?

Back at my car, I sit behind the wheel and let out a long breath. That meal wasn't unpleasant, but it was tiring. I close my eyes for a beat, then start the engine.

Instead of driving to my place or my office or even Lily's place, I find myself in front of my grandmother's bookstore. All is quiet inside when I push the door open, and then I find myself face-to-face with my cousin.

"Jared," I say, half-startled. "I didn't know you could read." The words are automatic, a barb that always seems easy to reach for whenever my cousin's sneering face is near.

Jared puts three books on the counter and glances at me. He looks...tired. With a breath, he turns to face me. "Can we not do this?" he finally asks.

A frown tugs at my brow. "Do what?"

"I know it's my fault we don't get along. I... I'm sorry."

I blink. "Oh."

"That's it? Just 'oh'?"

My throat feels itchy, so I clear it. "Where is this coming from?"

"I was always jealous of you, you know," he says, a palm leaning against the counter. "Everything comes so easy to you. Women, money, success. And you always just toss it away like it means nothing."

A hot, prickly feeling spreads through my chest. "Excuse me?"

Jared closes his eyes. "Never mind."

We both turn toward the stacks when my grandmother comes toddling down toward us. She glances at me, then Jared, then back at me, and starts punching the prices for Jared's new books into her antiquated cash register. "You nearly done with the audit?" Grandma asks me without looking my way.

"Nearly," I tell her. "Only a few loose ends to tie up now."

She grunts, then tells Jared his total. I walk away as he pays for his new books, letting my feet carry me the few blocks toward Lily's place. It's not a conscious decision to go there, but at the back of my mind, I know I won't be able to stay away.

My cousin's words rattle around my brain. Is he right? I've never felt like things came easy to me—I always felt like I had to work for everything I have. My business didn't fall into my lap; I built it. Women are attracted to me, sure, but I haven't had a successful relationship in years. So where does he get the idea that I've got some kind of divine luck?

Before I can stop myself, I press the buzzer to Lily's apartment. Her name is written in black ink on a little sticker next to the button. She lives in a four-story building made of brown brick that was probably built in the seventies. Balconies jut out of the building at regular intervals. The nearest one has a few old pots filled with dry dirt and dead plants.

"Yeah?" Lily's voice says through the intercom speaker.

"It's me," I say. "Rudy."

There's a pause, and I wonder if I should have stayed away. Why am I here, anyway? We already decided to take the day off from working on my grandmother's audit. I had no plans to see her. I haven't even called her. She probably thinks it's weird for me to show up at her place.

It *is* weird for me to show up at her place, but I came here without even thinking, like I was drawn here by some external force.

Then the buzzer sounds and the door unlatches, and I push it to step through.

It smells musty inside. There are mailboxes lining one wall, with junk mail piled in the corner. An old elevator is to my left, but I choose to take the staircase directly in front of me. The stair treads are so worn down that they've been tarnished to a dull brown color in the middle.

It feels wrong. Not being here—but this being where Lily

lives. She should be in some gorgeous log cabin nestled in the woods, or a house made of steel and glass perched on a cliff. She should be in an ashram in India or a shack on a beach somewhere. She should be living some glamorous, beautiful life.

Not in some dull, boxy apartment on the edge of the downtown of Heart's Cove.

She should be with me.

The thought clangs through me, and I pause on the second-floor landing, staring at the worn linoleum. Somewhere in the distance I hear a door open above me, and my feet start moving again. I make it to the fourth floor and realize I don't know Lily's apartment number. The buzzer outside just had black buttons beside the names. But there's a door propped open with a shoe wedged in the opening, and I recognize Lily's sneaker.

I knock on the door before pushing it open. "Hello?"

"In here," Lily calls out.

I step inside and pause.

Lily's apartment is a small one-bedroom space, with a tiny U-shaped kitchen that opens onto a medium-sized living room that only has a desk and a chair in the corner, with a laptop sitting on the desk. There's an old sofa on the opposite wall. Through the bedroom doorway, I spy a tidy bedroom with a double bed. There are approximately seven thousand cushions and pillows on the bed. The only other pieces of furniture I can see are two barstools on the far side of the kitchen's peninsula counter.

The whole place is beige. Beige carpet, beige walls, beige linoleum in the kitchen, beige countertops, and slightly-darker-than-beige cabinets. The desk is brown.

Lily straightens up from the kitchen sink, yellow rubber gloves pulled over her hands. She wipes her brow with her bicep, the bandana on her head nudging back over her dark hair. "Hey," she says. "I wasn't expecting you."

"I should have called," I say. I smell the sharp, astringent scent of cleaning products and notice the mop and bucket propped next to the stove. The windows are open, and a vacuum is waiting to be used in the middle of the living room. Lily pulls off her gloves, drops them on the edge of the sink, and opens the old relic of a fridge (also beige), to pull out a jug of cold, filtered water.

She catches me scanning the room and grins. "I'm still working on decorating the place. Obviously."

"It's very..."

"Beige?" she supplies, then laughs. "I know. The owner used the words 'blank canvas' when I came by to sign the lease. It's temporary."

"Should you be cleaning so hard in your condition?" I hear myself say.

The hard iron mask that falls over Lily's features is the first hint I get that I said something wrong.

"My condition?" she answers carefully.

I shake my head. "I just mean... I didn't..."

Lily lets out a harsh breath that might be a laugh, and hands me a glass of cold water. "I have cancer, Rudy, but I'm not dead yet."

"I know." My fingers wrap around the glass, barely brushing hers. I take a gulp while Lily stares at me. "What?"

"I'm waiting for you to tell me why you're here," she says, cocking a brow.

The discomfort that had been churning in my gut slows, and I find my lips curling. This is what I love about Lily. The sass. The attitude. The total and complete irreverence.

"I hadn't really thought it through," I admit.

"Thought what through? Showing up at my house uninvited?"

"Exactly," I say, finishing the water and setting my glass on the counter. "One minute I was at the bookstore having the weirdest conversation I've ever had with my cousin, next minute I'm ringing your buzzer."

Lily pauses, her eyes sliding away from me. She takes a sip of water and backs up to lean against the edge of the sink, her head tilting. "Your cousin?"

"He was buying books from my grandmother."

"Does he live in Heart's Cove?"

I shake my head. "No. Lives in Edgeville."

"Huh," she says, brow knotting. She sucks in a breath. "I ran into him too. At Cantina."

"The taco place?"

"The one and only." She meets my gaze, eyes narrowing. "He told me he saw you at the yacht club. Said you were on a date."

"It wasn't a date," I answer automatically.

Lily turns her back to me. "None of my business."

"It wasn't a date," I repeat.

"Even if it was, it still wouldn't be any of my business." She slides her gloves back on and starts scouring a pot again. "I told you I wanted things to be casual, and they are."

I watch the way her shoulders bunch as she moves to scrub the pot soaking in sudsy water. She pauses when I slide my hands over her hips and bring my lips near her ear. "It wasn't a date. It was a business lunch. I haven't wanted to date anyone since the moment you walked into my grandmother's bookstore."

A shuddering breath passes through her, and I slide my arms all the way around. My hand slips under her shirt and I feel the warm skin of her stomach against my palm, and a deep feeling of *rightness* trills through me. I lean my chest against her back, then hook my chin over her shoulder.

This is where I want to be. This, right here, is why I rang her buzzer. Because I'll never be able to feel calm unless my arms are wrapped around her.

I sweep my hand up from her stomach to her waist with slow, careful movements, as if she's an animal that might spook.

Lily's breaths turn shallow when my hands span around her ribs, so I ask, "Is this okay?"

She nods, her rubber-glove-covered hands leaning against the edge of the sink. Her body feels edgy until I sweep my thumb over her skin in a slow, steady circle. The urge to squeeze my arms around her and protect her from everything that hurts is so strong, I nearly crush her to my chest and keep her there.

"Rudy," she starts, her voice so soft I hardly hear it. "You and I... It's not a good idea."

"I don't care about the cancer," I say, and I'm surprised to realize it's true. I'm usually the first one to put distance between a woman and me. I have a bad habit of dating women who are emotionally unavailable—like, for example, Lily's sister Candice—and backing away at the first sign of resistance.

An ex-fling once told me I was so afraid of commitment that I'd probably die alone in my house and no one would find the body for days. She was angry, obviously, but her words stung because they rang of truth. I keep everyone at arm's length. I've done it since my last relationship fell apart and I lost the family I'd worked so hard to build.

So why do I feel like I need to be close to Lily? Why this urge to protect her from everything wrong in the world?

Closing my eyes against the onslaught of unfamiliar feelings, I widen my stance so my feet are on either side of Lily's. I inhale the smell of her shampoo, a floral scent with a familiar thread that can only be described as Lily. Settled by the scent of her, I open my eyes again.

"I have a proposition," I say, my lips moving against her ear.

She shivers as my breath skates over her skin. "Oh?"

"How about for the next twelve hours, we forget about the outside world? No past, no future. No talk of exes or cancer or anything else. We just stay with each other"—I inhale softly, my thumb still sweeping over her skin—"and see what happens."

Lily's lips tug ever so slightly, her body relaxing against mine. I nearly groan when she leans into me, the length of her pressed against me from shoulder to hip. She's wearing faded jeans and an old tee, and she's never looked better.

"Twelve hours," she repeats, her head tilting slightly to rest against my shoulder, her lips half an inch from mine. "I might be convinced to forget about everything for twelve hours."

I glance to the side, where the microwave proclaims the time to be just past four o'clock. "At 4:17 a.m. tomorrow morning, we rejoin the rest of the world." My left hand slides down from her rib to her hip, coming to rest in the hollow between her pelvis and her thigh. I can feel the heat of her there, and all other thoughts leave my head.

EIGHTEEN
LILY

RUDY'S FINGERS are weaving some kind of spell on me. He has one arm across my stomach, with his hand tracing slow circles over the hollow of my waist. His other hand is flat against my jeans, fingertips inching closer to a very dangerous area.

He wants twelve hours, but I'd give him everything. He's dangerous. He makes me forget all the bad things that have happened.

He makes me hope.

The hand on my waist starts a slow, torturous exploration of my skin, fingertips sliding up my ribs to tease the side of my breast.

A sharp inhale sounds next to my ear as Rudy's hand cups the underside of my breast, his thumb sweeping over my already-peaked nipple. "You're not wearing a bra," he growls.

I let myself lean into him, into his touch. "I'm home alone

on a Saturday afternoon," I say. His hand caresses my breast, fingers tweaking its peak, and my voice goes a bit breathless. "Of course I'm not wearing a bra."

A very masculine sound comes from Rudy's throat, and his other hand slides from my hip to the space between my thighs. Even over my jeans, the touch feels electric. I know he can feel the heat of my arousal through the layers of fabric, because he cups his hand around my core and pulls me hard against his body. I melt into him, reveling in his touch. His hands do something funny to my brain, my body, like everything is firing at once. Maybe it's the way his hand moved—no hesitation, no pause. Just pure possession.

The hand on my breast sends tendrils of heat racing through my core, and the hand between my legs holds me tight to him. I close my eyes as he touches me softly, slowly, and force myself not to think about tomorrow.

The only thing that exists is Rudy's warm body behind me, the feel of the counter gripped in my gloved hands, the breathlessness squeezing my lungs, and those hands.

There's the hand that explores the places of my body that I haven't been able to look at in the mirror since my diagnosis. His fingers trace the outline of my nipple before tweaking it, teasing it, caressing it. His fingers wrap around my breast and knead before moving to give the other breast the same treatment.

I moan, head falling against his shoulder, and realize with a distant sort of haziness that I've started rocking my hips against his other hand. The heel of his palm presses against me just so as Rudy whispers soft encouragements in my ear, and the rasp of my underwear against my sensitized skin is almost too much.

"Rudy," I breathe.

His lips press over the pulse thundering in my neck. "You are so fucking hot," he groans, grinding his hand between my legs.

I let out a breathless laugh. I can feel the hardness of his arousal against my ass. It's not the most eloquent compliment anyone has ever paid me, but it might be the most genuine one. And damn it, it feels good to feel sexy. To feel wanted.

And it helps that need is curling tight in the pit of my stomach, that my skin feels hot and tight over my breasts, that my legs are shaking as I grind my hips against his touch.

Didn't take much for me to agree to twelve hours, did it? I just wish we'd done this sooner.

"Are you wet for me?" he asks, his voice low and sultry.

Another harsh laugh falls from my lips. "I'm surprised you can't feel it through my jeans."

There's a sharp breath behind me, and Rudy's spinning me around. His hand tears at my shirt and pulls it off over my head, and I realize with a laugh that I'm still wearing rubber gloves. They get tangled in the T-shirt and for an awkward moment, I'm pinned in a tangle of fabric and rubber. With a growl, Rudy pulls the shirt free.

I pant, rubber gloves resting on his shoulders, feeling deliciously exposed and loving every minute of it. I don't remember the last time I was this turned on.

Instead of undressing me further, Rudy curls an arm around my back and angles my head toward him, then he kisses me.

Our kisses in the car, at the gala, and at his house were frantic and hot and full of need. This kiss is different. It's consuming. He plasters my body to his and explores my mouth thoroughly, mercilessly, until I'm worried I won't be able to hold myself up without his arm banded across my back.

I only realize I've twisted my fists into his hair when he gasps, eyes flashing, then nips at my bottom lip. "Your gloves are pulling at my hair," he growls, and I can't help it. I laugh.

"I've never made out with anyone while wearing rubber gloves," I admit.

"I never thought I'd find it hot, but here we are."

Rudy leans back, his hips still glued against mine, as his hands slide over my shoulders and down my arms. He finally tears his gaze away from mine to help me tug the rubber gloves off one hand, then the other. He tosses them aside and they land beside the sink with a wet slap.

"I'm not sure twelve hours will be enough for all the things I want to do," he says.

The counter bites the back of my hips as I lean into it and arch my back.

And Rudy lets out a low, masculine growl.

His fingers find the zipper at the front of my jeans, and I can almost feel each of the zipper's teeth spread apart as he tugs it down. My hands seem to have a mind of their own, sliding over Rudy's arms and tracing the hard lines of his shoulders. I tug at the top few buttons of his crisp white shirt as he works to unzip my jeans, but stop when his lips descend on mine again.

We don't talk, but our bodies do. Desire rises in me so fast I feel dizzy. All the fear, the dread, the worry that I've felt over the past few months is burned away with white-hot lust. In the dark recesses of my mind, I wonder if my worry will come back with a vengeance in the light of morning tomorrow, but I'm too far gone to care.

I have breast cancer. I'm pregnant. And I'm going to sleep with Rudy.

All three of those things are true.

The zipper finally conquered, Rudy wastes no time in sliding his hand exactly where it was moments ago—minus a few layers of clothing. We both gasp hard when he does, his fingers exploring the wetness of my arousal.

"You weren't kidding." Rudy's voice is full of smoke, his lips taking mine once more.

I moan into his kiss as his fingers move over me, finding that hard bud at the top of my sex to tease and pinch and touch.

"Stop me any time you need to," Rudy says, his voice so full of gravel it's a wonder I can tell the words apart. He pulls away and looks down to where his hand disappears into my pants.

For a brief, biting moment, I think about what I'm doing. I realize I'm nearly naked with a man in my kitchen, pretending nothing else exists. As the cool air of my kitchen kisses my skin, I fight the urge to cross my arms over my chest.

This is my body, and it will change. This time next year, I'll have scars and stretch marks and puckered skin, and for the first time in seven weeks, the thought doesn't terrify me.

It's still my body.

My breast will be removed, but for a few weeks longer, it's still part of me.

Rudy's fingers do something a bit magical between my

thighs. Heat floods low in my stomach as my legs tremble. I blink up to meet his gaze and catch the satisfied male smile tugging at his lips.

"So fucking hot," he repeats, then dips his head down to kiss me. The scrape of teeth against my bottom lip makes me gasp, just as Rudy uses the moment to slide a long, talented finger inside me.

I nearly lose my mind.

After the first time, I'd half-convinced myself I imagined how incredible it felt to have his fingers inside me. It couldn't possibly feel this good. But it did, and it does. Distantly, I wonder if this is a mistake—but how could it be, when nothing has ever felt so right?

His palm is angled expertly so it hits that bundle of nerves every time he pumps his fingers inside me. With trembling hands, I manage to unbutton most of Rudy's shirt and push it off his shoulders. I want to feel his skin against mine, but when I nearly have the damn thing off, Rudy slides his hand from my pants and catches my wrists with his. His eyes are dark, hooded. His lips are glistening from our kisses. There's a bulge in his pants that makes my heart skip a beat.

Even yesterday, the thought of standing in my kitchen, topless and with my jeans undone, with Rudy's eyes tracing every line of my body would have terrified me. Hell—even a couple of hours ago I would've run away screaming.

But right now, the only thing that terrifies me is that this moment might end. That I might have to live my life without Rudy's eyes on me making me feel like the most beautiful woman in the world.

"Are you okay?"

I blink. "What?"

"You have a habit of acting like a scared rabbit when I touch you. Just checking in." His breaths are harsh and when I slide my hands over his chest, his muscles are rock hard—as if he's holding himself back with every ounce of strength.

"I'm fine," I answer with an arched brow. "Why so worried?"

His lips quirk. "When dealing with a scared rabbit, one needs to be careful."

"One needs to start removing one's clothing, otherwise the rabbit might grow teeth and bite."

"I don't mind biting," he says, but he finishes undoing the button I'd gotten to. That's as far as he gets, though, because Rudy buries his face in my neck as his hands glide over my skin to cup my breasts. I gasp at the gentle scrape of his teeth on my pulse point, mind reeling at the intensity of his touch.

And when his hands cup my breasts, thumbs teasing my pebbled nipples, I melt. Rudy leans down and takes one breast in his mouth, his other hand diving back down underneath my panties, and all I can do is lean against the counter and hang on for dear life.

I don't remember the last time I was this turned on. I don't know if I ever have been. My hands go wandering again, this time curling around Rudy's neck and holding him to my breast. He growls in response, scraping his teeth over my stiffened peak.

It feels good. Better than good. It feels like *me*. Not some alien body that has betrayed me, not some husk that will wither and die before I'm ready. I'm still me. Turning forty didn't turn me into a pumpkin, nor will cancer. Nor will childbirth.

I'm still me, and I always will be.

His fingers move faster inside me, reminding me that I want something more. Then his thumb circles my clit in just the right spot and—

I cry out, every muscle stiffening as the tension leaves my body in a rush. Rudy straightens up suddenly, then picks me up and throws me over his shoulder. I yelp and laugh, delirious from my orgasm, as he marches toward the open bedroom door. Without warning, I'm flying through the air and landing on my bed. My head immediately falls between some of my throw pillows, and they're ripped away.

"So many damn pillows," Rudy growls. "Why? Why so many?" There's a sharp tug, and my jeans are pulled from my legs.

"I'm nesting," I say on a giggle, and am surprised to realize it's true.

"Too many," Rudy growls.

"Quiet, you. My throw pillows never did anything to you." I'm grinning when he sweeps the whole lot of them off the bed. My jeans fly over the pile of pillows and land with a soft thump. "Neither did my pants, for that matter."

Rudy gives me a light smack on the side of my rump in response, and I let out a yelping laugh.

I haven't had this much fun in ages.

Rudy toes off his shoes, eyes on my body. I might arch my back a little for his benefit, and I might stretch my arms in a way that shows off my curves. Sue me. I feel beautiful and sexy for the first time in far too long.

I turn on my side and prop myself on my elbow to watch Rudy fight his cuffs for a moment, until I swing my legs around and sit up to help.

It's oddly intimate. Rudy stands still, his belt buckle gleaming near my face, and presents his wrists to me one at a time to deal with. Once I've freed him of his cuffs, he starts on the rest of the shirt buttons while I attack the belt buckle. I finish first, and before Rudy has half the buttons off, I've pushed his pants, underwear and all, down to the ground.

My heart is in my throat as I see the hardness of his arousal so close to my mouth. I reach for it as my eyes flick up to meet his, but he catches my wrists and uses his weight to pin me back on the bed, hands clamped on either side of my head.

I laugh, surprised more than anything. "Hey! I was busy." I can feel his erection pressed against the crook of my hip, and my voice comes out breathier than I'd intended.

Instead of answering, Rudy grabs me by the waist and manhandles me up the bed and onto the much-reduced pile of pillows. Another laugh escapes me. I can't help it—I'm enjoying myself. There's none of the awkwardness there was with Phil, my apparently married ex. I don't have to try hard to be sexy for Rudy, because even braless in an old T-shirt and rubber gloves, he couldn't keep his hands off me. Now that I'm nearly naked, it feels like he can barely control himself, and that turns me on more than anything.

And when Rudy kneels between my legs and tugs my panties off, I decide I *am* allowed to have unlimited fun for the next twelve hours. His hands slide up my thighs, thumbs brushing the softness between my legs. When he dips his head to taste me, my knees fall apart. I moan as he touches me, licks me, devours me, my hands once again reaching down to twist into his hair.

What turns me on most of all are the rough sounds coming from Rudy's throat, as if he's enjoying himself just as much as me. Heat curls in the pit of my stomach and the tightness of an impending orgasm starts to build. I arch my back, gasping, and Rudy takes that as an invitation to delve into me with his fingers.

This is probably wrong. Scratch that—this is definitely wrong. I'm pregnant with another man's child, and even though that man walked out on me without looking back, I know I shouldn't be doing this with Rudy without telling him the truth.

But...

Is it selfish to think I deserve to feel good? The past weeks have been a quagmire of doctors' appointments, stress, and weighty secrets. Since my first dinner date with Rudy, those stresses have slowly been stripped away, and whatever happens when the clock strikes four o'clock tomorrow morning, I'm here now.

Rudy lifts his head, his lips glistening as he crawls up toward me. When he kisses me deeply, I taste myself on his mouth.

"Your mind wandered just then," he says, tucking his head by my neck to kiss the soft skin below my ear. "What's up?"

I close my eyes. Am I really that easy to read?

"I want you here with me when we do this, Lily," he says,

his voice barely more than a low growl. I feel the vibrations of it in my throat and find myself nodding.

"I'm here."

"You'll make me feel self-conscious about my skills in the bedroom if you're so quick to be distracted."

I roll my eyes as his hand starts a torturous journey south. "Wouldn't want to hurt your poor, fragile ego, now would we?"

Rudy grins as his eyes flash, then I'm on my stomach before I can blink. He gives me a sharp smack on the ass that makes me yelp in surprise, then I stuff my face in the pillow and laugh again. "Hey!" I turn my head to look over my shoulder.

With his knees on either side of mine, still wearing his half-unbuttoned shirt, Rudy looks undone and wild and beautiful. He grins at me, smoothing his hand over my curves to soothe the sting of his smack. "You deserve that for being a brat."

"A brat!" I cry, hiding my laugh with mock-outrage. I don't remember ever laughing this much while being intimate with a man. "Do you get off on calling a forty-year-old woman a brat?"

In response, Rudy prods me with something that proves that yes, he does indeed get off on that.

I giggle again, twisting around beneath him.

His palms land on the bed on either side of me and he dips his head to kiss me softly. "I love hearing you laugh," he says.

Turning around completely, I pull him down for a deeper kiss. We fumble to arrange our legs so his hips are cradled against mine, then Rudy is reaching over the side of the bed for his pants. I scrape my fingers through his hair as he pulls out his wallet, revealing a condom from one of the compartments.

I arch a brow. "Don't you know you're not supposed to keep condoms in your wallet? It can wear them down and tear them."

Not that I can get pregnant tonight—that ship has sailed.

Rudy sits up to kneel between my spread legs, tearing the wrapper open with practiced ease. His eyes flick to mine. "Don't worry, Lily. I only put it in there a few days ago." A faint blush sweeps over his cheeks. "The night of the gala."

"So sure you'd score, huh?" I curl an arm behind my head. "That's a bit presumptuous of you."

"I'm a man who likes to hope for the best," he responds, and I watch as he rolls the latex over his shaft. It's erotic, watching him do this. Watching him touch himself, knowing that he'll be inside me in mere moments.

But Rudy doesn't seem to be in a hurry. Turning his attention to his shirt, he takes his time to open the last of the buttons, then lets the shirt slide off his broad shoulders.

His body is magnificent. I'd feel self-conscious if he wasn't looking at me like he felt the same way about me. One of his palms slides over my thigh, gently spreading it wider. It continues over my hip, his thumb brushing my stomach before reaching up for my breast.

I'm like any other woman. I've had insecurities about my body, my stomach, the extra softness in parts of me that aren't as thin as they were in my twenties. I'm extra insecure about all the ways my body is about to change in the not-too-distant future. But when Rudy touches me, he lets out a rough noise that tells me he likes those parts of me. I watch his other hand wrap around his cock, and he guides himself inside me.

For a few beautiful moments, we say nothing. His eyes

move from between my legs to meet my gaze, and I feel a sizzling connection form itself between us. He moves over me, his elbows near my shoulders, and I tilt my hips to accept more of him.

My breath catches.

Slowly, inexorably, Rudy pushes inside me until he's seated between my knees, bottoming out inside me. His lips brush over my neck, my jaw, my cheek. "You okay?" His voice is harsh, as if he's holding himself back with every ounce of control.

I wiggle my hips a bit, smiling at the noise it elicits from him. "I'm good," I answer. "Really good."

It doesn't take long for me to come once more. A few deep thrusts from Rudy, and I'm already on the edge. A dirty word or two whispered in my ear, a rough palm gripping my body so hard it feels like he can't help himself. The hardness of his muscles beneath my palms. The way he sits up and lifts my legs onto his shoulders to get just that little bit deeper inside me. And when he angles his body so he can reach between us to touch me just the way I like, I explode.

When he stiffens on top of me and his movements get jerky, I wonder if it's the feeling of my own orgasm that sends him over the edge. The thought of him enjoying my pleasure that much makes another wave of ecstasy wash over me, and I wrap my arms and legs around him to keep him close.

Panting, we collapse in a heap on the bed, and I open my eyes to stare at the ceiling. My arms are wrapped around his shoulders, hands pulling him close.

"Mm," he says, face buried in the crook of my neck. "I'm sorry. I couldn't last. I'll hold out next time."

I laugh. "I didn't exactly hold out very long either."

He tilts his head and kisses my neck, and for the first time in a long, long while, I feel totally at peace.

WE ORDER takeout for dinner and have sex three more times. I fall asleep sometime around one o'clock in the morning, wrapped up in Rudy's arms, wishing we'd said twenty-four hours instead of twelve.

I LEFT Lily in bed this morning, then ducked out to grab the fixings for breakfast. When I got back, she was still snoring lightly, the bedsheet crumpled around her waist and her dark hair splayed over the pillows.

I could get used to sights like that.

Instead, I got to work making bacon and eggs. It's when I pull bacon out from under the broiler that I hear footsteps behind me.

"Morning," I say, putting the baking sheet on a trivet. "I made coffee if you want some." I nod to the gurgling coffee machine in the corner of the kitchen.

Lily has a silky bathrobe wrapped around her body. It's light pink with fluffy white clouds dotted all over it. Her dark brows tug together as she takes in the kitchen, then she puts a hand to her stomach.

"Oh no," she mumbles, then shuffle-sprints toward the bathroom.

"Lily? Hey!" I follow, but only fast enough for the bathroom door to slam in my face. From the other side, I hear the lovely sounds of her throwing up into the toilet. Leaning against the frame with my forehead on the door, I wait a few moments before rapping my knuckles on the door. "Lily? You okay?"

The toilet flushes and the sink starts running for a second. Then, I hear an electric toothbrush whirring. I wait by the door until the sounds stop.

When she finally opens it, Lily looks...well, she looks like she just puked.

Curling my arm around her shoulders, I pull her close. "You feel sick?"

She nods, head buried against my chest. "I'm sorry. I'm sure the bacon's delicious."

"Go back to bed," I tell her. "Can you manage some eggs?"

She freezes, a hand climbing up to her stomach.

I huff. "No eggs, then. A piece of toast?"

A slow breath slips through her lips, and Lily nods. "Yeah. Toast would be good."

"Butter?"

She nods. "And a little sprinkle of salt."

I tilt my head, then nod. I've never tried salt on buttered toast. Kissing the top of her head, I guide her back to the bedroom and get her settled. When I get back to the kitchen, I'm too worried about how she's feeling to care about the food. The smell of the bacon is obviously what got to her. I find a container and pop the pieces inside, then wrap up all the grease-covered foil I'd used to line the baking sheet. Smelly things disposed of, I leave the beaten eggs beside the stove and start slicing some of the fresh French bread I bought this morning.

It's when I'm waiting for the toaster to do its thing that I realize I like this—taking care of her. Glancing over my shoulder toward the bedroom, that same, unfamiliar feeling or rightness comes over me. This is exactly where I'm supposed to be.

I want more of this. Not that I want Lily to be puking every morning, but I want to be the one there to take care of her.

Then a chill walks down my spine, because I remember the last time I felt the need to take care of someone like this. It ended with me alone, wallowing in my own misery. Do I really want to go through that again?

When I bring Lily a plate with buttered toast and a cup of peppermint tea, she rubs her eyes with the heels of her hands and gives me a shy smile. "I'm sorry about that, Rudy. Thank you for cooking breakfast."

"Don't apologize." I wait until she's taken a bite of the toast, chewed, and swallowed before speaking again. "You think it was the takeout last night? I feel fine, but I didn't have any of the soup."

She shakes her head. "Just a bit of nausea. Doesn't feel like food poisoning." She opens her mouth, then closes it again, choosing instead to take another bite of toast. There's something she's not telling me.

I frown. "You sure? What else would it be?" I reach over to touch her forehead, which feels a bit clammy but not hot.

"I'm fine, Rudy."

I sit on the edge of the bed until she nods at the door. "I'll go eat out there. You should have bacon and eggs since you went to all that effort. I didn't even know I had bacon and eggs in the fridge."

I huff a laugh. "You didn't. I went to the store, but I'm not going to eat anything that has you running to put your head in the toilet." I arch a brow but get up anyway. Lily and I make the bed. She places all the throw pillows just so, which makes me smile and convinces me that she isn't that sick.

Some tightness between my shoulder blades eases, which makes me wonder just how far under my skin Lily's gotten. It's only been a few weeks—and only one night together. How far gone will I be after another night?

When we're back in the living room/kitchen area, Lily slides onto one of the barstools and nods to the stove. "Eat, Rudy. You need the calories after everything we did last night."

"Says the woman who just threw up first thing in the morning."

"Yeah, well, it happens." She doesn't meet my eyes, but finishes her toast. Maybe she's right; it was just a bit of nausea. If she's eating and she cared enough about her pillows, it can't be that bad.

By the time the eggs are done and my coffee is poured, Lily has finished her toast and tea. I eat quickly, perched on the barstool next to hers, keeping one foot on the rung of Lily's barstool and one hand on her thigh. I can't help it. Any time this woman is near me, I feel like I need to touch her. Her presence calms me, centers me.

"So it really doesn't bother you that I have breast cancer?" Lily asks out of the blue. "That I'll have to get a mastectomy?"

I glance at Lily, then at the time, then back at Lily.

She grins. "We missed the twelve-hour mark, so I'm allowed to ask."

Huffing, I finish my bite to give myself time to think. Once I've swallowed, I shrug. "No, doesn't bother me."

"I'm going to lose my breast, Rudy."

"As magnificent as I think your breasts are, there are lots of other things about you I enjoy just as much, if not more." I grin.

Lily's eyes are sad.

I take a sip of coffee, then say, "How are you feeling?"

"Terrified."

"That's understandable."

She lets out a snort. "Yeah. Doesn't make it any easier."

"So your treatment...you said something about chemo?"

Lily nods. "I get a mastectomy, and they do a breast reconstruction in the same operation. Then I need some chemo to follow up on the surgery."

"One of my employees had breast cancer," I say, getting up to refill my mug. "She said her doctors did everything they could to save the breast tissue. Did radiation, and she was grateful she didn't need to do any chemo."

Lily nods. "Yeah. I have...separate medical issues that mean I'm not eligible for radiation or hormone therapy, or even breast-conserving surgery. They have to take the whole thing." She cups her boob and pouts.

"That sucks," I say, sliding back onto the barstool. "But hey —at least there's a second one." I reach down and lay a kiss on top of her breast to emphasize the point.

I laugh when Lily punches my arm. She can't keep the

scowl on her face too long, though, and just shakes her head at me.

I tuck a strand of hair behind Lily's ear. "You look beautiful in the morning."

Lily's cheeks flush, and she nods to the bathroom. Her voice is quiet, almost shy when she speaks. "I feel like I need a shower. Would you like to join?"

Suddenly, my throat is tight. A gorgeous woman just invited me to shower with her. I nod. "Yeah," I manage to answer. "I would."

AFTER RUDY AND I HAVE—*AHEM*—SHOWERED, I stand under the stream of water and let him run my loofah over my back. He lays a soft kiss on my shoulder as a rumble passes through his chest. Strong arms wrap around my waist as he pulls me close, something hard nudging at the small of my back.

"You're insatiable." A laugh escapes my lips along with the words, and I lean into his warmth.

"Only with you."

His words make my breath catch. So it isn't just me who feels this way—like there's something between us that's differ-ent, special. I've never actually enjoyed showering with anyone else. It's usually awkward and inefficient, and I don't care what anyone says—the lubrication situation downstairs during shower sex makes the whole thing vaguely uncomfortable. But with Rudy, it's intimate and special and yes, *fun*. Just like everything else with him.

I turn around in his arms and let the water run over my hair.

He smiles, dipping down to kiss my lips. "I have a confession," he says softly, hands sliding to rest on my ass.

"Mm?" I answer, tracing patterns on his wet skin. "What's that?"

"I never wanted this to end after twelve hours." When I open my mouth to answer, he puts a finger on my lips. "Don't, Lily. Don't tell me that you have too much baggage, that you don't need my help, that you don't want to burden me. I know you feel this between us. I want to see where it goes."

My chest hurts.

I should laugh, really. For nearly a year, I dated a man who was literally married to another woman. He promised me everything and gave me nothing. He strung me along, and I clung on like a fool. It was only when I told him about the baby that he finally made a choice—and he didn't choose me. Less than a year isn't much to waste on a man, but it still makes me hesitant to jump in again.

Now, mere weeks later, I'm standing until the stream of a hot shower with another man—a better man—telling me he wants to choose me despite my baggage.

The problem is, he doesn't know the half of it.

Can I really trust him to stay by my side when he finds out about the baby?

I guess there's only one way to find out. Before I can stop myself, I let my mouth run away with me. "Jared said something else."

Rudy freezes, a hard wall of muscle in front of me. "Oh?"

"Something about a stepkid." Even I can hear the odd note

in my voice, but I just close my eyes and tilt my head into the stream of the shower to hide it. When I straighten up again and meet Rudy's eyes, I've regained control over my own body.

Rudy hesitates, then lets out a huff. "A girl," he finally says. There's a pause, and he pushes a strand of wet hair off my forehead. "I had an ex with a daughter, and it...didn't work out. If you think breast cancer is baggage, you have no idea of the complications that come with dating a woman with a kid."

And just like that, my hope crumbles to dust. With great effort, I unwind the tightness in my muscles and busy myself running a washcloth over his pectoral muscles. "You didn't like the girl?" I'm proud of how neutral my voice sounds, even if my pulse is pounding.

"I loved her," Rudy says, his voice distant. "Thought I could be the best stepdad ever."

Hope blooms inside me. He *wanted* to be a stepdad. He didn't care that the kid wasn't his blood. Maybe... Maybe he wouldn't care about my baby being another man's, either. "But...?"

He shrugs. "We broke up. She refused to let me see her kid, even though I was the only father she'd known for over half her life." There's a bitterness in his voice that I've never heard before.

I keep my eyes on the washcloth, letting the fingers of my other hand drift through its wake of suds. "What happened?"

Rudy watches me for a moment, then lets out a humorless huff. "You know, I've never told anyone about my past, but when you look at me like that, it makes me want to share it all with you."

Is it normal for my chest to ache like this? I force my expression to remain neutral. "Oh?"

Rudy spins us around so he's under the water. The soap rinses off his body, and his hands move to make slow sweeps over my skin. "I understand, you know. She was the girl's mom, and I was just an ex-boyfriend. I had no legal or biological ties to her daughter. Logically, I know I had no right to be her father. But..." He shakes his head. "I love kids. I mean, doing the bookstore's story time is sometimes the highlight of my week. I'm just not sure I could go through that again. Felt like it was my daughter I lost."

The water is turning colder, but neither of us makes a move to shut it off. "It hurt you," I say a little uselessly.

Rudy blinks, his eyes focusing on me. "Yeah. After that, I decided no stepkids. It's not worth the pain."

There's nothing inside me. My heart has stopped beating. My blood has stopped pumping. I'm just...empty. The water from the shower hits my skin like a thousand icy needles. Shivering, I shove my head under the spray to hide the moisture in my eyes.

Rudy might want kids, but he doesn't want stepkids. I heard the hardness in his voice, the surety. Once I tell him about the baby, he'll be gone.

But didn't I always know that?

It was stupid of me to go on a date with him after our initial dinner. When I felt the chemistry of our kiss, I should have known it would be more than physical between us. It was never going to be just scratching an itch. I lied to myself about keeping things casual, and I knew this would end in disaster.

There had always been this tiny kernel of hope, though. A dim, flickering flame that I kept alive in the darkest parts of my soul, thinking I'd found my white knight. Thinking I could be saved.

Maybe I really am living in one of the Grimm brothers' stories. I sure as hell am blind.

I stare at the tile in the shower, then reach over to shut the water off. Neither of us moves to get out, since the shower stall is still warm and steamy. A cocoon.

Rudy keeps his hands on my hips, our bodies close. "It was for the best, you know. After we broke up is when I started the brokerage and went from a realtor to a business owner. I wouldn't have half of what I have if I'd been part of their family. I'm not mad at her for taking the kid." As if he suddenly realizes what he's saying and who he's talking to, Rudy jerks away from me and shakes his head. He drops his hands from my hips. "I've made a good life now," he tells me, the words coming out hoarse. "Tracey did me a favor. I realized after that happened that I never wanted kids. Not even my own. They're fun to be around, and I'm sure if I had siblings I'd make a great uncle, but fatherhood just isn't for me. It's too much of a burden to bear."

Throat tight, I nod. "At least now you know." It comes out as a croak.

Maybe what I mean is, at least now *I* know.

I should have told him about the baby when he asked me out for dinner that first time. Now the words stick to my throat, and all I can think is that I'm naked in the shower, exposed, vulnerable. I need to wrap myself in armor before I can tell him. I haven't even told my family, for crying out loud.

So, instead of being responsible, telling him the truth, I just give him a stiff nod. "Well"—I suck in a sharp breath—"I'm sorry you went through that."

Rudy opens the glass partition and a billow of steam exits the shower stall. He grabs a towel and hands it back to me. "What about you? Kids would hamper your travels around the world, no?"

I wrap it around my chest, feeling slightly more protected. Still, I force a wry grin. "Not much traveling happening these days."

My world feels off-kilter, but what did I expect? I shouldn't be dating anyone when I'm staring down the double barrel of cancer and a new baby.

I've always known I can't pursue a relationship with Rudy. Now I know for sure.

I've been a fool, clinging to the first man who gives me attention. I'm going through the hardest time of my life, facing things that terrify me down to my marrow. Rudy rode in on his damn white horse, and every fiber of me wants to cling to him and let him save me.

How utterly pathetic.

Rudy is a good man, and he deserves a woman who won't drag him down into the mud. He deserves a woman who can give him a childfree life. He deserves a future free of surgery and chemo and caring for someone he barely knows.

He deserves someone better than me.

As I sort through my tangled feelings, trying to find the right words, Rudy kisses me. He curls his hand around the back of my head and tilts my head to meet my lips. I cling to his wet shoulders, too weak to push him away.

When we pull apart, Rudy stares into my eyes and opens his mouth—and I know I need to stop him. I need to tell him about the baby, and I need to do it right now. This can't go on a single minute longer, because it's wrong. I'm lying to him now, and I need to tell him the truth. He deserves that.

I open my mouth to tell him—and someone knocks on my door.

"Lily," Nora's voice calls out. "Open the door!"

"Coming!" I answer, then turn to wrap a second towel around my head. I glance at Rudy, who has an eyebrow arched and a smile tugging at his lips.

"We're not done talking," he informs me. "You're supposed to open up to me about the cancer and why you're so terrified of letting me help."

"Uh-huh." I speed-dry myself off as Nora knocks on the door again. "I was in the shower," I call out. "Just throwing on some clothes. One second."

The knocking subsides as I tug on some sweatpants and my silky bathrobe. I open the door to see Nora standing on my doorstep with a foil-covered plate.

"I brought you my mother's carrot cake. She insisted on me picking her up when I drove back from Reno last night, and I'm pretty sure she just used the cake as an excuse to come back. As I'm sure you remember from last time, it's delicious, and it's most definitely a bribe so that you'll tell me about what's been going on with"—her eyes widen at something over my shoulder—"Rudy."

She's already thrust the plate into my hands, so I'm holding it when I turn around to see Rudy standing in the bathroom doorway in a cloud of steam, my fluffy pink towel wrapped around his slim hips. Water runs down the carved lines of his stomach and chest. He holds the towel closed near his crotch, but it doesn't hide the line of pale hair traveling from his navel down beneath the towel.

Every dark emotion that had been gripping my body just... melts away. For a moment, I forget why, exactly, I'm not supposed to want him.

"Hey, Nora," he says casually, as if he doesn't look like some kind of female fantasy come to life. "Did you say carrot cake?"

She squeaks, then clears her throat. "Yeah. Ma's recipe. Lily can vouch for it. It's delicious."

"Yum," he says.

"I was just thinking the same thing," Nora replies.

I throw her a sharp glance, and she grins at me.

The plate in my hand moves when Rudy takes it from me. He lifts the foil and lets out a little noise. "This smells amazing. Cream cheese frosting?" He dips a finger into the frosting and brings it to his lips.

Nora and I might as well be watching a tennis match, our eyes moving in sync from the plate up to his mouth. Then I meet Rudy's laughing eyes just as he wraps the tip of his finger with his lush lips. I scowl. He's doing this on purpose.

"You know it!" Nora says brightly, blinking away her stupor. She makes a beeline for my kitchen and pulls out the drawer holding my utensils. "Cream cheese is a breakfast food, right?"

I laugh and accept a fork. Thankfully, the smell of carrot

cake doesn't set my stomach off. I've been lucky with the morning sickness so far, and I don't want it to start now that I'm almost done with my first trimester. Puking with Rudy on the other side of the door was embarrassing enough.

Finding out our relationship was doomed made me feel just as bad.

Carrot cake will fix that, right?

Rudy disappears for a moment and returns wearing his pants and nothing else. It looks almost as obscene as the towel, but at least there aren't a thousand droplets of water glittering in the early morning sun for me to stare at.

The three of us stand around the kitchen counter and dig into the cake. It tastes divine, just like the last one did.

"You know, I'm not usually a fan of nuts in cake, but these walnuts definitely add something," Rudy notes.

I pause. "You don't like nuts in cake? What about brownies?"

He wrinkles his nose. "No way. Nuts are a great way to ruin an otherwise good brownie."

Nora snorts. "Next thing, you'll say you prefer cakey brownies over fudgy ones. You're probably one of those freaks that likes the edge pieces."

Rudy takes a bite of cake and tilts his head from side to side. "Well..."

I make an outraged sound, and he just laughs. His arm curls around my shoulders to tug me close, and Nora's brows climb upward. Unease tightens my stomach. I really shouldn't be enjoying his touch as much as I am.

"You think your mother came back to Heart's Cove in the

hope she'd go on another motorcycle ride?" I ask Nora as I scrape a bit of frosting off the plate.

My friend laughs. "I wouldn't be surprised. She asked me about Dorothy's new bike on the drive over."

"Careful," I say. "Next thing you know, your mother will be moving to Heart's Cove and falling in love with someone."

Nora grins. "That wouldn't be so bad. Fallon seems to be enjoying her company. They've been planning to cook together most nights. He said he regretted never learning any Indian dishes growing up, and Mom took that as an invitation to have a whole week-long masterclass with him." She takes another forkful of cake, then pauses. "You know, that day she went for a ride... There was another man there, riding a motorcycle." Her eyes are glued to the lump of cake on her fork. "He looked like he might be related to Mac." Her words are casual—almost too much so. "Do you know who that was?"

I glance at her, but she doesn't meet my eye. Maybe Candice's plan to pair the two of them up isn't so far off base...?

"That's Lee," Rudy replies, scraping a bit of frosting off the plate with his finger. I miss the next few words because my brain short-circuits at the sight of him licking it clean. He's definitely doing it on purpose. "...and I can introduce you if you want."

"Oh, that won't be necessary," Nora rushes to say. "I was just wondering, is all. They look so similar." I arch a brow, but Nora just grabs the now-empty plate. "I better go."

"Want to grab lunch this week?" I ask almost desperately. I like Nora a lot, and the thought of talking to her about my predicament with Rudy appeals a whole lot more than spilling my guts to the Heart's Cove Rumor Machine, a.k.a. my family.

Nora pouts. "Can't. I have to drive to Reno tomorrow morning—boss wants me in the office in the afternoon."

"Again? Didn't you just get back? I thought you said you'd be working from home permanently." I put the used forks in the dishwasher, then glance over my shoulder.

Nora huffs. "That's what he promised. So far, he's asked me to come back every week for useless meetings. I'm looking for something new—either a local job or a fully remote position."

Rudy's hand slips over my hip as I straighten up, the touch sending heat blooming over my skin. "Well, drive safe, and let me know when you get back to town."

"Should be back by the end of the week," Nora says brightly. "I'll be at Candice's housewarming next weekend."

I smile. "Good."

Nora nods, then waves goodbye.

I watch her go until the door closes behind her, then glance at Rudy. The carrot cake turns to stone in my stomach as I think of what I need to tell him.

His arms encircle me, and despite my best intentions, I find myself melting into his embrace. I'll break it off with him—I will. He deserves better than someone who's broken and complicated.

Just...in a bit. Once I'm able to pull myself away from his arms.

TWENTY-ONE
LILY

WHEN RUDY GETS ready to leave, his last kiss lingers on my lips. "I know we said our fun ends after twelve hours," he tells me, "but I'm not sure I'm ready for it to be over."

I take a deep breath. "Rudy..."

"I know. I know. You have a lot going on and you don't want to start a relationship."

I give him a tired smile. "Exactly." Sort of.

"Just...think about it, yeah?"

"I need time." I close my eyes for a beat. "There's a lot going on, and I don't want to cling onto you because it feels good to have someone to lean on."

His finger drifts over my cheek. "I don't mind you leaning on me."

Damn it. This feels really good, and he's saying all the right things. I've been alone for so long. When Phil left after I told him I intended to keep and raise my baby no matter what he thought, I was freaking out but I was ready to be a single mom. I've lived an adventurous, varied life, and I was ready to move on to the next chapter.

Then I got my diagnosis.

And now...Rudy is making me think of all the things I'll miss.

But he doesn't want to be a stepdad, so this is all a moot point, isn't it?

"Let me be there for you, Lily." His voice is soft, and something weird happens in my body. My chest spasms and softens at the same time. Half of my brain screams at me to throw my arms around his neck and say, *Yes! Yes, I'll let you make everything better!* and the other half just wants to crawl into a hole and never come out.

I huff. "Easy to say after last night. What about when I'm puking my guts out from chemo? When my breast gets cut off and I only have one nipple?"

"To be fair," he starts, eyes glimmering, "you were puking your guts up this morning too."

I punch him in the arm, which draws a deep, tender laugh from him that warms me down to my toes.

"Fine," Rudy says, leaning in for another quick press of his lips. "I'll back off. Just...don't write me off so quickly."

I force a smile and resist the urge to put my hand on my stomach. The cancer is one thing—the baby is quite another.

I'll just tell him right now. It's the right thing to do. He'll find out within a couple of months one way or another, and it'll be easy. All I have to do is open my mouth and say two little words. *I'm pregnant.* That's it.

But I must be weak, because my lips stay sealed until the door closes behind him. I'm enjoying his affection too much to throw it away. It could be the last time he looks at me like it means something.

Footsteps echo in the stairwell outside my door, and when I hear the exterior door close behind him, I let out a long breath.

I'm in trouble.

I really like him—and I know without a shadow of a doubt that I can't have him. Once he's out of my apartment and the press of his presence is gone from my skin, my head clears. It's like a veil lifting from my eyes, and I can see just how stupidly I've acted.

The man has a hard rule against dating women with kids, and I'm having a kid. Why the hell am I wasting his time? Why the hell am I wasting *my* time?

I'll tell him about the baby next time we go out. If we go out.

God, I want to go out with him again.

Groaning, I scrub my face, then square my shoulders. I just need to do what I do best—push all my problems to one side and ignore them and get ready for the day. It's Sunday, which would usually be a day off for me, but I'm feeling strung out and stressed, and the only thing I can think to do instead of pacing my apartment or tearing my hair out is work.

Going over to Rudy's house to finish up the audit is obviously out of the question.

Dressed, hair dried, and skin moisturized, I sit down at the small desk in the living room when my gaze catches on a little square of cardboard sticking out of my purse.

Dr. Melissa Gardner's name stares back at me in big, black,

bold letters. I run my fingers over the slight indent of the text and blow out a sigh.

Nerves tighten every muscle in my body, but I force myself to open my laptop and type in her name. Her website is sleek, and there's a big button right there on the front page that says, *BOOK NOW*.

Twenty-four hours ago, I probably would have closed the website and looked at a spreadsheet instead. I'm not sure what's changed. Maybe it's the conversation I had with Rudy—hearing about his past and knowing we can't be together. Not with a baby growing in my womb. I can't lie to myself any longer and pretend I'll be swept up in a fairy tale.

My life has always been more like the Brothers Grimm's stories, anyway. At least I still have my eyesight.

No, I'm on my own, and that's okay. I've traveled the world and created a business for myself. I've stood on my own two feet since I was a teenager. This is just another bump in the road.

Squaring my shoulders, I click the big orange button on Dr. Gardner's website and start typing in my information. I'm alone, but I'll survive. Maybe Dr. Gardner can give me advice on telling my family. She can tease out the tangled knot of emotion inside me and help me come up with a plan.

A plan that doesn't include clinging to the first available man who gives me a second look.

By the time I've confirmed my appointment for this coming Tuesday, my shoulders relax, and a real smile drifts over my lips.

Then someone bangs on the door.

"I know you're in there," Trina's voice calls out. "You can't hide from us forever, Lily!"

Us?

The worn carpet scratches against my bare feet as I make my way to the front door. When I pull it open, an avalanche of female energy nearly knocks me back.

Simone's red hair is tied up in a messy bun. She grabs me by the shoulders and grins in my face. "We're here for a rescue."

"A rescue?" I frown.

My sister Trina comes rushing past me as Candice beams from the doorway. Simone drops her hands from my shoulders and huffs. "Don't pretend you weren't working, Lily." She thrusts an arm toward my laptop which, thankfully, is no longer showing the therapist's website. "It's Sunday! You can't stay cooped up in here forever."

What was I just saying about being on my own and surviving? Maybe I'm not so alone, after all.

I close the door behind them. "You guys ever hear of calling ahead?"

"We did," Candice says, picking my phone up from the counter and turning it toward me. I have seven messages and eleven missed calls...all from the past ten minutes.

I purse my lips to hide my smile. Despite myself, that ball of emotion in my stomach starts to unwind. "What's this about?"

"Did you talk to Rudy yet? Was he on a date?" Trina leans against my kitchen counter and arches her brows at me. "You never called us back after lunch yesterday."

"Do I need to get my garden shears?" Candice asks, then makes a snipping motion with her fingers.

My lips twitch. "It was a business lunch."

"See?" Simone says, throwing her hands out. "I told you Rudy wouldn't do that. That man is looking for love."

"That makes one of us," I grumble.

Candice arches a brow while Trina's eyes narrow. I avoid both sisters' gazes. Feeling cooped up in my tiny apartment all of a sudden, I ask the girls if they want to walk and talk. We end up power walking the tree-lined streets of Heart's Cove for the better part of an hour while I do my best to field their questions. Somehow, I manage to avoid mentioning that Rudy slept over last night. These women *really* like to gossip, and that is a grenade I don't want exploding in my face.

We end up near the new community garden, where Dorothy looks up from one of the flower beds. "So?" she calls out. "Was it a date?" Then she picks up *actual* garden shears and closes them with violent enthusiasm.

"Business lunch!" Simone calls out. "I told you not to worry about him."

"Good." Dorothy nods, putting her shears down.

"You guys told Dorothy about Rudy's lunch?" I ask. The four of us have drifted into the garden, and Dorothy is thrusting gardening gloves into our hands. "When? Why?"

"Shh," Candice says, patting my arm. "We're just looking out for you."

"With a grandmother like Agnes, you can never be too sure. Rudy must have taken after his father's side," Dorothy says, pulling a few intrepid weeds from the rich, dark earth.

"Dorothy, is that a new dress? It's beautiful," Trina cuts in, and I get an urge to kiss her for changing the subject. Then I notice that my glamorous middle sister isn't sweating in the midsummer sun. She's glistening while I wipe another fat droplet of sweat off my brow. Then I feel less like kissing her and more like asking her why the heck she won the genetic lottery.

Surrounded by my friends and family, I end up spending a few minutes with the sun warming my back, weeding and raking and mulching and doing a thousand little things to keep this garden pristine. I have to admit, it's better than sitting at my computer staring at a spreadsheet.

As I stand up and stretch my back, I meet Trina's eyes. She gives me a smile and a nod, and it feels like an injection of strength.

I don't need Rudy, or any man. His attention is nice, but I can do this without him. I *have* to do this without him—and I will.

Once Dorothy dismisses us from our gardening duties, the four of us continue down the street toward the café. The tables outside the Four Cups Café are full of people, with two dogs lapping at bowls of water and a baby in a stroller cooing at her mother.

That will be me soon.

My hearts squeezes and Trina must notice because she grabs my hand where no one can see it. The touch settles me, and once again I feel the support of these women propping me up.

"Candice, are you ready for your housewarming?" I ask her, just to say something. I gently pull my hand away from Trina's, and she lets it drop.

"Mom ordered seventeen cases of wine," Candice says with

a flat stare. "*Cases.* Don't even ask me why. I'll be drinking chardonnay until I'm sixty."

Laughing, I open the Four Cups Café door. Fiona is standing behind the till with her stepdaughter Clancy and the regular barista, Sven. The three of them are in matching pink T-shirts with glittery *Heart's Cove Hotties* written on the front. Sven's shirt has the sleeves ripped off, and his colorful tattoos climb up his arms like vines. Something softens in my heart at the sight of them behind the till, and I'm not sure why. Maybe this place is feeling a bit more like home every day.

Fiona's eyes cut to me, then Simone. "So? Was he on a date?"

"You are all insatiable," I mock-grumble, then let Candice pull a chair out for me as Fiona bustles over to get the gossip.

As it turns out, I don't get any work done that day at all.

RUDY and I finish preparing for the audit late Monday afternoon. When I make up an excuse about having to get some work done, he gives me a soft, tender kiss that sets my blood on fire, then tells me he'll see me soon.

It makes me feel like dirt. I don't deserve him, and the longer I string him along, the worse it'll be when I tell him about the baby. Resolving to ask my new therapist about it, I leave Rudy's house with the taste of his lips lingering on mine.

Tuesday comes around faster than I can blink, and I find myself sitting in a brown cushioned chair in Dr. Gardner's waiting room. My fingers worry at the strap of my purse. There are magazines stacked in the corner, and the middle of the waiting room is dominated by various toys and children's books. The walls have faded posters about pregnancy, postpartum depression and anxiety, and pictures of happy women holding happy babies.

It's all a bit too real, but before I can jump up and run away, my name is called.

A woman about my age—maybe a bit younger—stands at the mouth of a hallway holding a clipboard. When I look up, she smiles and gestures down the hall. Stomach in my throat, I follow. Her expertly highlighted hair is twisted into a neat bun at the nape of her neck, right above the collar of her pale pink silk blouse. The material is tucked into straight-leg brown pants, giving her a soft, professional look.

"I'm Dr. Gardner," she tells me, gesturing to an open door. I step inside a comfortably furnished room. There are four soft-looking chairs angled toward each other. On the opposite wall is a desk with a computer chair tucked in. The screen is dark.

"Take a seat," the doctor tells me, and I choose the closest chair. I put my purse down on the seat next to me. Dr. Gardner takes the chair opposite, crossing one leg over the other. Her eyes skim my file for a moment, then rise to meet my gaze. "So," she starts.

"So," I repeat.

"What brought you here?" Her voice is neutral, but kind. Her tortoise-shell glasses have a slight cat-eye shape, and they emphasize her brilliant hazel eyes. She's a very beautiful woman, elegant yet approachable.

"My doctor recommended you," I hear myself saying.

Dr. Gardner nods, waiting for me to go on.

"I…" I clear my throat. "I'm pregnant, and I…have breast cancer." The words come out slowly, their jagged edges ripping at my throat. But I get them out, and I realize it's the second time I've told the truth—and the first time I've told someone both secrets.

"I see that you're going to get a mastectomy," Dr. Gardner says, her hand on my file, eyes on me. "And you'll be getting chemotherapy once the surgery is done."

"Is that safe for the baby?" I blurt, my hand sliding over my stomach.

Dr. Gardner nods. "It is. Does that worry you?"

All of a sudden the dam bursts, and I can't stop the words from coming. I tell her how terrified I feel about the surgery, the safety of my baby, what will happen during the birth, if I'll even survive long enough to see my baby grow up. I tell her how alone and isolated I feel, but that I'm even more terrified of telling anyone what's going on.

With gentle, open-ended questions, Dr. Gardner coaxes the truth from me. She guides me to the hard ball of feelings that's sat like a weight in my chest for weeks.

It's painful, saying these things out loud. When tears start leaking from my eyes, Dr. Gardner pushes a box of tissues across the coffee table toward me. We do a breathing exercise that softens the knife-edge of my terror, and I slowly regain control over my own body.

By the time our hour is up, I feel exhausted, but for the first time in a long time, I don't feel alone. I don't feel like some freak of nature going through this horribly complicated medical drama. Many other women have been through what I've been through, I'm told. I'm not doomed. My baby isn't doomed.

But it still scares me to death.

"I can see you at the same time next week, if that works for you?" Dr. Gardner says from the chair at her desk, her computer lit up with an appointment calendar.

I nod. "Sure."

When I walk out of her office a few minutes later and tilt my head up to the blue sky, I feel...lighter. Still terrified, of course, but ever so slightly less alone.

Then I go home and sleep for three hours to recover. When I wake up in time for dinner, I feel a tiny step closer to opening up to my family and friends about what's going on. A little worm of doubt has wiggled inside me, whispering that my silence is hurting them—and me. I know I'll be better off once everyone knows the truth.

Realizing that and acting on it, though, are two very different things.

CANDICE'S new house is incredible. The fourteen-acre property has over a mile of coastline, and the architects did an amazing job with the design. It's a single-story building with so much glass, it almost disappears into the surrounding forest. Large, leafy trees line the winding drive before opening up to reveal the house. I have no idea how the landscapers got such large trees planted, but I suppose I don't have movie-star funds to make that kind of magic happen.

The house itself is just as beautiful. My mouth hangs open as I'm ushered inside and welcomed like an old friend.

"It's smaller than I expected from a movie star," Simone says before popping a corn chip in her mouth. She crunches down, then walks out onto the patio that extends so far it feels like it floats above the ocean below. The drop to the water is steep, with a narrow strip of sand to catch the lapping waves.

"I had no idea you thought so little of me," Blake responds, the grin apparent in his voice. "You don't think movie stars can do subtle?"

Simone just gives him a *look*. Before she can sass him, Wes drops his arm on Simone's shoulders and whispers something in her ear. Judging by Simone's blush, it's probably best that the rest of us can't hear.

I tear my eyes away from them. Last time a man whispered something in my ear like that, I was so wrapped up in loving him that I forgot about myself. Now I keep my distance. Mostly.

"It's gorgeous, Blake," I say, letting my eyes drift over the deep cherry hardwood, the tasteful navy furnishings, the elegant finishes. It's luxurious, but not ostentatious. The place feels like it's always existed on the property.

"The yoga studio should be done in two weeks," Candice cuts in smoothly, handing me a glass of wine. She pours another and gives it to Fiona, who has joined us on the patio. "I'm going to do an inaugural class with just us girls."

The way she says it makes me think I'm included in the "just us girls," which sends something warm gliding through my chest.

It's only been a couple of months since I showed up in this town, and already it feels more like home than Reno did. As soon as the thought pops into my head, I hear the familiar sound of my phone's ringtone. "Sorry," I mumble, then shuffle back to the couch to hunt through my purse. I should have put it on silent before I got here.

When I see my boss's name on the screen, my shoulders tighten.

"Everything okay, Nora?" Margaret asks, dressed in an

elegant cream pantsuit with a cowl-neck silk camisole underneath. She's arranging hors d'oeuvres on the tables dotted around the living room, but her eyes are on me. "You look a bit ill."

"Boss," I explain, waving my phone as I ignore the call.

"Is he expecting you back in Reno *again?*" Fiona asks from the balcony. "You just got back a couple of days ago."

"Terrible bosses will not be spoken of in this house!" a voice says from the entryway, and Trina appears, trailed by her two kids. "I'm making that a rule."

Candice laughs. "I can get behind that." She greets her sister with a hug, and the two of them restart the partial tour of the house that I've already gotten. I hear Candice tell her sister about the kitchen with large gas range, the home office, the gorgeous view from the spare bedroom. After greeting the kids, I give Mac a smile, then freeze in shock when he puts his arms around me in a hug.

"Good to see you, Nora," he says, as if we're best friends. Then he moves to Simone and Fiona and gives them the same treatment before shaking hands with Wes and Grant.

Yep. I'm one of "us girls." When did that happen?

My eyes drift to the door again, and I almost open my mouth to ask Mac whether his brother is coming or not. Just in time, I realize I haven't officially met Lee, and it would be monumentally weird for me to ask about him. Instead, I busy myself helping Margaret and Dorothy put out food and offer drinks to people.

"I'm supposed to be the host here," Candice chides, then laughs as she tosses a cherry tomato in her mouth.

"Oh, hush," Dorothy responds before topping up her wine. "Let us help."

A crash sounds from the kitchen, and everyone stops talking. After a pause, Jen's voice floats through the room. "We're okay! But, uh...Candice, you might need to replace a few plates."

"What happened?" Candice calls back as she moves toward the kitchen. It's around a corner. The house isn't quite open plan. The kitchen is attached to a casual dining room, but the balcony opens onto this bigger formal living room which is clearly designed for entertaining. That's where we are, all heads turned in the direction of the kitchen.

"Um," Jen answers, a bit more quietly, "Fallon was... clumsy."

I look up and meet Simone's eyes, who has a grin playing over her lips. "Clumsy, huh," she says quietly. "Maybe they need a chaperone in there."

"Eww," I answer. I may be a grown woman, but I don't need to think about my big brother doing things a chaperone wouldn't approve of.

Fiona just laughs at my reaction. The doorbell rings and Margaret says she'll get it, so Fiona glances toward the entrance. "I wonder when Lily will get here."

"Maybe she's coming over with Rudy. He was at her place last weekend when I stopped in, so I assume they've been spending weekends together," I answer, inspecting the fancy-looking hors d'oeuvres on the plate in front of me.

Another, more curious silence settles over the women in the room, and all eyes turn to me. Even Candice reappears from the kitchen and looks at me with keen interest in her gaze.

"My sister was with Rudy last weekend?" She tilts her head at me. "They were at Lily's place?"

"Did he sleep over?" Simone asks, taking a step toward me. "Wait. This was the morning after he had his business lunch with that other woman?"

"Oh my goodness," Fiona says, grabbing a bottle of wine to top us all up. "They hooked up? What time did you go over? Did it look like anything happened? I can't believe she didn't say anything! We spent all day together... That little hussy!"

"I'm going to kill her," Candice says. "She held out on us."

"Um..." I cringe. "I probably shouldn't have said anything."

"Oh, stop." Simone waves a hand. "Now spill."

"You want me to stop or spill? Seems contradictory."

"Stop stalling," Candice says, gripping my wrist as her eyes dance. "Tell us everything! You've been sitting on this news for a whole week!"

I laugh, then shrug. "I went over with a piece of cake, and we ate it. That's it." Sort of. Biting my lip, I glance over my shoulder at the door, then turn back to the women gathered around me. When I speak, my voice is low. "Rudy was just getting out of the shower when I arrived. He was wearing nothing but a towel. Lily's hair was wet too."

A high-pitched squeal rings out from every female mouth in the room, right before an avalanche of questions comes my way. Laughing, I throw my hands up. "I've said too much."

"Oh, no way, Nora," Fiona huffs. "You're not leaving us hanging like that."

"She's new," Simone says in a conciliatory tone, patting Fiona's arm. "She hasn't learned the rules yet."

"The rules?" I ask.

"Gossip must be shared at the earliest opportunity," Candice says solemnly. "Especially when it pertains to one of us girls."

I'm starting to like the sound of "us girls" more and more each time I hear it. It makes me feel like I've found a place where I can settle, and I haven't felt that way in a long time.

The doorbell rings again, and a shiver of anticipation runs through all my new friends. I can almost feel them bursting with questions about the new pairing. But when Blake moves to open the door, it's not Lily and Rudy who step through.

It's Lee—and his eyes land straight on me.

TWENTY-THREE

LILY

WHEN I ENTER Candice's living room, I'm immediately mobbed by a horde of women.

"So, we hear that Rudy looks good in a fluffy pink towel," Simone says, cutting straight to the important stuff, as usual. "Would you agree?"

Nora arches her brows at me. "I'm sorry. This is my fault."

"Oh, quiet, you," Simone says, waving a hand in Nora's general direction. "We'll deal with you holding back on break-ing-news-worthy gossip in a minute. First, Lily has to talk. How big is his dong?"

"Excuse me?" My eyes bug.

Fiona cackles. "Don't mind her. She asks everyone that."

"And do people actually answer?" I stare at Simone, who just shrugs. "Don't you all have something better to do than gossip about me?"

"Lily," Candice huffs, "you didn't even *mention* Rudy

sleeping over. You kept it a secret, which means..." Her voice drifts off as she wiggles her eyebrows.

Which means things are serious, she's saying.

When in doubt, play dumb. "Which means what?"

"Would you look what the cat dragged in!" My mother's voice carries from the entryway in the way that only a mother's voice can. Briefly, I wonder if I'll gain that ability within the next few months.

My mother's full name is Charlotte Anne Viceroy, but everyone calls her Lottie. I don't think my mother has been a Charlotte since the minute she was born. Too rambunctious, never demure. Today, she's dressed in neon-pink pants and a polka-dot top. Her glasses and lipstick match her pants, and it looks like she just got her pixie hair cut today. It sticks up in funky silver spikes.

Spreading her arms, my mother enters the living room. "Candice, it's gorgeous."

"You saw it this morning, Mom," Candice says with a wry smile. "You helped me set up the patio furniture."

"Yes, but I was saying that for everyone else's benefit." She turns at a scuffing sound in the hallway, and my throat tightens at the sight of Rudy and his grandmother arm-in-arm.

I haven't seen Rudy since Monday, and somehow, I'd forgotten how good he looks. He's wearing navy pants and a fitted white shirt. The top few buttons are undone, and the shirt clings to every hard muscle slabbed over his frame. He looks like a magazine advertisement. He looks like sex. He looks like my dream man.

Meeting my gaze, his eyes heat. He looks me up and down,

taking in the airy summer dress I'm wearing before his eyes soften on mine. Those lush, kissable lip tilt into a smile that I know is meant just for me.

I want to bulldoze everyone as I run and fling myself into his arms. I want to pull him into a broom closet, flip my skirt up, and beg him to screw me. I want to feel his arms wrapped around my body. I want to growl at any other woman who comes close to him so she knows he belongs to me.

Uh oh.

Those are *not* good feelings. Those are not the type of feelings one gets when one is about to drop a bombshell on a budding relationship.

My mother hooks her arm into Rudy's free one and gives his bicep a squeeze. "Isn't he just gorgeous?" She looks at me. "Isn't he, Lily?"

Oh no.

Somehow, my mother knows. She knows about last weekend, about everything. She might not know she knows, but she *knows*.

I squeeze my eyes. That doesn't even make sense. I need a drink.

No, I don't. I'm pregnant. And I have cancer. And I'm in a room full of people and no one knows the full truth but me. They all think I'm free to date Rudy and give them things to gossip about, but how will they react when I tell them what's really going on?

How will *Rudy* react when I tell him what's going on?

I turn my back on the new arrivals and stride to the nearest door. I'm startled to find it's a storage closet, then my brain helpfully provides images of me and Rudy together in a dark closet with my skirt bunched around my waist.

What the hell is wrong with me?

"Bathroom is down the hall, Lily," Candice says, her voice strangely muted.

"Thanks." I find the bathroom behind the next door I open, and lock myself inside. Flipping the toilet cover down, I sit and bury my face in my hands.

Last weekend was a mistake. A very fun, very pleasurable mistake, but a mistake nonetheless. The sight of Rudy makes me want to forget about all my issues, but my issues aren't going away. I'm already in my second trimester, and I have a doctor's appointment early next week where I'll schedule my mastectomy. Within a month or so, I'll have a baby bump.

I. Cannot. Date. Rudy.

Ever.

Especially not now.

But the thought of him standing there, being a doting-grandson-cum-male-model as he led his grandmother into Candice's house makes my body heat. I'm sitting on a toilet, horny as hell, feeling like world is ending.

This has got to be hormone related. My feelings are not normal. Everything just feels so...*big*. Big emotions, pulling me apart limb from limb. How the hell am I going to go back out there and face them all?

I don't know how long I sit there, but it's long enough for a knock to sound on the door and make me jump. My butt has gone numb.

"I'll be out in a minute!"

"It's me," Rudy's deep voice says from the other side of the door. "Will you let me in?"

Glancing at myself in the mirror, I'm glad to see I only look a little frazzled. Apparently, the hurricane of worry and stress and lust within me has stayed right where it should be—buried deep inside. I unlock the door and open it, and Rudy enters without hesitation.

The powder room is a good size, but it still feels too cramped for two people. I back up until my legs hit the closed toilet, keeping my eyes averted. The door closes. Rudy hooks his hand around my waist and pulls me close. Catching myself against his chest, I let out a shuddering breath.

"Iliana."

Not many people use my full name. The sound of it on Rudy's lips makes something twist and tighten in my gut. I'm not sure if it's lust or dread.

"Talk to me." His voice is patient, but his eyes are searching.

When I say nothing, he spreads his hand over my jaw and neck. Tilting my head up, he kisses me long and deep. He tastes like sunshine and sex, feels like silk sliding over my sensitized skin.

My panties are drenched. Damn it.

Rudy's kiss is unyielding. He kisses me like he's trying to tell me something—or maybe like he saw it in my face outside how much I wanted him. When his hand slides down my ass and dips under the hem of my dress, I let out a moan.

There's a tiny Iliana on my shoulder gripping my ear and screaming, "STOP RIGHT NOW, YOU IDIOT," but she's surprisingly easy to ignore as Rudy's hand climbs up the back of my thigh. His touch is pure heat and desire as he palms my ass and tugs me closer.

We could have sex right now. Candice would fucking kill me for desecrating her bathroom, of course, but Rudy and I could do it. My body is practically begging me to let him in, and that voice in my ear is getting softer and softer as the seconds tick by.

"You've been avoiding me," Rudy says, the words sounding ripped from his throat. Desire rides his voice like a low growl, and he drops his lips to my jaw. "All week, I've been needing you." He nips at my bottom lip. "I don't think you understand what I feel for you, Lily."

I blink, his words snapping me back to the present. I stiffen in his arms, and Rudy backs his head up to meet my eyes.

"The scared rabbit is back," he says, but he doesn't remove that palm from my ass—and damn it, but I like it there.

But I suck in a breath, and the fog clears from my vision. Rudy said he feels something for me. Rudy *feels* something for me. We've blown past the barriers of casual sex right into Feelings Land, which is nothing less than an unmitigated disaster.

And it's all my fault.

"I can't do this," I say, my voice raw.

There's a pause. Then, "Do what?" He moves his hand to smooth my dress back down, then replaces his hand on top of it right where it was before, smoothing over the curves of my rear.

I wish his touch didn't scramble my brain so badly. I can only manage one word in response to his question. "Us."

Rudy goes very still.

Squeezing my eyes shut, I shake my head. "There's too

much going on, and I need to focus on what I'm going to do. I can't deal with the gossip and the questions and feeling like I'm out of control every time I'm around you."

"I make you feel out of control?" The quiet in his voice doesn't fool me. He's not calm. Not even a little bit. The absolute stone-hardness of his body is anything but relaxed.

I snort, still not meeting his eyes. "You make me feel like nothing else matters, Rudy, but that's the problem. Other things *do* matter. It's all well and good to say you'll drive me to my surgery, but what happens then? What happens when I have one breast? What happens when I have to go through chemo for weeks and my hair starts falling out? What happens when I'm throwing up all the time and I have no energy to do...what we did last Saturday?"

What happens when you find out I'm pregnant with another man's child?

"You think I'm going to walk away because you won't want to have sex with me?" He sounds...hurt. "Lily, I'm not a fucking animal."

I shake my head. This is it. This is when I tell him about the baby and put this relationship to bed. He doesn't know what he's getting himself into, and the kindest thing for me to do is lay all my cards on the table and show him that things between us will never work. We've been dating for what, a month?

This relationship won't survive cancer, never mind a baby that isn't his.

But when the thought crosses my mind, my stomach tightens into a knot. Rudy looks so sincere right now. So patient and kind and caring.

What if I told him about the baby, and he broke his cardinal rule? What if he stayed?

I heard his voice when he talked about the child he treated as his own. No matter what he says, he wanted kids. That wound may be old, but it hasn't healed.

But if he promised me the world and then left me the same way my ex did, it would hurt so much worse. Leaving Phil was easy, because at the end of the day, I didn't need him. The problems heaped onto my plate were so much bigger, so much more important than a breakup with a man who lied and never truly cared about me.

Rudy is different. If I let him in and he left me...it would break me.

I can't give him that chance.

Instead, I straighten my shoulders and try to clear the pain from my face. "Rudy, I don't want this. I had fun with you, but I'm not looking for a relationship. I'm not going to date you."

He stares into my eyes for a moment, and it takes all my willpower to hold his gaze. It feels important, though, like I need to prove to him that I mean it. That by meeting his eyes, he'll know I'm serious.

It breaks my heart when I realize I'm right. His shoulders drop as his lips pinch, and he gives me a sharp nod. The hardness in his body remains, but he backs away from me. His eyes grow hard. "Fine. If that's what you want."

"It is," I answer, more to convince myself than to convince him.

When he flinches, I regret my words. All I can do is nod before I slip past him.

Once outside the bathroom, my mother is the first one to notice something's wrong. I mumble a few words about not feeling well, and she lets me go. Agnes is the next to accost me, and she tells me all went well with the audit. She says something about saving her thousands in back taxes, but the words sound all fuzzy. I can't focus. I just nod.

Candice walks me to the door and tries to meet my gaze, but I just wave her off. I'm already inside my car when Trina comes rushing out to knock on my window.

As soon as it lowers, she leans into the car. "You good?"

"Just feeling a bit under the weather," I tell her, and it's mostly the truth.

She searches my face for a moment, then nods. "You need me to come with you to any doctors' appointments? My schedule is flexible. I'll make time."

I start shaking my head, then pause. These past few weeks have felt good to have people around, to be able to lean on my family. So, instead of refusing, I nod at my sister. "Yeah. I'll let you know."

As my sister watches me for a moment, I try not to squirm. Then gives me a sharp jerk of her chin. "Good. Get some sleep."

When I back the car out of its parking space and get on the road that heads home, I let out a long sigh of relief.

I did the right thing. Even if Rudy had convinced himself he wanted to pursue something with me, he would've regretted it. I saved us both a mountain of heartache.

I'm better off without him—and he's definitely better off without me.

TWENTY-FOUR
RUDY

IT SHOULDN'T BOTHER ME. It *shouldn't.*

I've known the woman, what, a few weeks? Before that, I met her once at a Thanksgiving dinner years ago? Why do I care that she broke things off? We went on a couple of dates. Spent one night together. Big deal.

I should be thanking her for breaking things off. She did me a favor.

My fingers drum on my steering wheel as I make my way back to town, taking a circuitous route home—and I realize with a start that my path will take me past Lily's house.

Am I a stalker now? What the hell am I doing?

Shaking my head, I turn off on the next cross street and head straight home.

The housewarming party was fine. It would have been fun if I didn't have acid boiling in my stomach. I must have done a decent job of faking it after Lily left, though, because no one said anything to me about it. Not even my grandmother.

When I make it home, the old house feels drafty and cold. I keep the lights off and toss my shoes on the mat by the door, then pad toward the back of the house. When I pass my office, I see my laptop on my desk. Too wound up to do anything else, I power up my computer and decide to do some work.

There's an email waiting for me when I turn the laptop on. It's from Georgia Neves, who wants to introduce me to a friend of hers who's interested in buying a property in Heart's Cove. She's a shameless flirt, even over email. She insists on introducing us in person, preferably over a meal. Her treat.

Having interacted with Georgia a lot over the past couple of weeks, I know she flirts out of some sort of habit. She's mentioned her divorce a few times and isn't quite able to hide the pain in her eyes when she does. I don't think she's actually interested in me. She just uses sex and flirtation as a defense mechanism.

The email shouldn't make me feel bitter. It should make me want to return her flirtation, should make me want to fall into bed with her, because I need to shore up my defenses as much as she does—but all I want to do is find Lily and let me clear those shadows from her gaze. I have this undeniable urge to protect Lily from whatever's bothering her. I want to be the knight in shining armor for her dark and twisted fairy tale.

It's only when I've been sitting in front of a blank screen for the better part of an hour that I give up on work. I leave the email unanswered, marking it on my to-do list for Monday. I rub my stinging eyes and let out a sigh, tipping my head back to stare at the ceiling.

Lily got under my skin. Somehow, between fish and chips and a crushed champagne fountain, Lily burrowed into a part of me that hasn't been touched in a long time.

After my ex left me and took the daughter I thought of as my own, I shut a part of myself away. I vowed to never let someone hurt me the way she did. I told myself to live in the moment, to live for me. What use is it giving my all to someone, only to have it thrown back in my face?

How could I be so stupid to let that happen again with Lily?

I replay all our conversations as I lean back in my office chair, propping my feet on the desk and folding my hands over my stomach. There's got to be a way around this. This sick feeling in my stomach won't go away, and I can't convince myself that leaving Lily alone is a good thing. We got along. We clicked. We *had* something. When did things change? When did she decide she didn't want me?

She's terrified of the cancer. Understandable. She pushed me away because she doesn't think I'm up for it—or she doesn't want to burden me with caring for her. That's understandable too.

It's also fucking incorrect. Caring for her wouldn't be a burden; it'd be a privilege.

I stare at a spot on the wall, seeing nothing.

There's something else. There was a moment in the shower, when I told her I didn't want kids. I frown, staring at a cobweb in the corner of the room. She...wants kids? Maybe she never met someone she wanted to have kids with, and she feels like she's running out of time? And the cancer complicates everything?

Grunting, I drop my feet from the desk to the floor.

If we'd been dating longer—even as little as a couple of months—it would be different. Maybe then I'd have a chance at proving to her that I care. Maybe then, if I showed up at her door and begged her not to push me away, it'd be less "psycho stalker" and more "worthy partner."

So what are my options?

I can respect Lily's decision and back off. Let her deal with her own demons and keep my distance. The thought makes me ill. I want to be beside her. If I could pick up a weapon and fight her cancer in her place, I would. But what right do I have? We weren't even officially together. From the start, she was clear that she didn't want anything serious.

Alternatively, I can try to convince her that I don't care about the illness, and she's worth the effort and heartache and care that it'll take to get through it together.

If she wants kids, I...

I squeeze my eyes shut. I feel like I lost a daughter already, and that pain hasn't faded in the years that have passed. If Lily wanted kids, would I be willing to open that part of my heart to her?

I don't think I can. A breath leaves my lips and my mouth tastes sour. If Lily wants children, I'm not sure I'm ready to be the man for her. Years ago, I decided I wouldn't be a father. Nothing has changed.

The phone rings. I glance at the screen and see Lee's name.

When I put it to my ear, he doesn't even wait to hear my voice. "I'm outside," he says. "Taking you out to the Grove."

Huffing, I agree and hang up to grab my shoes. Lee's father owns the Grove. Hamish doesn't drink, and claims he bought the bar years ago so he'd have an excuse to hang out with his buddies without having to get drunk. If you ask me, it sounds like a recipe for disaster and relapse, but to each their own. Sometime over the past year or so, it's not just his buddies that sit in the old dive bar full of grizzly, wannabe bikers. Candice and all her friends regularly have girls' nights there, and even the older generation make regular visits.

It helps that Margaret, one of the twins who owns the hotel, has Hamish wrapped around her little finger. I never thought I'd see the old man in love until I saw the way he treats Margaret.

Maybe there's hope for us all.

Lee is sitting on his big, gleaming Harley Davidson motorcycle outside. I jerk my head to my car. "I'll take my car."

With a nod, Lee starts the engine and pulls out of my driveway, then waits for me to follow. The parking lot is mostly empty, which makes sense, because the only days it's full is when there's a girls' night going on. I pull into an oil-stained parking space and get out, locking the car behind me.

Lee meets me at the door, the soft leather of his jacket creaking as he pulls it open. "You looked like you needed a drink when you left Blake and Candice's."

I snort. "That obvious?"

Lee just grins and enters the bar behind me.

Three regulars who are as much fixtures as the stools they sit on glance up as we enter. Recognizing the two of us, they turn back to their drinks without so much as a greeting. I follow Lee to the bar and take a seat, accepting the beer that's placed in front of me.

I brace myself for Lee to ask me about Iliana, but he jerks his head at the television. "You catch the game?"

Not being a huge fan of baseball, I shrug. "Nah."

We slide into easy conversation, talking about nothing at all. Certainly not my love life—or lack thereof. It's not until a long while later that Lee clears his throat and says, "You know Fallon's sister?"

"What about her?" The basket of fries I ordered a few minutes ago slides across the bar as the bartender nods at me. I bite one in half and exhale when it nearly burns the skin off the roof of my mouth.

When I finally look at Lee again, he just shrugs. "She seems nice."

I blink. I've been so caught up in my own life that I never even noticed Lee talking to Nora. Did they talk? Is this why he asked me here? Not about Iliana at all, but about his own issues?

Grinning, I lean back in my stool and pop another too-hot fry in my mouth. "Yeah," I say. "She does."

"I heard she met up with you last weekend. Something about you looking good in nothing but a towel?"

I can't help it. I laugh. Clapping Lee on the shoulder, I shove him until he scowls. "You jealous?"

"Fuck off." He bites into one of my fries and has the same

reaction at the temperature of them, breathing out aggressively to stop his mouth from burning.

"I was at Lily's place," I finally say to put Lee out of his misery. "Nora brought some cake over. I think she was surprised I was there and was coming over to gossip with Lily about me."

My mouth twists. Not much to gossip about anymore.

Lee's shoulders relax ever so slightly. If I hadn't been paying attention, I would've missed it.

Behind him, the door to the bar opens, and Hamish appears with Margaret on his arm. Her twin, Dorothy, trails behind them while my grandmother brings up the rear.

"Rudy!" Dorothy exclaims, gliding over to me. "You came here and didn't even invite us to join!"

"Oh, leave him be," my grandmother grumbles. "Why would he want to spend time with an old cow like you?"

"Go find a bridge to guard, troll," Dorothy replies, keeping a bright smile on her face and her eyes on me. "Did you enjoy the housewarming, Rudy?"

"It was great, Dorothy," I reply. "You ladies want a drink? It's on me."

"On the house," Hamish corrects, ducking behind the bar to get us all a round.

"Hey, Hamish," the bartender says from the other end. "We got a booking for one of the rooms." He jerks his head toward a door that leads to the three tiny rooms on the second floor above the bar. To my knowledge, bookings are exceedingly rare. Only a few guests per year have stayed in them since the Cedar Grove opened over a decade ago—but Lee might have been exaggerating when he told me that. All I know is a booking is rare enough to be unusual.

Hamish still lets out a whoop. "How long are they staying?"

"Guy named Phil," the bartender says, clicking something on the computer behind the bar to pull up the booking system on the screen. "He's booked a week. Gets here next month—early September."

Hamish glances over his shoulder, then nods. "I'll get the cleaners to prepare the room."

"Let's celebrate!" Dorothy exclaims. "Shots! From one hotelier to another."

"Dorothy, you're an old woman," her sister groans. "Don't you think you should have stopped drinking shots fifty years ago?"

"She only pretends to drink them," my grandmother cuts in. "Gets everyone else drunk and takes pictures for blackmail."

"That was *one time*, Agnes," Dorothy replies with a roll of her eyes. "It happened in the eighties, for crying out loud. I would've thought you'd let it go by now."

I rap my knuckles on the bar and slide off my stool. "I'm out," I say. "I can't keep up with you ladies when you get going."

"Don't think we won't corner you and ask you what's going on with Lily," Dorothy says, pointing a finger at me. "We'll let you off easy tonight, but the interrogation is coming."

I force a grin. "Can't wait," I lie.

When I step back outside, I suck in a deep breath and let it out slowly. I love this town, but sometimes its residents can be overbearing. I understand why Lily chose to travel the world for so long—and why she might not want to tie herself to a place like this—or a man like me. Maybe it's better for me to be unattached too. I might be the one who needs to take off on an international adventure to escape the weight of this town, the gossip, the lack of privacy. It's better to be unattached. I've known that for a long time.

But no matter how many times I tell myself she did us both a favor by breaking things off, it doesn't help the fact that I don't believe my own lies.

TWENTY-FIVE
LILY

MY SECOND TRIMESTER trundles on without me noticing. I have more energy than I did before, and I end up throwing myself into my work. For two weeks, I keep to myself, finding a few new clients from local businesses who need help with their accounts, plus a few other remote clients that should keep me busy until tax time comes around.

I don't think about Rudy. Mostly.

It's the middle of August, and I'm once again in my obstetrician's office listening to a prognosis that doesn't sound too good.

My oncologist is here too.

"We'd like to schedule your surgery as soon as possible, Iliana." My oncologist, Dr. Gilmore, is a distinguished-looking man in his early fifties. He's done many mastectomies and is confident he can treat me while I'm pregnant. "Normally, with your type of cancer, I'd recommend a breast-conserving surgery. The tumor is still small, and there are no signs it has metastasized. However, BCS would require us to give you radiation as an adjuvant treatment post-surgery, which isn't safe for the baby."

I nod. They've told me this before, but by the patient tone in Dr. Gilmore's voice, I know he doesn't mind re-explaining it.

"There are some chemotherapy drugs that are safe for the fetus," he continues. "So what I would recommend is that we perform the mastectomy and follow up with chemotherapy. Although it's safe for the baby in terms of development, there is a very small risk of early delivery."

Dr. Alder, my obstetrician, says something to agree with Dr. Gilmore. They both rattle off more information than I can absorb about safety of procedures and outcomes and prognoses. I can feel my anxiety ratcheting higher.

"Can we wait until after the baby is born?" I ask, my voice smaller than I'd intended. "I know you said chemo is safe for the fetus, but it just... It makes me uncomfortable."

Dr. Gilmore purses his lips. "Iliana, if we wait, there's a risk the cancer could metastasize—it could spread. The absolute best way to treat this is to remove it as soon as possible. Survival rates for your type of cancer drop dramatically when intervention is delayed. Taking into account the progress of your tumor since you've been under our care, leaving adjuvant therapy until after you give birth is a risk I strongly, strongly advise you not to take."

I know he's right. Despite my grumbling, I've read all the pamphlets. I've been going to see Dr. Gardner every week, and the terror choking me has receded with every passing day. I know the doctors have my best interests at heart, and my hesitations come from a place of irrational fear.

I can't put this off any longer; I need to just face my demons and move on with my life. Plus, after the surgery, after the chemotherapy, I'll finally get to meet my baby—if that's not a reward for staring down cancer and surgery, I don't know what is.

But when the doctors book my surgery for two weeks from now, it takes all my self-control to keep my face steady. Inside, I'm panicking. I still haven't told anyone. I've been holed up in my apartment working, eating, and sleeping, only leaving to go exercise or do groceries. My sister Trina has stopped by a few times, but my mother and Candice seem busy with her new house. Nora's called me regularly, but she's been shuffling over and back to Reno all the time and we haven't had time to catch up.

That's probably mostly my fault, though.

Now, my reprieve is ending. No matter how much I want to carry this burden on my own, I know my family would never forgive me if I went into surgery without telling them. I've had a few weeks to prepare with my therapist, I've done the breathing exercises and the journaling and all the homework she's given me. I broke up with Rudy and I'm determined to face these things from a place of strength.

The final thing I need to do is tell my family.

I'll do it today.

Decision made, appointment over, I thank the doctors, stop at reception for payment and my next booking, then leave the office. Once I'm in my car, I sit for a few moments before grabbing my phone.

"Hello, stranger," Trina says when she answers my call. I can hear the hiss of an espresso machine and the chatter of a few people, and I know she's at the Four Cups Café.

"Hey, Trina," I say. "What's up?"

There's shuffling, and the background noises die down. "Lily! Where are you? We're all at Four Cups. Mom was just saying we should go break down your door for a welfare check, because she hasn't seen you in nearly two weeks." Her voice drops. "You okay?"

"I..." I pause. I don't want to lie. "Do you think you could get everyone up to the library? I need to tell you all what's going on, and I don't want to do it more than once."

There's a slight pause, then Trina lets out a breath. "Yep. Of course. We'll all be up there in ten minutes. Is that good?"

My heartbeat picks up, but I force myself to nod. Then I remember Trina can't see me. "Yeah," I say. "That's good. I'll see you there."

"I'm proud of you, Lily," my sister tells me, her voice oddly muted as if she's tamping down a wave of emotion. "It'll feel good to tell everyone about the baby."

I almost laugh. She doesn't even know the half of it. Instead of blurting it out over the phone, I tell her goodbye and hang up, then lean against the headrest and close my eyes.

I want to call Rudy. How crazy is that? We haven't talked to each other since the housewarming party, when I told him I wasn't interested in pursuing anything with him. He respected my decision and hasn't tried to rekindle anything between us, which makes me feel good and awful at the same time.

So why do I have this urge to call him to stand next to me when I tell my family what's been going on? Why do I want to feel his palm against mine and draw on his strength when I face my uncertain future?

Shaking my head, I brush the thought away. This right here —this need to lean on Rudy—is the whole reason I broke it off with him. How can I trust my feelings when they could just as easily be neediness? I don't care about Rudy, I'm just using him for his strength and support.

That's not fair to him. It's not fair to me.

I need to face this on my own.

Turning the car on, I back out of my parking space and make my way to the Four Cups Café. I park down the road and take a deep breath, then start the long walk to the library.

It's not really a long walk, but it feels like I'm about to face the gallows. When I pass the new community garden, Dorothy glances up from a garden bed. She's got a wide-brim straw hat on, and she gives me a wave and a big smile. "Gorgeous Lily! Come help me lift this tree into the hole."

The garden is taking shape beautifully. It seems like thousands of plants have been added, benches have been installed, and a beautiful mural has been painted on the brick wall lining one side of the property. There are big handmade pots that I know were donated by Mac. I recognize his style, the sweeping glazing and dramatic shapes that are all his own. The garden feels like a tiny, beautiful world that encompasses all of what Heart's Cove really is. Home, community, family, and growth.

And I live here now, right alongside everyone else.

Angling toward the older woman, I force a smile onto my lips. Dorothy tells me about Hamish's guest, who will arrive in a few weeks, then jokes about him being the hotel's new competition. Then she cackles, as if it's a huge joke. She waves at the small tree with its root ball still wrapped in burlap. "Lift that up so I can cut the burlap away," she tells me.

Obliging, I grab the trunk and lift it up. Distantly, I wonder if she'd ask me this if she knew about the pregnancy. Will everyone treat me like I need to be wrapped in bubble wrap? Will they understand that I just want to be treated normally?

Dorothy prepares the roots and then directs me to the hole in the ground. I place the tree in and keep it straight while she shovels some dirt around it to keep it in place.

"Any chance you could help me plant a few more?" She nods to the half-dozen saplings leaning against the wall.

"I'm supposed to meet my family at Four Cups," I say apologetically. "I'm already late."

"Fine," Dorothy says with a put-upon sigh. Then she grins. "Maybe I can call young Rudy to help me."

I force a smile. I know she's trying to be nice, but the sound of Rudy's name just makes my stomach tighten. I excuse myself and wave goodbye, then continue on my way to the café.

I wish things were simple. I wish I could enjoy the gentle teasing from Dorothy and the rest of the ladies in town, and that the worst thing in my life was a bit of embarrassment about a budding—and failed—relationship.

Instead, I have to face down my family and tell them all my

darkest fears, all the while knowing I have no right to want Rudy at all.

Palms slick with sweat don't dry when I wipe them on my pants. My heart beats an unsteady drum in my chest, and it's all I can do to put one foot in front of another. When I make it to the café, I peek inside and note that my sister isn't inside. She must have succeeded in herding everyone upstairs.

With trembling hands, I push the red door open and make my way up to the library. The chatter of many voices floats down the stairs, cranking my nerves a little tighter. When I open the door, all eyes land on me and the voices die.

"Lily," my mother says after a moment of heavy silence. "What's all this about? Are you okay?"

"Mom," Trina admonishes. "Let her walk in the door, at least. You promised you'd let her speak."

Lottie ignores her completely, moving to wrap her arms around me. She pins my arms to my sides as she hugs me tight, and even though my mother is four inches shorter than me, her embrace still makes me feel like a little girl. I nearly break down and cry right then and there.

Instead, I pull myself together and back away, squeezing my mother's arm as I straighten up.

That's when I notice that it isn't just my sisters in the room. Fiona, Simone, Nora, and Jen are there, too. I almost turn right back around, but a deep breath steadies my nerves. They're my friends now, and if I tell everyone at once, it's one less explanation I have to make.

My mother shoves me closer to one of the couches and

forces me to sit down. She waves her hand until everyone else is seated. Candice is beside me and Fiona is in the armchair to my left. Jen leans against the counter of the small kitchenette next to Nora, and Simone perches on the arm of Fiona's chair. My mother takes the seat on the other side of me and grips my hand while Trina pulls out an office chair and sits across from us.

Silence settles over us like a heavy blanket. I need to say something. I spent the whole drive here thinking of how I would tell them what's going on, but the words seem to die in my throat.

The seconds drag on a little too long because my mother finally huffs. "What is it, Lily? Are you pregnant?"

"Mom!" Trina cuts in, widening her eyes at Lottie.

Our mother shrugs. "What? Look at her face." She thrusts her index finger at my cheek. "She looks like she's about to puke, and don't think I haven't noticed that you're not drinking," she says, turning to me. "You forget that I gave birth to all three of you. I know a pregnant woman when I see one. What are you, twelve weeks along?"

"Fifteen," I answer meekly.

Everyone sucks in a breath, except my mother, who rolls her eyes. "Well, there you go. Will you pick up the phone and call me once in a while now that that's out of the way? You fly halfway around the world to come to Heart's Cove and then you ignore us all. Makes no sense."

"Mom, give her a break," Candice cuts in, patting my knee. "Pregnancy is overwhelming."

"You think I don't know that?"

"I wish I hadn't gotten rid of all my baby stuff," Candice says.

"I've got a garage full of it," Trina cuts in. "I already told her she was welcome to it."

"You *knew?*" Mom looks outraged.

"Uh-oh," Simone mumbles, voicing what everyone else is thinking.

Mute, I sit in my seat, head whipping from one person to the next. I've lost control of the conversation.

"I found out a few weeks ago," Trina answers with a wave her hand. "I found out by accident."

"A few *weeks* ago?" my mother screeches.

"And you didn't tell anyone?" Candice is the one who looks upset now.

"It wasn't my secret to tell!" Trina stands, picking up a mug from the coffee table and bringing it over to the sink. Jen shuffles out of the way. Nora gives me a sympathetic arch of her brows.

"How are you doing, hon?" Fiona leans forward to rest her elbows on her knees. "I've never been pregnant, but I'll help in any way I can."

"Me neither, and same," Simone agrees with a nod. "Candice, you know how to do prenatal yoga, right? Maybe we can have regular sessions until the baby gets here."

"That's a good idea," Candice says with a nod. "The studio is getting a final coat of paint today, but we could start in a couple days, once the smell of paint clears out."

"Do you have a nursery?" Simone asks. "We could help prepare your apartment for the baby." She tilts her head. "Are you going to stay in that apartment? You don't think you should get something a bit bigger?"

"Babies don't need much room," Trina says. "The apartment will be fine for the first year at least, and it'll be one less stress for Lily to worry about. The last thing she needs to be doing right now is moving all her stuff again."

"True," Simone says. "We should have a baby shower! Jen, you could make baby-themed cupcakes. Do we know if it's a boy or a girl?"

As if they've remembered I'm here, all eyes turn to me. My head is spinning from the conversation, and I feel a weird mix of gratitude that I have such a support system, and sheer terror at what I need to tell them. "Not yet," I start slowly, then clear my throat. "I, ah... There's something else."

My mother's eyes narrow. Candice's hand reappears on my knee. Silence crashes over the room, and I have to close my eyes.

I told Rudy. I should be able to say the words once more without puking all over myself.

The thought of Rudy's reaction centers me, and I take a deep breath. "I have breast cancer," I say in the silence. When no one answers, I open my eyes and keep going. "I was diagnosed a couple of weeks after the doctor confirmed I was pregnant. I'm getting surgery in two weeks. A mastectomy." I point to my left boob. "They need to take the whole thing because radiation isn't safe for the baby, which I would need to have if they weren't removing the entire breast."

Everyone is frozen. My mother makes a little squeaky noise, and I don't have the courage to look at her. If I do, I might cry.

A deep breath buoys my courage. "I'll have at least one

round of chemotherapy, which will be once a week for six weeks following my surgery. It's safe for the baby, but there's a small risk of me giving birth early. My medical team assures me that everything is safe and it's likely I'll make a full recovery, but I, uh"—I gulp—"I'm just telling you because I don't know how my treatment will affect me. I might need some help over the next few months."

To my surprise, the first person to react is Simone. Exuberant, brash Simone, who always has a quip and a sarcastic remark. She jumps off the arm of Fiona's chair and leans over me, planting a big kiss on my cheek. "You are so brave," she says quietly, both hands on either side of my face. "Thank you for trusting us with this."

Candice's hand is clenched over my knee. I meet Trina's eyes across the room and see them filled with tears. Oh no. She's going to start me off.

Gathering my strength, I look at my mother. "Mom," I say gently when I see her stricken face, "I'll be fine."

She snaps out of whatever stupor was holding her and gives me a sharp nod. "I know. Of course you will, honey." Her smile is fierce and more than a little forced. "You *will* be fine."

I have a feeling she's saying it to convince herself more than me, but I manage to nod before the first of my tears spills over my cheek. From there, the library turns into waterworks central. Every single one of us turns into a blubbering mess. Even Jen, who I don't know very well, has wet cheeks as she passes tissues around the room. I'm smothered in hugs and kisses and promises to help.

And...a weight lifts off my shoulders.

I was terrified that I'd be burdening them, that my fear and illness would drag them down with me. Instead, as we try in vain to dry our eyes, a strange, beautiful sort of lightness fills the room. For the first time—maybe in my whole life—I realize that friendship has a touch of magic to it. My soul feels lighter than it has in a long time.

Opening up to these women wasn't a mistake. I've been shutting myself away for fear of dragging them all down, but I hadn't considered that it could actually bring us closer together.

What if I'd trusted Rudy the same way I've trusted them? What if I was wrong, thinking he would've eventually walked away? What if there *are* people who will stick by you through thick and thin?

The father of my child walked away, but that doesn't mean everyone else will. What if I don't have to live the rest of my life alone?

"Well, look on the bright side," Simone says, plucking another tissue from the box Jen thrusts at her. She dabs her eyes before giving me a watery smile. "At least you'll have an excuse to get a boob job."

"Simone," Candice chides, but her lips twitch.

"She's got a point, honey," my mother says, shrugging, and for the first time in many, many weeks, I find myself laughing about my future and my fears. "Once you have kids, it's all downhill from there. Literally."

"Actually, they're doing a reconstruction in the same operation as the mastectomy," I say.

"Any chance they'll plump up the other one while they're at it?" Simone grins. "I know I'd be asking for it."

A few agreeing grunts sound in the room, and I let out another laugh. Leaning back against the couch, I meet my mother's gaze.

She pats my knee, her eyes still shining. "You'll be fine, honey."

This time, it sounds like she believes it.

TWENTY-SIX

RUDY

GEORGIA HAS her arm hooked into the crook of my elbow from the time we leave my office to the time we reach her car. She jingles the keys to her new home and gives me a coy smile. "I won't be able to use this excuse to talk to you anymore."

Despite myself, I let out a laugh. At least she's upfront about it. "I hope you didn't buy a five-million-dollar property just as an excuse to talk to me."

"If I did, it would be worth it." Smooth words from a woman who doesn't mean them. She clicks the fob in her other hand to unlock the Mercedes SUV behind her, then gives me a look. "I bought champagne to celebrate my first time stepping through the doors to this house. It would be a shame to drink it all by myself."

I'm a professional. I've never slept with a client, and I have no desire to sleep with Georgia. I open my mouth to reject her as diplomatically as I can when a door opens behind me and women come spilling out.

"Rudy!" Lottie calls out behind me. "Long time no see. Have you been hiding along with Lily all this time?"

I turn to see the older woman exiting the door that leads to the library above Four Cups. Beside her is Lily, and the sight of her takes my breath away.

For the past couple of weeks, I've thrown myself into my work and given her space. I wanted to respect her wishes and show her I care what she says—and sometime in the past few weeks, I convinced myself it was the right decision. We shouldn't be together. I don't need to care for someone with cancer, not when I've made it my mission to keep my relationships short and casual.

But she tucks a strand of dark hair behind her ear and blinks those bright eyes at me, and all I want to do is fall to my knees in front of her.

"Lily," I choke out.

She inhales sharply, and that's when I notice the redness of the tip of her nose, and the wetness gathered on her lashes.

"Have you been crying?" I take a step toward her. Just like that, the past few weeks disappear from my mind. I can't walk away from her. I can't leave her be. All I want to do is tug her close and wipe those tears from her face.

"We were all crying," Lottie announces. "Absolutely ridiculous. Bunch of blubbering messes, every one of us. Weren't we?" She turns to Candice, who snorts and nods.

"Went through an entire box of Kleenex," Simone says. "Literally the whole box."

"Absurd," Nora adds.

"Are you okay?" I ask Lily, not once taking my eyes off her. There are lines around her eyes that weren't there before, but her shoulders are relaxed.

"Oh, I'm just peachy," she responds, and for some reason, everyone bursts out laughing. Even Lily's lips twitch and twitch until she's leaning on one of her sisters and laughing along with them. I look at the group of women, frowning. I don't understand what's so funny...

And then the penny drops. I look at all the faces of her closest friends and family, and I realize she told them what's going on. "They know?" I ask softly.

Lily's eyes widen slightly. She straightens off her sister's shoulder and gives me a single, sharp nod.

Then Lottie makes a noise and throws her hands up. "Hold on. Wait, wait, wait." She whirls on Lily. "Rudy knew too? You told *Rudy* before you told me? Your own mother, Lily?"

"Mom," Lily starts, eyes flicking from me to Lottie and back again.

"I'm hurt. Shocked. Offended!" Lottie thrusts a finger in the air. "My own daughter won't confide in me! My own baby daughter goes *weeks* without telling me that she's—"

"*Mom.*" Lily's voice is hard. "Please. Not here."

Lottie takes a deep breath and drops her hand. "Fine." She glances at me, then over my shoulder. "And who are you?"

With a start, I realize Georgia is still standing behind me. She takes a step forward and slides a hand over my forearm. Lily's eyes zero in on the touch, but there's no space for me to pull away. I try to gently move my hand, and Georgia drops the touch. It's one of those moments where I think she acted out of habit without thinking. Fell back on her defenses and used the fact that she's an attractive woman to build up her strength.

"I'm Georgia Neves. I just bought a property, and Rudy and I were about to celebrate."

"Celebrate?" Candice asks, eyes narrowing.

Anger is a blade slicing across my chest. They're mad at *me?* After Lily pushed me away and ignored me for weeks, they're treating me like I'm some kind of asshole for doing my *job?*

"Yeah," I hear myself saying. "We were just heading out to her new place."

"Just the two of you?" Fiona asks, tilting her head. She frowns, then glances at Lily.

My chest feels hot at the look that passes over every woman's face. Do they not realize that *Lily* broke up with *me?* That I told her I actually *wanted* to be by her side, and she turned around and pushed me away? That she was the one who insisted we keep things casual?

And now they're looking at me like I'm a piece of shit?

Please.

The edges of my vision go red. Yes, I know they're thinking I'm going to sleep with Georgia and hell, maybe I will. Who the fuck are they to make me feel like I shouldn't? Lily and I were never an item. She made that perfectly clear. I was the fool who clung to the hope that something could happen between us. I was the idiot who followed her around like a pathetic puppy in need of affection.

"We better get going if we're going to catch the sunset," Georgia helpfully supplies.

Lily's face is blank, and she gives me a pinched smile. "Well, have fun. Should be a nice one tonight."

"I'm sure it will be," I hear myself say, and I turn to Georgia. "Shall we?"

"Would you like to drive, or should I?" She dangles her fob between two manicured fingers.

I grab the key. "I'll drive."

When I walk around the car and get behind the wheel, I don't look at the group of women still standing on the sidewalk.

TWENTY-SEVEN
FIONA

GRANT IS in the kitchen when I get home. He has his back to me and calls out a hello without looking, his eyes on whatever he's chopping on the cutting board in front of him. I say nothing as I make a beeline toward him and wrap my arms around his waist, shoving my face into his back. I inhale the scent of him and let his chuckle sink into my bones.

"Everything okay?"

"Lily's pregnant," I say, my voice muffled in his T-shirt.

He spins around, leaning against the counter and pulling me close. "Oh," he says softly, wrapping his arms around me and resting his head against the top of mine. "Are we happy about this news?"

"Yes," I say. "But she also has cancer."

He blows out a breath. "Damn."

"*And* we saw Rudy, and he was just about to hook up with a client of his who just closed on a house."

Grant freezes against me, and I glance up to see him frowning. "That doesn't sound like Rudy," he notes. "He dates a lot of women, but he's serious about his business. Doesn't mix the two."

"Trust me," I say. "I saw it with my own eyes."

He leans down to press a soft kiss on my lips. "Were he and Lily together?"

I chew my bottom lip. "No."

"So why are you mad at him?"

I huff. "He and Lily were supposed to end up happy together. I asked her if he ran away when he found out about the cancer, but she said she's the one who broke it off. I don't know. I just don't believe it."

Grant kisses me again and leans his forehead against mine. "What kind of cancer is it?"

"Breast," I tell him. "She'll lose her breast and have to get chemo, all while being pregnant. I don't even want to think about how hard that'll be."

"What can I do to help?"

The words are soft, but they warm me all the way to my toes. This is why I fell in love with Grant. He's such a strong, steady presence in my life. The past few years have been so full of joy that if I had tried to imagine this life when I was married to my ex-husband, I wouldn't have thought it was possible. My past feels like a distant story that happened to someone else.

Glancing at the diamond ring glittering on my finger, I snuggle into Grant's chest and let out a sigh. "I don't know. Just hug me."

He chuckles, then presses a kiss to the top of my head.

"That, I can do." His hands sweep over my back before moving lower. "And maybe we can ask Miss Fifi if she needs some company later."

I freeze, pull away, and stare up at him. Horror floods every inch of me. "Miss Fifi," I whisper, remembering that mortifying conversation I had with Simone about my own freaking vagina. Grant walked in on us talking about it, and I just about exploded from embarrassment. "You *knew*? You knew what we were talking about?"

Grant's lips twitch. "She's not so shy anymore, is she?" His hands slide around to my front and I yelp, laughing. I bat his hands away until he wraps me up in a hug and pulls me tight to his chest. "Don't push me away," he growls, pressing a kiss to the corner of my lips. "I've become quite fond of Miss Fifi."

"You're unbelievable."

"Would you say Miss Fifi is having more fun than she had in college, or less? Just for reference." His hands slide over my curves again and squeeze.

I bark out a laugh. "Stop it."

Pausing, Grant pulls away and gives me one of the crinkly-eyed smiles I love so much. "Never."

TWENTY-EIGHT
LILY

THE GIRLS SPLIT up shortly after Rudy drives away, and I end up having dinner at Trina's house. My mother attempts to drive me home, but I insist on walking, telling her in no uncertain terms that no matter what's going on with me physically, I will not be coddled.

That's how I end up walking home and stopping in the community garden. Dorothy has gone home, and I have the place to myself. It's become a bit of an oasis for me, like all the hours of community and joy poured into the soil here now soak into my skin. As I sit on one of the benches and stare up at the night sky, I let out a long breath.

Today was hard, but it was also wonderful.

Well, it was wonderful until I saw Rudy driving away with another woman, but what did I expect? I told him I didn't want to be with him. I can't exactly blame him for moving on. That's what I wanted, isn't it?

Still, if he were in front of me right now, I might punch him right in his stupid, handsome face.

"Lily?" Rudy's voice sounds behind me.

I turn to see him at the entrance to the garden. As soon as my gaze lands on his broad, masculine features, the urge to punch him is replaced with an urge to kiss him. I close my eyes. Maybe I should book an extra appointment with Dr. Gardner this week, because I think I need professional help.

"What are you doing here on your own?" Rudy's footsteps move closer.

I open my eyes to see him standing next to my bench. He nods to the open seat next to me, and I shrug. He sits, and every inch of me wants to melt into his warmth. Instead, I lean on the arm of the bench to put more space between us.

Silence settles over us, but it's not uncomfortable. It's never uncomfortable with Rudy. Even though he was with another woman earlier, I still can't quite ignore the desire to lean my head on his shoulder and inhale the scent of his skin. Being wrapped up in his arms feels like home, and how many homes have I had in my life? How many times have I felt as content when I was drifting from country to country with all my possessions in two suitcases?

Not many.

"You told your family about your diagnosis today?" he finally asks. His voice settles over my skin like velvet, and my shoulders relax despite myself.

I really shouldn't enjoy his company as much as I do. I can't be with him. Sitting beside him and talking to him is just a gentle form of torture.

I nod. "Yeah." A soft breeze ruffles the leaves in the new trees around us, bringing the scent of the summer night. It's not quite chilly outside, but not quite warm. Rudy's legs spread wide as he slouches down slightly on the bench, his arm stretching out across the back toward me. I can feel the heat of his leg next to mine, and it chases the night away.

"How did they take it?" His fingers stretch out, resting half an inch from my shoulder. I could lean into his touch with barely a movement right now.

But I don't need a knight in shining armor.

And Rudy doesn't want kids.

And no matter what he says, he won't want to carry me on his shoulders for the remainder of my treatment.

"They were great. I should have done it weeks ago." I give him a tight smile. "I'm not very good at asking for help, though."

"I noticed," he deadpans.

I snort, body softening toward him, then freeze. I can't do this—I can't fall into the comfortable, intimate conversation that's so easy when Rudy's around. So, I force myself to ask, "How was your date?"

Even though I'm not looking at him, I can feel Rudy's eyes on me. "Lily," he says quietly. "That was business."

I nod. "Business. Right. I also have sunset champagne with my business associates. Just out of curiosity, is that the same woman you had a business lunch with before?" My eyes are trained on the tree directly across from me. It's the one Dorothy and I planted together, and I'm pretty sure it's a little crooked.

Rudy lets out a bitter snort. "So, what, now I can't talk to anyone? I can't do my job? You broke up with me, Lily. Actually, it wasn't even a breakup, because you insisted on never having anything with me in the first place. Why are you mad at me right now?"

My heart pounds, but no words come. He's right, of course. I pushed him away. I've done nothing but push him away when he made promise after promise to me. He said he'd take on my illness, that he wanted to be with me so badly he'd brave the cancer alongside me.

How the hell could I possibly believe that? The last time I trusted a man, it turned out he had a whole other family complete with wife and kids waiting for him at home. But a few weeks after that happens, I'm supposed to believe the perfect man truly exists? Please. I may have made my share of bad decisions in my life, but I'm not a complete idiot.

I turn my head to meet his gaze, and I see nothing but hard steel in his eyes. Ice pours down my spine, and I know this is the end of whatever existed between us. This is my chance. When he's mad—buoyed by his anger—I can tell him about the baby and show him that he doesn't really want me at all. I'll put the final nail in the coffin of our romance. I'm having a baby, and that's exactly the thing that will push him away. He'll walk away from me, and we'll both be better off.

"Rudy, I'm—"

"I'm not doing this." He stands up. His fingers just avoid brushing my shoulder as he moves. "I saw you here and I thought we could talk, understand each other, but you're convinced you'd rather be alone. This isn't worth it."

His back is a broad shadow as he stalks away from me,

pausing at the entrance to the garden. Glancing over his shoulder, Rudy's features look carved from marble in the moonlight. His hair is so pale it looks like spun silver, but his eyes are black as night.

"For the record," he growls, "nothing happened with Georgia. I handed her the keys to her new home, had half a glass of champagne, and I left." His eyes are hard when he lifts them to meet mine, and I see nothing of the Rudy I know in his gaze. "I left because I was thinking of you. I see now that was a mistake."

Mute, I sit there until he's out of sight. I sit until the air raises goosebumps over my skin, and the chill of the night settles into my bones. I sit until I have the strength to drag myself up to my feet again, knowing something changed forever tonight.

It was inevitable, really, but it still sends pain spearing through my chest. I did this. I pushed him away, I withheld the truth and dragged our relationship on much longer than I should have. Any pain I feel is my own fault.

My legs feel like lead as I heave myself from the garden to my apartment building. Body numb, I fumble with my purse and manage to get the key fob pressed up against the sensor to unlock the building door. By the time I make it up to my apartment, I'm barely able to stand on my own. My body feels like it's breaking down.

One look at the pillow-covered bed is enough to turn my stomach. That's where Rudy and I made love. It's where I had one last night where I felt like a woman. For those few hours, I was more than my pregnancy, more than my illness.

That's over now too. The next few months—years, even—

will most likely strip away all the things I thought I knew about myself

I sleep on the couch that night. The bed reminds me too much of Rudy.

TWENTY-NINE
CANDICE

MY NEW YOGA studio is big enough for about ten people. The back wall is lined with mirrors and a small dais where my own yoga mat is laid out. I light a few candles and put on my favorite yoga playlist, then let out a long breath.

Someone clears their throat behind me. I turn to see Blake leaning against the wall next to the door, a small smile playing over his lips. "Happy with how the studio turned out?"

"Blake," I answer, crossing the hardwood floors toward him. He wraps his strong arms around my body and pulls me tight to him. "Thank you."

"Nothing to thank me for, Candy Cane."

I pull away and pinch the underside of his arm until he yelps, laughing. "You know I hate that nickname."

"You mother says it all the time!" He rubs the back of his arm.

"Those things are not mutually exclusive."

Blake just laughs, then ducks down to kiss me. I part my lips and am about to get lost in his kiss when the sound of an engine coming down the driveway makes us pull apart. Blake lets out a sigh. "Guess we'll have to pick this up after your class."

"I'll come find you," I say with a smile, and I watch him walk away until he disappears into our beautiful new house. Turning to see the first arrival, I'm surprised to see Nora.

She smiles. "Hey. Am I early? I hope I didn't interrupt anything."

"Right on time. Everyone else is late." I step aside to let her walk inside, then grin when she lets out a whistle.

"Blake didn't hold back, did he? This place looks sleek."

"Wait until you see the shower and bathroom. It looks like a luxury resort." I walk across the space and open the door to the shower, all gleaming stone and fancy finishes.

As someone who lived in the same house for the better part of twenty years, with mostly hand-me-down furniture and old memories, moving somewhere new has been interesting. After my house burned down, my daughter Allie and I moved to a small rental in town, but this new house with Blake feels more... permanent. It's the start of something beautiful.

"You certainly landed on your feet," Simone says from the doorway, brows arching high as she takes in the space.

"Says the woman with a coastal property that she calls her own woodland fairy tale," Fiona quips, gently shoving Simone inside so she can enter.

Jen arrives next, looking a bit flushed. "Sorry I'm late. Fallon and I were planning the autumn menu for the café. I lost track of time."

Simone's eyes narrow. "Girl, you have sex hair."

Jen's eyes widen as she pats her bird's nest down. Her cheeks flush, and I can't help the belly laugh that tumbles out of me. I've known Jen a long time, and seeing her with Fallon is something special. She's never been so relaxed. The other day, she burned a batch of cranberry-orange muffins and *laughed*. Jennifer Newbank *laughed* about messing up her baking. Unheard of.

There's a bit of bustling as everyone removes their shoes and lays their yoga mats on the ground. As everyone talks and laughs while we wait for Trina and Lily, I grin. This is a far cry from the normal yoga classes I teach, where people relax and lie down to meditate for the minutes before the class—but I know trying to get these women to stop chatting and giggling would be near impossible. I wouldn't want to silence them, anyway.

Trina and Lily arrive together, and I immediately know something is wrong. Lily has dark smudges under her eyes, and her steps are labored. Immediately, my plan for a vigorous session to get everyone sweaty goes out the window.

"Let's all get bolsters and blocks from the shelf by the wall," I say. "We're going to do an easy Yin yoga class today."

Lily lets out a sigh of relief. "Thank God. I was worried you'd work us until we collapsed. I almost didn't come."

"I had to threaten her with calling Mom to keep her company before she agreed to join me," Trina says, grabbing a couple of bolsters from the stack on the shelf.

Smiling, I steal one last glance at my little sister, and head to the front of the class. First, yoga. After that, we can talk.

THIRTY
LILY

IT'S funny how time can be fast and slow at once. My days feel torturously sluggish, like every task is an effort. I do yoga with Candice and I keep myself busy with work, but my thoughts always drift back to Rudy. The hours tick by, and I know in the depths of my heart that if our situation had been different, we could have had something great.

But at the same time, the days whip past so fast I can hardly keep track. It's not until Candice is helping me into her car to drive me to the hospital for my surgery that reality comes crashing down.

"Did you pack an extra pair of underwear?" Candice asks, grabbing my bag to put it in the back seat.

I huff. "I pretty much only packed granny panties and socks."

She nods, satisfied, then slides behind the wheel. "Mom and Trina will meet us there."

"You guys don't need to come. I'll be wheeled into surgery this afternoon and probably home tomorrow or the next day. It's no big deal."

Candice turns the car on before facing me. "Okay. Listen. You're my sister, and I love you, and you're getting a major surgery. It is a big deal, and we're going to be there whether you like it or not."

I blow out a breath. "Fine."

"'Thank you' also works," Candice says with a grin.

I jump when someone bangs on the window next to me. It's Jen, and she holds up a paper bag. "Made you some snacks for tomorrow," she says, her voice muffled. I roll the window down and she repeats herself. "I know you can't eat today, but I made some things in case the hospital food is gross. It'll all keep at room temperature for the day. Fallon's making your dinner tomorrow."

"He is?"

Jen nods. "Yeah. We'll either bring it by your place or take it to the hospital, if you're still there for another night." She shoves the paper bag through the window, then nods. "Good luck."

I watch her stride diagonally across the street toward Four Cups, her white chef's uniform smeared with various types of batter. She has a floury handprint on her butt, which looks very large and very male.

I hold the bag of treats on my lap and feel a suspicious prickling in the back of my eyelids. Candice smiles at me and pats my knee. "Let's get you to the hospital, yeah?"

"Yeah," I croak.

. . .

I'VE NEVER HAD general anesthesia before. I've actually never had any kind of surgery at all. But the nurses are kind, and the doctor explains everything in detail, and before I know it, my mother and sisters are saying goodbye and an orderly is wheeling me down to the operating room. He's an older man with tattoos snaking all the way up his arms, his long, gray hair tied in a ponytail at the back of his head. He tells me a story about his granddaughter taking her first steps this morning. For some reason, the story calms me. By the time he wheels me to the ward right outside the operating room, I'm ready.

This cancer will be cut away, and then it'll be me and my baby against the world. I slide a hand over my stomach and stare at the tiled ceiling, feeling a rush of warmth and love fill me up. I can do this. This first hurdle is terrifying, but within just a few short hours, I'll be on my way to recovery. My baby needs me healthy and happy.

It's while I'm lying there, waiting to be wheeled into the OR, that I really think about my baby for the first time in my pregnancy. I'd thought about the baby before, obviously, but it had always seemed like this hazy future that I could get to if I crossed a deadly minefield.

But in those few minutes when time stops and all I can do is wait for surgery, I realize that I'm going to be a mother. I'm going to have a tiny human with tiny little fingernails and soft, soft skin, and they'll be relying on me for everything. I'll get to watch my baby grow and learn and explore the world.

Suddenly, the cancer seems surmountable. Surgery, then

chemo, then the reward is a child I get to call my own. Why have I been worried about my ex turning his back on me? Why have I been thinking about Rudy and a budding romance that went nowhere?

The biggest change in my life will happen in a matter of months, and it's going to be *great*. I'll be like that orderly soon—seeing a child of my own take their first steps and telling anyone that will listen about it.

A team of nurses approaches, and a sense of calm settles over me. This is just a challenge I have to get through for my baby. It's just a test of my strength that I need to pass in order to get the reward of a full and happy life. For the first time since I found out about the baby, I realize what a gift this really is. Not just the baby, but the fight against this disease, too. My priorities are being muscled into place and I can finally *see* what's important to me.

It's not some guy. Not my ex, not Rudy, not anyone. What matters is my kid. My recovery. My family.

I'm moved, prepped, and put under. Then I blink, and I'm awake again, with a nurse behind me welcoming me back to the real world.

For some reason, the first thing I ask her is if my teeth are okay. In the pre-surgery briefing, they told me there was a risk of damage to the veneers I have on my two front teeth during intubation and extubation, and my anesthesia-addled brain decided that was the most important thing to verify.

Forget what I said about priorities. Apparently, mine are all out of whack.

The nurse smiles. "Your teeth are fine. The surgery went

well. The baby is healthy. We're going to bring you up to your room in a few minutes and the doctor will come see you there. Just relax. You did great." She pats my arm, checks the various bits of equipment near my head, then walks away.

I WAKE up again in my room to a blurry shape sitting in the chair next to me.

"Rudy?" I rasp, then blink a few times to see Candice standing up from the chair.

"Hey," she whispers, patting my leg. "What did you say?"

I gulp past painful dryness in my throat and shake my head once. "Nothing. Hey."

"Your surgery lasted just under three hours," she says. "Mom and Trina had to go back to town to pick up the kids from daycare. They're dropping them off with Mac, but they'll both be back soon with some more supplies. Doc said you'd probably be here more than a day. Mom went through your bag and decided you hadn't packed properly." My sister winces. "She went back for fresh toiletries and more comfortable clothes for you. She wasn't sorry about snooping."

I huff. "No worries." My lids are heavy, and the last thing I know is Candice is readjusting the blanket over my waist and patting my leg before I doze off.

THIRTY-ONE
RUDY

I SIT on my brand-new hardwood floor and lean back against my aching arms. In the past few weeks, I've repainted the entire downstairs level of my house and installed all-new flooring. My fixer-upper is finally getting fixed up. Today, I just finished installing the last of the baseboards and re-hung the freshly painted doors. I glance around the room and let out a sigh.

This is where Lily and I worked on my grandmother's paperwork. Down the hall, where new kitchen cabinets are about to be installed, is where we kissed right before Grandma interrupted us and spooked Lily.

Instead of smiling, the memory makes me feel bitter. I've spent the last couple of weeks burying myself in work and renovations. I've taken on three new clients personally and pushed my sales team hard. Then evenings and weekends, I've worked on the house.

Last weekend, Lee came over to help me paint and I'm

pretty sure he was just checking if I was still alive. I refused his offer to buy me a drink at the Grove and watched him drive away on his bike with a sigh of relief. It's been good to be alone.

My stomach growls, and when I peel myself off the floor and shuffle to the kitchen, I realize my fridge is completely empty. The pantry isn't any better, unless I want to open a dusty can of chickpeas that came with the house.

Grabbing my keys, I head into town to grab some dinner. I park near the Heart's Cove Hotel and walk toward a little Thai place just diagonally across from the Four Cups Café. When I get closer, I glance across the street at the dark windows of the café and wonder how Lily's doing, then kick myself for even caring.

Our evening in the garden still lingers at the forefront of my memory. Lily wants nothing to do with me, and I shouldn't even be thinking about her anymore.

I pause when the café door bursts open. Out of the Four Cups Café come spilling most of the members of Lily's family. Before I can stop myself, my feet carry me closer.

"I've got the food," Trina says. "Jen says she already gave her a few things, but I grabbed more. Mom, did you get Iliana's overnight bag? You said she forgot her toothbrush?"

"Who do you think I am?" Lottie huffs, then thrusts an arm toward a waiting vehicle. "It's all packed and ready to go. You must have forgotten that I'm your mother, Katrina, and that I'm more than capable of caring for my daughters."

Trina seems content ignoring her mother as she glances at her phone. "Candice just texted me," she says. "Lily woke up a couple of minutes ago. The surgery went well."

I stumble on a crack in the pavement. That was today? Lily's getting her mastectomy *right now?* I frown, hurrying forward. It hasn't been that long since the housewarming...has it? I keep telling myself that Lily was right to push me away, that it's better for us to go our separate ways.

But this acid burning in my stomach disagrees.

"Well, what are we waiting for?" Lottie throws herself at the passenger door and clambers inside.

I cross the street in time to help Trina with the boxes of food she's hauling into the trunk of her car. She looks up when I grab one end of the box before it tips over and gives me a relieved smile. "Rudy, hi! Thank you. I almost lost the sandwiches there."

"You feeding a football team?"

She grins, but the edges of it are tired. "No, just the visitors that will be stopping in to see Lily." Trina glances at the box and bites her lip. "We may have gone overboard."

My throat is tight, but I manage to respond. "She got her mastectomy today?"

She studies me for a moment, then nods. "Yeah. It went well."

My throat feels raw, and I only manage to nod. "That's good. She was nervous about it, I think."

"She actually *talked* to you about how she felt?" Lottie's head pops up above the roof of the car. "Am I *always* the last to hear about these things? First she tells Trina, then you know how she's feeling—I'm starting to think Lily is trying to keep me in the dark about everything. Next thing, I'll find out she's already married or maybe she's decided to become a nun!"

Trina plants her hands on her hips. "Mom, you saw her when she told us. She was terrified that we'd have a bad reaction to the news. It doesn't exactly take a rocket scientist to figure out she was scared. Rudy just happens to be more perceptive than your average Neanderthal. Yesterday, she admitted to me that she couldn't stop thinking about the months before Dad died, and that's why she was nervous to tell us. She didn't want to burden us with the news."

"I know, I know." Lottie huffs. "Silly girl."

I frown, remembering Lottie's words—she said Trina knew about the cancer. I could have sworn Lily told me she hadn't said anything to her family...but maybe she misspoke, or maybe she told Trina about the cancer after she told me.

It's not my business. Either way, Lily broke it off with me, and it's for the best.

"I'd better get going," Trina says, squeezing my arm.

I step aside and let her get in her car, standing on the sidewalk to watch them go.

I feel...useless. And guilty.

Why do I feel guilty?

The car engine turns over...and dies. Trina tries it again, and even through the car door I can hear Lottie's voice barking out instructions. When the car fails to start a third time, I bend over and knock on the window.

It rolls down and Lottie turns toward me. "You got jumper cables?"

I shake my head. "No, but I have a car."

"Good enough. Katrina, get out. Rudy is driving us to the hospital."

I straighten up and take a step back as Lottie exits her daughter's car. "Give me a couple minutes—I'll get the car and be right back. It's parked just down the road."

"Screw that," Lottie says. "We'll come with you, then we can drive straight to the hospital."

And that's how I end up carrying a box of sandwiches, muffins, and treats under one arm with Lottie and Trina in tow. Trina is carrying a small overnight bag that must have Lily's stuff in it.

I should have done more for Iliana. Even now, seeing the help she's getting from her family makes me feel like I've failed her. I walked away when I should have stayed.

We hurry to my vehicle, and when it starts without any issues, Trina breathes a sigh of relief from the back seat.

Once we're on our way, Lottie leans over to pat my thigh. "Whatever happened between you and Lily? I was sure you two would end up together."

My hands tighten on the steering wheel. "It didn't work out."

"She pushed you away because of the cancer?" Trina asks.

When I glance at her in the rearview mirror, her head is leaning against the window. I nod. "Yeah. How did you know?"

Trina lets out a bitter snort. "That's our Lily. I used to think she was jet-setting around the world all the time because she was afraid of being a burden on anyone. Needing help with the cancer—and everything else—is probably her worst nightmare."

Everything else? What does that mean?

Lottie grunts in agreement. "You can say that again. When your father died, she couldn't wait to run away to Peru. She called it wanderlust, but I knew what it was—she just didn't want us to see her pain. She's always been that way. Private. Your father was the same way. Damn near had to tie him to the bed to get him to rest and accept my help when he could barely make it to the bathroom on his own."

"Maybe we'll get away without tying her down," Trina answers. "At least she let us drive her to the hospital this morning."

I keep my eyes on the road as a lump forms in my throat, and I just keep repeating the truth to myself: Lily pushed me away. She broke up with me. We split up, and it was for the best.

So why do I feel sick?

THIRTY-TWO

RUDY

"ARE you sure you don't want to come up? I'm sure Lily would be glad to see you when she wakes up again." Lottie leans on the window opening to speak to me from outside the car. Katrina is already through the sliding glass doors and at the reception desk inside.

I shake my head. "I'll give her a few days. I'm probably the last person she wants to see when she's laid up in a hospital bed."

"I wouldn't be so sure." Lottie gives me a wink, then totters after her daughter.

I'm in a drop-off zone, so I don't give myself any time to dawdle. I get back on the road and head to the office. When I pull into my parking space, my stomach grumbles. I never did get any dinner. The thought of sitting by myself and eating while I stew about the fact that Lily is in surgery and there's not a damn thing I can do about it doesn't exactly appeal to me, though, so I find myself heading to the Grove.

The bar is located in a strip mall just outside the Heart's Cove town limits. It's nestled between a barber shop and a now-vacant store that has been a Chinese restaurant, a nail salon, a pharmacy, and a weird vacuum repair shop—all in the last couple of years. I guess the few motorcycles that are permanent fixtures outside the Grove scare away the scant customers.

The Grove isn't exactly a biker bar, but it's a convenient stop on a nice drive, and Hamish and his sons have ridden motorcycles for as long as I can remember. As such, it's become more of a biker-friendly bar. I park across from the four bikes parked outside and comb my fingers through my hair, a weight in the pit of my gut.

When I walk inside, I'm greeted by a dim interior that smells of stale beer and musk. Motorcycle memorabilia hangs on the walls, along with old photos and a few fizzing neon beer signs. Along the right side of the long, narrow room are some old vinyl booths upholstered in green, with the bar taking up almost the entire left wall. A few tables are dotted in between, but right now—as they are most weekdays—the tables and chairs are mostly stacked along the back wall.

Lee works the bar for his father a few times a week. I have no idea why. He either enjoys the company of grouchy old bikers or he has a soft spot for his father that he works hard to hide. It's not for money—Lee makes enough of that on his own. I don't even know if Hamish pays his son for the hours he works here. When I enter the old dive bar, Lee glances up and gives me a chin jerk.

There's a guy I don't recognize sitting at the bar, and I take a seat two stools from him. It's not exactly unusual to see new people here, but this guy looks different. He's wearing a shirt and suit pants, and both items look custom tailored. Shiny black shoes are hooked over the rung of his barstool, an odd contrast of old and new.

Glancing from him to the grubby old regulars whose faces are mostly scruff and wrinkles, I arch a brow at Lee.

"What're you having?" he asks, eyes twinkling. Clearly, he's curious about the new arrival.

"Beer," I answer. Lee gives me my usual drink and I take a long drink. It's bitter, cold, and frothy, and it makes something tight in my gut relax.

I'm not usually one to self-medicate. I like a social drink once in a while, but I've never been the type of guy to turn to alcohol to numb my problems.

Today, though, I feel like I could get lost in the bottle. I can't stop thinking of that hospital, of Lily there on her own. I should be beside her. I should be the one who was carrying her overnight bag, who made sure she had enough to eat. That's *my* responsibility.

I blink and take another gulp of beer because I know that's a lie. Lily was never my responsibility. Even when I was buried inside her, not an inch of space between her skin and mine, she kept me at arm's length. I wonder how long it'll take for her to take off on another international trip, once her treatment is done? How long until she's gone forever?

No matter what Lee says to me whenever he leans against the bar across from me, my mind drifts to the hospital bed where Lily is lying. I wonder if she's awake. If she's in pain. If there's a damn thing I could do to make her life any easier.

Then I remember her face when she told me she didn't want me, and I finish the rest of my beer. Lee pours me another.

"Rough day?" the suit sitting at the bar asks, leaning both arms against the sticky wooden surface. He nods to the empty glass Lee takes away as he replaces it with a full one.

I nod. "Yeah. You?"

He grunts. "Rough couple of months."

I huff. I can relate. It feels like ever since Lily arrived in town, my world has been thrown off-kilter. I've never felt this kind of burning need before. It's not sex. It's the need to care for someone. I could call Georgia Neves and have her on her back within the hour. I could call any number of booty calls to scratch an itch—but I don't want to. I want to be sitting in a chair next to Lily's bed, holding her hand and listening to her breathe.

What the fuck is up with that?

"Woman?" The man beside me nods to the now-half-empty pint glass in front of me. I hadn't even realized I'd drank any of it.

I arch a brow.

He snorts. "The only time a man downs a drink as fast as you did just now is because he's thinking of a woman." He lifts his empty glass and arches his brows meaningfully.

I grunt. "You too?"

"She's fucking gorgeous," he says. "And she wants nothing to do with me."

My next sip of beer goes down easy, and I nod. "I know the feeling."

"Phil," the man says as he extends a hand. "I'm staying here for a week." He points to a stairwell, and I nod, remembering the day I heard about the booking. "Trying to win her back."

"Rudy," I answer. We shake, and Phil moves one stool closer, so there's only one seat between us. I'd rather drink alone —even Lee has stopped trying to talk to me—but I say nothing. Maybe this guy needs to get something off his chest.

"I used to like that she was independent, you know?" Phil lifts his glass to ask for another. Lee nods, pouring out the golden liquid with expert movements. Phil waits for his drink, then takes a long sip before continuing. "I thought it was a good thing that she wasn't needy."

A bitter smile tugs at my lips. "It's all good until you realize you *want* her to need you."

"Fucking exactly." He shakes his head. His fingers play with the damp coaster under his beer. "She's carrying my kid, you know."

I arch my brows. "Rough."

"I fucked up, though. Made her think I didn't want it. My ex-wife—the woman I was with before her..." He shakes his head. "It's complicated, but I'm here now. She's not answering her phone, though." He glances over at me. "What about you?"

"Not talking to me either," I admit. "She's sick, and she's convinced she wants to deal with it alone."

"Shit," the man says, sympathy written in his eyes. "She won't let you help?"

"I'm completely powerless," I admit.

"Screw that," Phil grunts. "You should go to her. She might tell you she doesn't want your help, but she sure as hell won't refuse it if you give it without asking."

My brows arch. "I'm not so sure. This woman...she's something else."

Phil lets out a bitter laugh. "Sounds like my woman. Mind of her own. I told her I couldn't do a relationship, but she fucking sucked me in. Next thing I knew, I was traveling hours out of my way just to get a taste of her."

Now it's my turn to laugh. "I had the opposite experience. She told me she only wanted casual sex, and I was the idiot who wanted more."

Phil shakes his head, then calls for a few shots.

Lee pours them, then pours one for himself. "You two are pathetic, you know that?"

I laugh, and it feels almost foreign as it leaves my lips. When was the last time I laughed? The three of us take our shots, the alcohol burning on the way down. I grimace. Sambuca. I shake my head and huff at Lee. "I know how pathetic I am. Don't need reminding."

"Why don't you just go find these women and tell them exactly what you just told each other?" Lee leans against the bar, glancing at each of us in turn. His arms are crossed over his broad chest, brows arched. "What the hell are you waiting for?"

Phil slams a hand down on the bar. "You're right. I'm going to go find her. She's got to answer her phone at some point. I'll see her tonight. I *need* to see her tonight."

I blink, nodding. "Same. Fuck this. I'm not drinking on my

own when I could be beside her," I say, sliding off my stool. "I gotta take a leak."

By the time I return to the main bar, Phil has disappeared and Lee is cleaning up his glass. He gives me a grim smile and nods to the door up to the rooms above. "Your new best friend went to go harass his girl until she tells him where she is."

Groaning, I slide back onto my barstool. "I can't go see Lily tonight. I'll go tomorrow."

"I think you should." Lee leans against the bar across from me. I've known him most of my life. We met in ninth grade on the first day of high school. We were two scrawny kids in the same homeroom who fought over the hottest girl in our year. Chastity Jackson did not live up to her name, and neither her two-week relationship with Lee nor her two-day relationship with me ran the distance. Obviously. My friendship with Lee, though, has been just about the only constant in my life.

"You do?" I ask honestly, wanting to hear what my friend has to say. "I mean, I know Philly-boy wanted to go claim his woman, but the truth is, Lily told me to back off. I'm thinking maybe the right thing to do is listen to her."

"You've been moping around for weeks, and she's laid up in a hospital bed recovering from major surgery. Even if she told you to stay away, you have to go see her. You don't have to go profess your undying love, but you need to show your face, Rudy." He shakes his head. "Don't be a fucking idiot. She'll remember if you don't come see her."

"She might throw me out," I note.

"Yeah, and then you'll be exactly where you are now. What have you got to lose?"

"When did you turn into an expert on women?" I snip. "Last time I checked, Drea left your ass at the altar. You haven't exactly lived happily ever after."

Lee's eyes grow shuttered. "Maybe I don't want you making the same mistakes I did."

Sighing, I close my eyes. "Sorry. That was uncalled for."

"Just..." Lee combs a hand through his hair. "Just get out of here, get some sleep, and bring Lily some flowers in the morning. Trust me."

My best friend sounds tired, but there's a ring of truth to his words. Even if Lily wants nothing to do with me, I can't just let her slip through my fingers. I can bring her a bunch of flowers and show her I still care.

I nod. "Yeah. I'll go in the morning."

AND I DO. The next morning, I wake up in my brand-new bed (including bed frame) and inhale a cup of coffee and some toast before jumping in my car and heading for the hospital. I consider calling Lily's phone to make sure it's okay for me to come visit, but decide against it. What's that old saying about it being better to ask forgiveness than permission? I can't afford to have her tell me not to come.

I *need* to see her. I need to make sure she's okay. I need to touch her skin and hold her hand and tell her that I'm there for her, even if she doesn't want me to be. If she pushes me away, I'll leave. But if there's a slim, infinitesimal chance that she actually wants me to be in that room beside her, and I can't afford to let it pass me by.

I stop in at the local florist to grab a bunch of flowers, then tear out onto the freeway like my life depends on it. When I arrive at the hospital, visiting hours are just starting. The nurse at the front desk gives me Lily's room number and directions around the huge, sprawling hospital complex. By the time I make it to the oncology ward, sweat is dripping down my spine and soaking the underarms of my shirt. It's not warm in the hospital, but my nerves are wound so tight my movements are jerky and uncoordinated.

I'm regretting the impulsivity of coming here. I'm thinking maybe Lily will throw me out, and that will actually feel much, much worse than I felt last night.

But just as I'm about to lose my nerve, I see her room number. The hospital has plain beige hallways with clean tile floors, and the fluorescent light in front of Lily's door is flickering gently. I pause, glancing at the name written next to her door, and blow out a breath.

Even if she throws me out, at least I'm here. At least she knows I'm not afraid to come to the hospital to stay with her. Her illness doesn't scare me.

I knock gently, then push the door open. My chest seizes.

Lily looks like hell, and she's still the most beautiful woman I've ever seen. She's pale, lying back on her bed dressed in a hospital gown with an IV sticking out from the back of her hand. Her dark hair is splayed over the pillow, her face free of makeup. Something tight unknots in my chest.

I can't believe I actually considered turning away. My feet carry me to the bedside, and Lily's eyes widen.

"Rudy." She grips the blankets and tugs them up slightly before patting her hair.

I realize the flowers I brought are hanging limply in my hand. I thrust them up and toward her, which makes her rear back. I pull them back to my chest. "Sorry. I brought you these." Then I thrust them toward her again.

Lily's lips twitch. "You mind putting them on the table?"

I look around for a vase, then feel stupid for bringing flowers to a hospital room without anywhere to put them. Giving up, I just lay them flat on the little table on wheels next to Lily's bed.

She gestures to a chair. "Sit, if you have time."

"I've got time," I tell her, my throat tight. I've got all the time in the world. I pull the chair close to her side and put my hand on the bed, half an inch from hers.

Her fingers extend slightly, barely brushing the side of my palm. I feel that touch in my entire body. My cock twitches, which is entirely inappropriate but there's not a damn thing I can do about it.

"How are you feeling?" I ask.

"Tired," she answers. "But okay. The doctor said the surgery went well. They're waiting on tests to see if they got all the cancer cells. Had to take my nipple, but the reconstruction went okay. I have what they call a breast expander, and I'll have to come back and get it pumped full of saline every few weeks before they can put an implant in." She snorts, then closes her eyes. "Sorry. I don't know why I'm telling you this. I'm sure you don't want to hear about my mutant boobs."

"I love your mutant boobs," I blurt out, which make her

laugh. It's a hoarse, tired sound, but it unfurls the tight knot in my chest.

"Well, that's good." Her eyes soften. "Thanks for coming," she whispers. "And thanks for the flowers."

"I was afraid you wouldn't want to see me."

"Well, I'm sure I look terrible and I'll probably be embarrassed about it later, but right now I'm glad." Her eyes are soft as they search mine.

"You look beautiful," I tell her, shifting my hand to cover hers. Deep, undeniable contentment suffuses my body at the touch, as if all I've ever needed was to have my palm laid over hers. This is right. This is exactly where I should be.

She smiles sadly. "I'm sorry I pushed you away, Rudy. I just needed to get through this, and I felt like I might not have the strength if I was distracted by a man."

"I'm here," I say softly. "I want to be here. I don't want to be a distraction, Lily. I want to add to your strength."

Her breath catches, and I wonder if this is it. All it took was me showing up with a bunch of flowers she hasn't even looked at, and I'm about to win her back. Sure, the past few weeks have been shitty without her, but I'd go through it a hundred times over if it means I get to see this look in her eyes—the soft, tender look that tells me this was never casual between us. My chest squeezes, and for a beautiful, brilliant moment, I think I might have won over the woman of my dreams.

Then the door opens, and Phil from the Grove steps in. His eyes move from Lily to me, and everything falls to shit.

THIRTY-THREE
LILY

I DON'T KNOW if the hospital has me on some strong painkillers or what, but I actually forgot about Phil. How crazy is that? He texted me last night about a million times before I finally told him where I am. I was surprised he was in town, obviously, but I think a part of me thought he was bluffing. How many times did he tell me he'd come see me before a last-minute "business meeting" came up? In all the time I dated him, he wasn't ever reliable.

How could he be, when he had a whole other family waiting for him at his real home?

Then I fell asleep, and I woke up to bright sunshine, feeling simultaneously like a Mack truck ran me over and like my life could finally begin. My first thought this morning was for my baby—and how for the first time since I got the cancer diagnosis, I actually feel like my baby is connected to me. It's like cutting the cancer from my body lifted a weight from my shoulders.

I'm no longer this sick husk of a woman who might not make it to see my child grow up, or who might not even be able to carry my child. Now I've faced the first big hurdle, and I'm almost through it. Sure, the recovery will be tough, and I still have chemotherapy to contend with, but I've gone under the knife and my baby is right here with me.

For the first time in months, I feel like my future is...well, maybe it's not bright, exactly, but I at least feel like I *have* a future. I hadn't realized how terrified I was of getting this mastectomy until I woke up and everything (including my dental work) had gone okay. I think I had this niggling fear that the baby wouldn't make it.

More than a niggling fear, actually. I was damn terrified of going under the knife. I thought I'd wake up with one breast and an empty womb, and I'd have to deal with the guilt of a miscarriage along with the scars on my body.

But everything went well. The surgery, the baby, the reconstruction. For the first time in months, I feel *hope*.

Then Rudy walked into my room, and Phil just flew right out of my mind because Rudy is so damn pretty and the soft, sensitive parts of my heart were just delighted he'd actually come to see me.

For those few moments, when the tips of my fingers brushed the edge of his hand, I felt like I'd been wrong to push him away. He came to see me even after I acted like I wanted nothing to do with him, and doesn't that mean there's something good between us? Doesn't that mean he cares?

But then Phil walked through the door, and time has slowed

right down. The seconds melt by, and both men look at me, then at each other.

At first, I think Phil is shocked that there's another man by my side. But when Rudy stands up, his chair clattering to the floor, I realize they've met.

Oh no. Oh no, no, no.

Listen. I know that this far, as you've read my story, it might seem like I make bad decisions. It might seem like I'm a grown woman who has no idea what the hell I'm doing. That's fair. I don't, in fact, have any idea what the hell I'm doing.

But this?

Rudy and Phil showing up in my hospital room not twelve hours after I've gotten major surgery?

This is bad, even for me.

This must be in the top ten worst moments of my life. My stomach bottoms out, and I just *know* things are about to get much, much worse.

Rudy freezes, standing awkwardly next to the bed, his hand still gripped in mine, eyes on the man in the doorway. "Phil? What the fuck are you doing here?"

"I was just going to ask the same thing." My ex-boyfriend is holding a bouquet of flowers, and I notice they look like the sad kind of bunch you get at the grocery store. Nothing like the gorgeous bouquet Rudy brought.

Then I feel like a maniac, because why the hell am I comparing flower arrangements when these two men are shooting daggers at each other?

"Um..." I blink as both men turn to face me.

Something horrible crosses Rudy's face. He glances down at my stomach, then back at my face. "You're pregnant?"

"Wait." Phil takes a step forward. "I thought they had you in the oncology ward because of a bed shortage or something. But...you have fucking *cancer*?"

I flinch, tearing my gaze away from my ex to look at Rudy. I don't know what I want to see in his gaze, but it's not the harsh coldness in his eyes. He straightens up, his hand dropping from mine. His brows tug together and he searches my face as I try to find the words to say what I feel.

"I wanted to tell you," I finally whisper.

Rudy takes a step back. "You've been pregnant this whole time?"

"Are you fucking this guy?" Phil asks, stepping up to the other side of the bed. The two men tower over me, and my eyes flick from one to the other. My heart starts pounding and I close my eyes, feeling trapped and claustrophobic and so fucking stupid.

This is my own damn fault. My fault for getting involved with Rudy. My fault for telling Phil where I am. My fault for getting pregnant in the first place. I knew my birth control prescription had run out, and I knew it had been three days since I'd taken a pill by the time I filled it again. But I still chose to have sex with Phil, didn't I?

I don't know if the cancer is my fault, but it sure as hell feels like it.

"Iliana," Phil snaps. "Answer the question."

I hate when he does that. He treats me like a child and

scolds me like he has a right to. I frown at my ex, wondering what the hell I ever saw in him.

"You left, Phil, so I'm not sure what business of yours it is who I sleep with. You have some nerve waltzing into this room telling me I'm wrong for moving on, when I was the other woman without even knowing it. Or did you forget that you have a wife and kids waiting for you at home?"

"Ex-wife," he spits.

I blink. "What?"

"I left her. I'm here, but I find you shacked up with someone new? Didn't take you long."

"You left your wife for me?" I whisper, more bewildered than anything.

In all the possible outcomes of my situation, Phil leaving his marriage to come raise my baby with me didn't even register on my radar. When Phil told me he wanted me to abort my child right before walking away from me, I thought that was the last time I'd ever see him. I was glad for it, too, naïve as I was at the time. I was convinced I could do everything on my own.

That was before the cancer diagnosis.

My mind reels, and I remember Rudy is there when I see him walking toward the door.

"Rudy!" I call out. "Wait."

He pauses at the door, eyes flicking from me to Phil and back again. "I shouldn't have come here," he says. "This was a mistake."

"So fucking leave, asshole," Phil spits over his shoulder.

"Phil, stop," I admonish. Typical. The man has always had a

temper. What the hell did I see in him, anyway? Maybe when we were in Italy everything just felt a bit more romantic.

I try to sit up to call Rudy back, then wince as pain radiates across my chest.

Rudy pauses, taking half a step toward me. Then his face hardens, and he turns away and walks out the door.

A nurse bustles in. Her name is Wendy, and she must be nearing the end of her shift because she's been taking care of me all night. She's kind and gentle and incredibly efficient, but she has a spine of steel. Her hair is a riot of curls barely tamed in a bun at the nape of her neck. Her rich, dark skin is set off by the blue scrubs she's wearing, and she lifts an eyebrow at the interloper in my room. There's none of the soft kindness in her gaze now. "Everything okay here?" Her eyes narrow on Phil. "Who are you?"

"I'm the father," he says, that hard, bulldog expression setting itself over his features.

The nurse doesn't even blink. She turns to me. "You want him gone?"

"She wants me to stay," Phil says, taking a step toward the nurse.

She lifts a hand. "Sir, one more step and I'm calling security. Now, Lily, you want this guy here, or do you want him gone?"

I take a little sip of a breath and lie back on my pillows. "Gone," I whisper. "I think I need to sleep."

Phil splutters, but the nurse extends a hand toward the door to my room. "You heard the woman. Out."

"I'm coming back later," Phil says, and it sounds a little bit like a threat.

I just close my eyes. I don't have the energy to deal with any of this.

Wendy closes the door behind him with a sneer. "He seems like a winner."

I huff a bitter laugh and blink my eyes open. I turn to watch her take my blood pressure and let out a long sigh. "I think I fucked up, Wendy. The guy I want didn't know I was pregnant until just now, and he told me he never wanted to be a stepdad. The father of my kid didn't know about the breast cancer. I don't want him anywhere near my baby, but he just told me he left his wife for me. Everything is a mess."

She grunts, making notes on my chart. "Don't worry about any of that now. You've got more important things to think about than some prissy little man with an ego problem, or some blond hunk who won't get his head out of his ass and accept you as you are."

My laugh is a bit lighter this time. "You know, that might be the most accurate description of him I've ever heard."

"Which one?" She arches a brow, grinning.

"Both of them." I laugh, then shake my head. "But I meant Phil. He is prissy, small, and he has an ego problem. I can't believe I ever had sex with him."

"I know his type. They turn on the charm like a faucet, and turn it off just as quick," she says, then slides my chart back where it goes in its slot at the head of my bed. "Doctor Gilmore will be here in a few minutes, and they'll be serving breakfast within the hour. Your mom and sisters coming back today?"

I nod. "I'm surprised they aren't here already."

"If they have another box of goodies today, tell them to save me one of those blueberry muffins," she says, then gives me a wink. Her hand squeezes my shoulder. "You'll be okay, Lily. Trust me."

I nod and watch the nurse leave, grateful to have yet another woman on my side. If there's one thing I've learned over the past few months, it's that women are a lot more reliable than men when the going gets tough. A *lot* more reliable.

MY DOCTOR CONFIRMS the surgery was a success and is confident I'll be able to leave the hospital within a couple of days. They think they got all the cancer cells, which is good news. My mom, Trina, and Candice ask about a thousand questions, and I'm glad they're here. I don't even have the energy to decipher words, let alone ask for details on medical procedures and follow-ups.

First, sleep. Then, home. After that, when I have the energy, I'll think about the upcoming chemo. Once that's done, I might even consider the looming prospect of labor and delivery. Actual motherhood is on the very distant horizon.

Rudy and Phil can go kick rocks for all I care right now. My mother fluffs my pillow as I drift off into a hazy sleep, a hand on my stomach to feel my growing bump.

I have more important things to think about now.

THIRTY-FOUR
RUDY

SHE'S PREGNANT.

Pregnant.

With another man's child.

I slam my hands on my steering wheel until my palms hurt, then glare up at the big, boxy hospital building.

What the fuck?

Sucking in a deep breath, I close my eyes for a beat. What the hell did I expect, coming here? That unicorns would fart rainbows and butterflies and I'd live happily ever after?

Now I know the truth: Lily really did do me a favor by pushing me away. It doesn't help the fact that her lie—a lie by omission, but still a lie—has the sting of betrayal. Even after I told her about my ex and the kid I treated as my own, she didn't have the decency to tell me what was going on. Why? Was she afraid of my reaction? Did she want me to keep clinging on like an idiot? She could have told me on our first date and saved us both a lot of trouble.

As I turn the key in the ignition, I wonder if that would have worked. If I'd known about her baby as we sat watching the sunset together, would I actually have refused to see her again? If she'd told me she was pregnant when she talked about the cancer, would I still have felt that deep desire to protect her, or would I have walked away?

I don't know how to answer those questions. My chest feels torn to shreds, because all I really want to do is go back up to her room and wrap my arms around her.

But then what?

I heard her voice when she learned that Phil had left his wife for her. She sounded *hopeful.*

She doesn't want me. She probably just wanted a man to lean on, and I was the fool who gave her the chance.

Tires squealing, I race out of the parking lot and head back to town. I park outside my office building and storm inside, locking myself behind my door and burying myself in work.

Iliana lied to me. She kept secrets from me. She did exactly what my ex did to me, which was make me feel attached before pulling the rug out from under me. It's better to end things now, because what the hell else is going to happen?

I won't be the fool who gets attached to another man's child before having fatherhood ripped away from me again. I'll never meet a woman and ride off into the sunset. I'll have one-night-stands. I'll fuck. I'll be a bachelor until I die.

Isn't that what I always knew would happen? Nothing has changed.

But as the sun goes down and I stay locked in my office, I can't help feeling like everything is different. This pain in my chest just isn't going away.

MY MOTHER RUNS interference like it's her job. I don't see Phil at the hospital again, but I think I hear his voice outside my door. When I'm discharged, Candice brings me home and stays with me until I'm settled, then my mother comes to stay the night.

I'd love some privacy, but it hurts to move and I feel weak and tired. No morning sickness, though, which is a good thing.

After three days at home, when the pain in my chest has gone down to a throb and an annoying itch, I finally answer one of Phil's many phone calls, bracing myself for his hostility. For once, I'm alone in my apartment. My mother has gone out to get groceries, and both my sisters are busy. Nora hasn't stopped in and I'm pretty sure she's in Reno again.

"Lily," he says, his voice soft. "I'm glad you answered." That charm faucet is turned up to full blast, and I'm too weak to put up my walls.

I lie back on my couch and close my eyes. "Hi, Phil."

"How are you feeling?"

"Great," I answer, feeling anything but.

There's a pause. "I'd like to see you. Talk to you. I'm sorry for how I acted at the hospital, but I just hated seeing you there with another man."

I'm not sure what to say. The last thing I want to do is talk to Phil, but he's the father of my child and he came all the way to Heart's Cove to see me. Don't I owe him a conversation?

I sigh. "We can meet tomorrow."

"Great," he says, a touch of smugness in his voice. "What about that café on Cove Boulevard? Four Cups?"

I grimace, then pause. On one hand, I know if we meet at Four Cups I'll have exactly zero privacy. Not only does my sister co-own the joint, but that's the congregation spot for all her—*our*—friends. My mother is always there along with Dorothy and Margaret, and there's no guarantee Rudy won't be there either.

On the other hand, Four Cups feels a lot like home turf. If Phil starts acting like an ass, it'll be much easier to kick him out.

"Sure," I hear myself saying. "Ten o'clock?"

"Can't wait," he says, then disconnects.

CANDICE IS behind the counter with the barista, Sven, the two of them wearing their usual pink *Heart's Cove Hotties* tees. Fiona is sorting through bags of coffee behind them with a clipboard resting next to her. The three of them look up at me and I wave before taking a seat in an armchair by the window. I let out a tired sigh.

Since the only medication I'm on right now is ibuprofen, I decided to prove to the world that I'm a strong, independent woman by driving myself to the café—and promptly realized this strong, independent lunatic should have waited a few more days post-surgery to have a conversation with her ex. It took a lot more effort than I expected to get myself the couple of blocks from my apartment to Four Cups. It hurt to use my arm on the steering wheel, and I was grateful I drive an automatic. I parked right outside and shuffled indoors, and I already feel like I need a nap.

"Here," Candice says, setting herbal tea down in front of me. "You want me to get you anything? Food?"

I shake my head. "I'm meeting Phil."

Her face hardens. I told my sisters about how Phil reacted when I told him about the baby, and let's just say my family is not a fan of him. Can't say I blame them. Apparently, Nurse Wendy told them all about the little stand-off in my room too. Because my family needed more ammunition.

But my baby should have a right to know his or her father, so I'm here. Being the bigger woman. Being strong because that's what I need to do.

The past few days since my operation have been filled with nothing but clarity. I still feel this bright, warm connection to the baby growing inside me, like a haze has lifted from my mind. I can *think*. And the baby's father is here, so I owe him at least a conversation.

A few minutes later, when I've mostly caught my breath

and my tea is cool enough to drink, Phil blows through the door looking as dapper and distinguished as the day I met him.

We met in a coffee shop just like this one, in Milan. I was sitting on a cobbled patio sipping espresso and going over one of my clients' accounts on my laptop when he walked by. Our eyes met, and I swear I could hear a string quartet playing in the background. The Italian sunshine warmed my back and lit his face in a golden glow, and that was it. We slept together that evening and he promised me the world.

Over the months that followed, Phil wove a story about his life that felt as surreal as our first meeting. He told me about growing up in the States, then moving to Paris to work for world-class couturiers when he was in his twenties before starting his own business a decade later. He pulled himself up by his bootstraps, he told me. He worked himself to the bone. Then he made it—and I was the lucky woman who got to enjoy the fruits of his labors with him.

He didn't mention the family he already had back in Paris.

I still don't know how much of what he told me was true and how much was pure fabrication. I probably never will.

"Lily," he says, his broad hand on the back of the armchair across from mine. "It's good to see you. The past week has been hell."

I give him a tight smile. Am I supposed to feel sorry for him? Did he forget that I'm the one who had surgery, and who still has a mountain of pain ahead of me?

He ducks to the counter to order a drink, then comes back to sit down. We watch each other for a moment. When Candice brings his mug over, he doesn't thank her. Doesn't even look at her, just flicks his wrist to wave her away.

I bristle. You can tell a lot about a person by how they treat people they think are beneath them. I wonder if he would've been polite if he knew she was my sister?

He steeples his fingers. "You should have told me about the cancer. I would have come."

I sip my tea, wrapping dignity around myself like a blanket. "I didn't need you to come."

"You need support."

"I have support."

"Who? That ass with the blond hair? Come on, Lily. You can do better. How old is he? Twenty-five?"

I don't answer. Rudy's age has nothing to do with his. In fact, Rudy has nothing to do with this at all. I set my teacup down and take a breath. "Why are you here, Phil?"

When Phil walked away from me, I felt heartbroken. I was overwhelmed, devastated, and scared. Then I got my diagnosis, and I fell down a deep, dark hole and I realized the heartbreak was nothing. From then on, I mostly felt a numb kind of terror. Rudy woke me up again, and now, for the first time in a long time, I feel like myself again.

I went through surgery with a child in my womb. If my kid can survive what I'm going through—if *I* can survive—then I don't need a man like Phil to inject me with false promises.

Phil takes a deep breath to gather himself. "Lily, I came here for you. For our child."

I nod. "I'd like my child to have a father," I answer neutrally. I narrow my eyes. "What's your plan?"

Phil leans back and slurps his coffee. That always bothered me. The slurping. Who needs to slurp every single drink? Water, coffee, alcohol—always with that disgusting noise. His eyes lift to mine. "My plan is to come here and make you see sense. Now tell me what's going on. Why did you go under the knife when you're pregnant? That can't be safe."

Under the knife? As if I had a choice? As if I was getting a boob job for cosmetic purposes? As if my entire medical team didn't strongly suggest I treat this cancer as soon as possible in order to *save my life?*

He must see the look on my face because that charm faucet opens a little. "That's my kid too, Lily."

I nod. "That's true." Technically. Biologically.

He spreads his hands. "So pack your things and come home with me." He says the words like they're the most natural thing in the world. Like my leaving Heart's Cove isn't just an option, it's an eventuality.

I stare at him, wondering how the hell I ever had sex with him. Sure, he's attractive. He's successful. He has a charm faucet entirely under his control. But he's just so...*arrogant.* And fucking condescending.

"Home?" I manage to squeeze out. "Where is home?"

"I'll set you up in my apartment in Milan, baby. It's all ready for you. There's enough room for a nursery too, and we can hire a nanny. You'll have help there."

I frown, trying to understand the audacity of this man. "You want me to leave my entire family and my medical team to go to Milan with you just months before my baby is born? You want me to give birth in Italy?"

"I want you to be where you belong."

I think I'm in an alternate universe. Is this guy for real? "You broke up with me, Phil. You told me to abort my baby, and you walked away. I haven't heard from you for months." I lean forward. "You have a wife and kids I never even *knew* about. Why the hell do you think I would leave with you? So I can be the other woman for the rest of my life?"

Phil's face hardens. "Of course not. I left my wife for you, Lily."

I pause. "You mentioned that."

"I'm here, aren't I?"

"You have houses in seven countries, Phil," I remind him. "Traveling here isn't exactly different from your usual life."

He glances around the room with an ugly sneer on his lips. "Trust me, babe, it's different from my usual life."

Right. Because he's the hotshot fabric supplier who rubs shoulders with all the haute couturiers in the world. How could I forget?

I take a sip of tea to give myself a moment to think. When I set it down, I search his eyes. "You really left your wife for me?"

A loud bang makes me jump, and I see Candice behind the nearest end of the counter, fiddling with one of the display cabinets. The door of one of the cabinets behind her is swinging open as if it's been slammed too hard to stay closed. She looks... angry.

Phil doesn't notice. "I did. I did it for you, for the baby."

Something isn't adding up. Narrowing my eyes on the man across from me, I lean back. "What about your other kids?"

"What about them?"

I put a hand on my stomach. "Why is this baby suddenly more important than your existing children? You told me to, quote, 'Get rid of it or get out of your life.'" My eyes harden. "Why the change of heart?"

The man bristles. He's not used to this. We met in Milan and I was just happy to have a companion once in a while. I thought I was in love, but what was it, really? He'd flit in and out of my life and take me to romantic dinners, then lie on top of me and stick his dick in me until he came before falling asleep. He didn't even know I was an accountant until we'd been seeing each other for two months. I'm not sure I've ever really questioned him. I always just accepted his presence.

Not anymore.

"That baby is my blood." He thrusts a finger at my stomach. "Now stop it, Lily. Pack your bags and come with me. I have flights booked. We could be in Milan by morning."

Another bang, but this time Candice holds the cabinet closed. She turns slowly, shoulders bunched, and starts rubbing a spot on the counter with a dishrag with vigorous intensity, clearly listening to every word.

My lips almost twitch. I can't believe this is my life—and is it bad I'm kind of enjoying this? I've been through so much. Faced the fear of my own death, of my baby's death...and I'm still in the thick of it.

Phil's arrogance and condescension are nothing.

"Why Milan?" I ask, because I like the way his face is turning red. "I thought you said your home base was in Paris?" My eyes widen as a realization hits me. "Did you really leave your wife? Or is this just a way to get me to stay in Milan and be your good little Italian side piece?"

Phil grips his coffee mug so tight his nail beds turn white. "I left my family for you, Lily."

"You divorced her? Truly?"

Phil shifts in his seat. "We just need to sign the papers."

My eyes narrow. "Who needs to sign the papers?"

"Both of us."

"So you're separated but not divorced?"

"What does it matter?" he explodes. "I'm here, aren't I?"

Candice is leaning against the counter nearest us now, not even pretending to work, and she goes very, very still. I can feel her gaze on us like a physical weight.

"I'm just trying to get a sense of the situation," I answer neutrally. "Does your wife know you're here?"

"Ex-wife," he bites out, and I decide not to tell him that technically, she's still his wife.

I arch my brows.

He shuffles uncomfortably. "She knows I met someone."

"Met someone," I repeat slowly. "And the baby?"

"What about it?"

"Did you tell your wife—ex-wife—that you'd fathered a child?"

"How the fuck is this relevant?" Phil spits, throwing his hands out. "Lily, I'm here, and now we can be together."

I almost start laughing. Phil is so far down my priority list, he isn't even a blip. A cancer diagnosis does that to a person. A baby does that to a person. Puts everything in sharp focus. I was his side piece for months without knowing it, and when I got pregnant, he wanted me to get rid of it. Then he walked away and didn't say a word to me for *months*. Now he wants us to play at being a happy family? Is he deluded? "We broke up, and I'm not interested in picking up where we left off. If you left your wife for me, you did it a few months too late."

Phil's lips lift in a snarl. "I'm here because you were too fucking dumb to take the pill properly and you got yourself knocked up."

My muscles lock up. There's something ugly in his eyes. I'm not enjoying the redness in his face anymore. This was fun for a bit, because I got to poke him and see the true asshole beneath the charming veneer. But I don't like the turn this conversation is taking.

"That wasn't a solo endeavor, Phil," I hiss, anger arcing through me. "Takes two to make a baby."

"Your fucking fault, Lily. And now that I know you're sick, I'm trying to figure out if you're even able to carry that kid to term. The doctor told me you need chemo, Lily. So you're planning on poisoning our unborn child as well as putting it through the trauma of surgery? Some fucking mother you'll make."

I freeze. In just a few sentences, Phil has managed to cut to the core of my worries. It's like he's been able to take a scalpel to me and dig through my insides to figure out exactly how to make me hurt. Isn't that what I've been telling myself? That I'm not good enough? That I'll fail? That even though my medical team assures me these things are safe, I can't quite shake the feeling that I'm starting this whole motherhood thing off on the entirely wrong foot?

Tears well up behind my eyes, but I will not cry.

I. Will. Not. Cry.

This asshole might have donated his DNA to make this baby, but I will fight tooth and nail to make sure he can't hurt it the way he's hurt me. If there's one thing I've learned since I found out I'm pregnant, it's that I'm strong. I'm so damn strong I wonder why I ever thought I needed to run away. I didn't find myself in all those international trips. I didn't need to wander from country to country to figure out what I wanted.

I just needed a smack across the head with a two-by-four to show me what's really important.

My baby. My family. My *home*.

I also learned that I have support. I have a whole army of women at my back that are there for me whether I need a laugh or a cry or food to stuff my face with.

"You're nothing," Phil hisses, his face twisted in a snarl. "A piece of ass I kept in Milan, and now I'm in this shitty town because you were stupid enough to get yourself pregnant."

Dozens of cups fall off the counter and smash on the floor beside us in a cacophony of breaking ceramic. Phil startles, rearing back, and Candice leaps over the counter like she's a teenager and not well on her way to her fifties. Her movement is graceful as she vaults over the edge, her face like thunder. My sister grabs a serving tray from the counter with both hands and holds it up near her shoulder like she's about to bring it down on his head.

"It's time for you to go," she says deliberately, in a soft, calm voice. The menace in her eyes is unmistakable.

Phil scoffs. "I'm a paying customer."

"I don't give a shit." Candice looks great and terrible and

furious, and I've never loved her more. She lifts the tray a little higher, and Phil has the decency to look concerned.

He pushes himself up to his feet. "I tried, Iliana. You're throwing away a good life. You and the baby could have it all, but you'd rather stay in this shithole. Don't come crawling to me when it falls apart, and keep my name off the birth certificate." He gives me one last venomous stare, lifts his gaze to Candice, then stalks out the door.

I feel...odd. A bit detached.

I'm relieved, of course. Relieved that he's walking away and he's not going to grab me by the hair and drag me across the world to a foreign country. But I'm also deeply sad. My kid won't have a daddy. Not to mention those hateful words swirling in my head, reminding me of all the things I'm most afraid of. What if he's right? What if I'm really not fit to be a mother? My body isn't exactly doing what it's supposed to do right now. I'm laughably unprepared for whatever comes next.

Candice's shoes crunch on all the broken mugs. Face red, hands trembling, she turns to me. "You want me to kill him? Jen knows a pig farmer who can get rid of the body."

Blinking at my big sister, I let her words sink in. Then Fiona ambles over with a broom and leans it against the wall before putting her hands on her hips. "I'll help. Grant has all kinds of tools in his workshop we can use to chop him up into itty bitty little pieces. He showed me how to use the table saw just last week. It's kind of fun."

They look at me, completely serious, and I feel my lips twitch. Then the three of us burst into inappropriate, raucous laughter, and all the tension in me drains away.

Nothing says friendship like homicidal intentions.

My tears soak into a scratchy napkin as I finally wipe my eyes, laughter fading into little leftover giggles. I lean back against my armchair with a sigh. My body feels broken and exhausted, but somehow lighter.

I wouldn't trade this sisterhood for anything. Least of all a flight to Italy with Sir Charming Fuckwad.

Then the café door flies open so hard it hits the wall and leaves a dent. Rudy strides in, face set with grim determination. He stares straight at me, completely ignoring Candice and Fiona and the rest of the patrons in the room.

He stalks toward me like a predator and I freeze in my seat. Gone is the happy, charismatic Rudy who doesn't have a care in the world. The man before me is dangerous. Determined. I blink, and he's in front of me. Then, without a word, he wraps his hand around the back of my neck, tilts my head up toward him, and crushes his lips to mine.

THIRTY-SIX
LILY

RUDY IS KISSING ME.

He's kissing me *hard*. It's less of a kiss and more of a claiming. He shoves his tongue into my mouth and grips the back of my neck so hard I'm trapped against him. Stupidly, my body heats up and lust floods my veins. I just had a mastectomy days ago, and now my body wants sex? What the hell is wrong with me?

Rudy breaks the kiss but doesn't move back very far. We're both panting hard, and his hand is shoving into the hair at the back of my head. I like the way it feels. I like the way he smells. I like having him here, a strong man whose shirt I can curl my fingers into when things get hard. He leans his forehead against mine and closes his eyes.

It feels good. So, so good to have him close.

"Lily," he sighs, as if my name is his salvation.

"Rudy." My breaths are still sharp, and there's a twinge in my armpit from sitting forward like this. I should take another painkiller before things get worse, but I still feel vaguely uncomfortable taking medication while pregnant. I feel like I've put my baby through enough. The poor thing will have to go through chemo with me, and I'll never even get the chance to breastfeed. Baby's not getting the easiest start to life. I shift again, and another slice of pain lashes from my armpit to my sternum.

When I try to extricate myself from Rudy's hold, he tightens his fingers in my hair. "I don't care about the baby," he says fiercely. "I want you, Lily. You're my woman. The only woman. I want you beside me."

He slides his other hand over my stomach, and suddenly I'm mad.

What is *up* with these men just coming over here and thinking they have a right to me? To my body? Suddenly, it doesn't feel so good to have his arm wrapped around the back of my head. It feels *stifling*. It feels like another offer of being shoved into an apartment in Milan behind a locked door, away from everyone and everything I know. It feels like someone shoehorning their way into my life when it should be *my fucking decision*.

I slap his hand away and pull my head back, glaring.

Rudy straightens, his thick brows tugging together. "What?"

"Did you hit your head?" I ask.

"What?"

"In what world is it acceptable to march in here and kiss me like that? After the way you acted at the hospital like some caveman who was angry that someone dared talk to his woman? After you walked away from me like my baby was a parasite?" Anger whips through me. Not only at Rudy, but at this whole situation. I don't have *time* for this! I want to laugh about burying bodies in pig pens, not deal with stupid men and their stupid egos.

"No, Lily—"

"Then you waltz in here and say you 'don't care about the baby.' I don't know about you, Rudy, but that's not exactly a ringing endorsement for fatherhood." I scoff, moving to cross my arms, then wince. Stupid operation. Stupid boob. Stupid cancer.

Stupid *Rudy*!

"That's not what I meant, Lily. I just meant that I'll be there for you. I was surprised, that's all."

"So?" I let out a bitter snort. "So what? You were surprised I'm pregnant. Great. So was I. I asked you for casual sex, Rudy. I didn't ask you to be my kid's stepfather."

He bristles. "It was more than casual sex."

"Fine. It was more. Then it ended. You can't just stride in here like I'm going to fall at your feet and ask you to save me. I'm *over* it, Rudy. Over men thinking they need to pick me up and be by my side. I'm *fine*. I'll be okay. I don't need you. I just want to be left alone!" My little speech ends on a shrill note, and I know my face is red with emotion.

Rudy's face goes utterly blank. He stands up straighter, taking a step back. His heel grinds into a shard of broken mug, but he doesn't even glance down. He just holds my gaze as his throat works to swallow. Then his chin jerks down sharply. "You're right. I shouldn't have come here."

I watch him turn on his heel and walk away, the cheery bells above the door ringing as if to mock me.

Candice and Fiona's eyes bore into the side of my head, but all I do is lean forward and pick up my teacup. I sip at it primly, pretending it doesn't taste cold and bitter after sitting on the table for so long. Swiveling my head, I meet the stares of my two girlfriends. "What."

Fiona clears her throat and grabs the broom she'd leaned against the counter. "Well, you told him where you stand," she says neutrally. "That's for sure."

Candice hums, still staring at me.

I turn my head and stare straight ahead, the last wisps of anger still burning through me.

Anger feels *good*, I realize. Sharp and astringent. I've spent the past couple of months drifting from crisis to crisis, feeling overwhelmed by everything the future holds.

But I made it through my surgery and yes, I'm still sore as hell, but I'm here. I drove myself down the block and sat myself in this chair and told not one but two men to leave me the hell alone. Which I sincerely hope they do.

Jen appears from the kitchen in the back of the café with a tray of fresh salted caramel brownies. She puts one on a plate and drops it in front of me, nodding without a word. Then Fiona starts sweeping, and Candice heads behind the till.

I eat every bit of that brownie, trying to forget that they're Rudy's favorite.

. . .

MY CHEMOTHERAPY IS SET to start four weeks from now. I have appointments with obstetricians and oncologists, and they all assure me that things are going well. I rest, eat, and even do some work. I go see Dr. Gardner twice a week, and she helps me center myself. My mother and sisters bring over so much baby stuff that my tiny apartment is overrun. The crib gets shoved between the wall and my bed, the rocking chair in the other corner of my cramped living room. There are diapers stacked all the way up to the ceiling in the corner of my bathroom.

Nora checks on me often, and even gets Fallon to cook dozens of meals for me, so my freezer is always stocked with home-cooked meals ready to be reheated. When I thank her, she just winks and tells me she used her super-special little-sister powers of persuasion to keep him coming back week after week, and I'm not complaining. The man can cook.

I'm lucky, I realize. And I'm nowhere near alone.

In those weeks, I don't think of Phil—but I do think of Rudy. I see him driving around town, and I see his company's real estate signs all over the place. I was rude to him. I know I was. He came over to tell me he'd stand by me and I pushed him away.

Again.

But I still feel like it was the right decision. The clarity I experienced after my mastectomy fades a bit, but I still feel more determined than ever. If I let Rudy sweep me away, I'm afraid I'll lose myself. He promised me the world, but I've spent my whole life traveling and I've seen enough to know that I don't need those kinds of promises. I need to know that my baby will be okay, that I'll be okay.

I might not have a perfectly healthy body, but I'm going to be the most kick-ass mother this town has ever seen.

THIRTY-SEVEN
RUDY

MY LIFE HASN'T CHANGED. As the weeks pass, everything is the same as it was before Iliana came to town, so it shouldn't bother me that she turned me down.

But it does.

I go to work, come home, work on my house, hang out with Lee, spend time with my grandmother, and it all just seems so fucking pointless.

Whenever I catch a glimpse of Lily, she's with her sisters, her mother, and her friends, and I'm on the outside.

Autumn has already painted the leaves in red and gold when I run into Georgia Neves again. She looks as glamorous as ever, and she gives me a broad smile.

"Rudy." She spreads her arms and gives me air kisses on each cheek. "You look very handsome today."

I glance down at my jeans-and-sweater combo, and grin. "You can't help yourself, can you?"

Her laugh is carefree, and for maybe the first time, I feel like she's genuine. If I were a better man, I'd wonder what was behind the shadows in her eyes. I'm not, though, and all I can think about is the fact that I still don't want her any more than I did before.

The only woman I can think of is Lily.

"I haven't seen you since you so rudely left my home after half a glass of champagne." She winks, and I know there are no hard feelings. "How are things with your girl?"

I shrug. "There is no 'my girl.'"

"Oh, honey." She squeezes my arm. "Well, I have good news for you." She brightens. "My best girlfriend is moving here, and she needs a super sexy agent to show her all the nicest properties in the area. I gave her your number."

I nod. "Much appreciated, Georgia."

"Do you have time for a drink?" Georgia smiles at me, her red lipstick shaping her full lips into a lush pout. "Cantina has a special on margaritas this afternoon."

"You never struck me as the type of woman who goes out searching for happy hour specials."

A sensual smile turns wry. "That's because you know nothing about me. Come on. Tequila fixes everything."

I'm pretty sure that's the exact opposite of the truth, but I let her hook her arm into mine and we walk down the tree-lined street toward the Mexican restaurant. It's a beautiful late-September afternoon, where the air is warm yet crisp and the whole world feels like it's holding its breath.

For what, I'm not sure. Maybe for me to get my head out of my ass.

"My new home was featured on an interior design blog, did you know that?" Georgia asks pleasantly, her head tilted to the sky. A curl of her hair falls onto my shoulder, an intimate caress of the silky strands.

"That's great," I say, eyes drifting to the side as we pass Lily's street. I do that every time I walk or drive by, because I'm a desperate fool.

"My ex-husband saw it, and it made his head explode." She laughs in a way that makes her sound just a little bit evil. "I think he's convinced I do things just to piss him off."

"Do you?" I tear my eyes away from the distant shape of Lily's building to glance at Georgia.

Her arm squeezes over mine. "I plead the Fifth," she says with a sly grin. "He tends to forget that we're divorced, which I don't exactly think is my problem. Ever since I glitter-bombed his bedroom he's had such a stick up his ass."

A surprised chuckle falls from me. "You did what?"

Georgia, the refined, elegant woman clinging to my arm, *glitter-bombed her ex-husband's bedroom?*

"You know," she starts conversationally, "if you sprinkle glitter on a ceiling fan it really gets *everywhere* when you turn the thing on. I laughed my ass off when I went to our arbitration at the lawyer's office two whole weeks after he left a very nasty voicemail on my phone. He still had a couple pieces of glitter in his eyebrow." She shifts her purse on her shoulder and glances at the distant horizon, sucking in a deep breath. "So did his hot young assistant, actually. Wonder what she was doing in his bedroom." Georgia's voice goes a bit tight at the end, but she turns a bright smile on me. "Oh well. Guess I'll never know."

"I'm sorry, Georgia." Voice muted, I give her arm a squeeze. I feel an odd sort of affection for Georgia. I know we'll never be close—she'd never let anyone, much less a man, get close to her—but I still feel like we could be friends.

She shrugs. "I'm here now, and I'm going to drink margaritas with a gorgeous younger man. You think we could get a picture for my Instagram? I got a suspicious new follower that I'm pretty sure is my ex-husband being a creeper."

I chuckle, something tight loosening inside me. I prefer this relationship with Georgia, I realize. She's not flirting shamelessly with me, she's just...lonely. Maybe we all are. "Sure," I tell her. "I'll take a photo with you."

"Marvelous," she says, and we turn down the street toward Cantina. "Maybe I'll unblock his phone number before we post it. We can take bets on how long it'll take him to call and screech at me. I'm thinking thirty seconds."

"Does he not realize the two of you are divorced?"

"Honey, he's got a stick up his rear. He probably can't think of anything beyond how much his asshole hurts."

I burst out laughing, and it feels like the first time I've laughed in weeks—just as we pass the Four Cups Café, and Lily walks out.

Damn. She looks incredible. I don't know if it's the autumn afternoon sunshine or the pregnancy, but the woman is glowing. Her chocolate-colored hair is shiny and thick, falling in loose waves down her back. She's smiling bright and wide, and it fades when she sees me.

I stop, Georgia's arm still hooked in mine, and all I can do is stare. There's a slight swell in Lily's lower stomach, and all I want to do is drop to my knees and press my lips to it.

I was such a fucking idiot for how I acted at the hospital. And instead of fixing it, I came barreling into the coffee shop and kissed her like a cat marking his territory. Not my greatest moment. No wonder she pushed me away.

Lily's eyes flick to Georgia, then to our clasped arms. Her mouth tightens for a moment, then she forces her face to relax. She nods. "Rudy."

"Hey, Lily. You remember Georgia." I drop her arm and nod to the woman at my side.

"Of course." She smiles at my former client, one hand moving to her stomach. My chest aches something fierce being here, close enough to catch a faint whisper of her scent, but too far away to touch.

"We were just heading to Cantina for their margarita special," Georgia says, surprising me. "Would you like to join?"

"Um, no," Lily answers without hesitation, and a little bit of me dies. "I'm good. Also, I'm pregnant. Margaritas aren't really enticing right now."

Georgia's brows jump up, and she glances at me. The question in her gaze is clear.

Lily rolls her eyes. "It's not his." She hikes her bag over her shoulder, but she only catches one of the straps. The other falls down, and a bulky item comes falling from her bag.

A book.

I lean over to pick it up, turning it around to see the collection of *Grimms' Fairy Tales* I gave her for her birthday.

She kept it?

Frowning at the cover, I lift my gaze to Lily's. She blushes, and it's the most beautiful thing I've ever seen. The fingers of my free hand curl into my palm, everything in me resisting the urge to reach over and sweep my fingers over that peach-colored flush.

"I've been reading them for the baby," she says, not quite meeting my eyes. "I'm thinking this kid is coming into the world with a bit of a rough start, so I might as well not kid myself with fluffy fairy tales. Better stick with the dark and twisted."

I can't help it as a grin tugs at my lips. Lily answers it with one of her own, and for a moment, I forget all about Georgia. I forget about the coffee shop and the margaritas and everything else.

The woman who holds my heart in her hands is smiling at me, and for the first time in weeks, I feel like I can breathe.

Then Lily clears her throat and takes the book from my hands, giving us both an awkward nod. "Well, I'd better..." Her voice drifts off, and she just shuffles past me to walk away. I watch her go, loving the way her leggings cup her ass. Even as my heart is slowly shredded by her leaving without looking back, I can't deny how much I want her still.

The sound of a throat clearing makes me look at Georgia, who has a gleam in her eye and a smirk on her lips. "There's a story there," she says. "And you're going to tell it to me over margaritas."

THIRTY-EIGHT

LILY

CHEMO SUCKS. Like, a lot. Knocks me on my ass when I get it, and takes days to recover enough to feel halfway normal. Next thing I know, a nurse is sticking another needle in my arm and hooking me up for another round.

Lying back in the chair in the hospital ward, I stare at the other half-dozen patients getting their treatment. One girl looks about fifteen. She's lost all her hair, but she's chatting happily with the nurse who's checking her IV. An older gentleman is in the chair beside her, and he just looks very tired and very, very sick.

So far, a month in, I've kept all my hair. I might be one of the lucky ones. Apart from the aches and nausea, I've noticed a lot of forgetfulness—like the time I called my mother because I'd lost my phone for the nth time, only for her to ask me how I was calling her. We laughed about "chemo brain" but I was still horribly embarrassed. But perhaps the most bothersome symptom I've had is what the nurses call peripheral neuropathy. I have no sensation in the soles of my feet or the tips of my fingers, and I feel flat-footed and awkward when I walk or try to do things with my hands like do up buttons or pick up small objects.

Maybe that's the reason I haven't removed the pendant hanging around my neck, the sapphire hard and cool against my breastbone. Or maybe its slight weight reminds me of my father's strength all those years ago.

"How's your niece liking college?" a nurse asks as she bustles around me. "Northwestern, right?"

I smile. "Allie's loving it. I think she's enjoying being away from Heart's Cove, but my sister Candice is gravely insulted that Allie isn't homesick. Her best friend, Clancy, is at the community college in town and she's hoping to transfer somewhere closer to Allie. They still talk every day."

The nurse—Caroline—smiles warmly. "It's got to be a strong friendship to last through distance."

"It is. Allie will be back for Thanksgiving," I say. "And I have a feeling once she feels how cold it gets in Illinois, she'll be missing our mild winters enough to be glad to come home."

Caroline chuckles. "You're all set," she tells me with a kind smile. "I'll be back to check on you in a few. You got everything you need?" She nods to my tablet, phone, and stack of magazines.

I nod. "All good."

"That's a beautiful necklace," Caroline tells me, nodding to my neck. "I've seen it on you every day and keep meaning to comment on it."

"My father gave it to me before he passed," I hear myself saying. "He had cancer too."

"I'm sure he's right here with you," she says before patting the back of my cushioned chair and walking away. I sink back into the chair and close my eyes, wondering if she's right. I haven't taken the pendant off since I started chemotherapy, and it does feel like it gives me strength. My father didn't make it, but he was still strong. A fighter.

Like me—and my baby.

Mac picks me up once I'm done. He's got a big pickup truck that is very difficult to get into when you've just had cancer drugs pumped into your body and a growing baby bump throwing off your center of gravity. I try to haul myself up, and Mac stands behind me to give me a boost. He waits until I'm clicked into the seat, head resting on the seat.

"I'm sorry," he says, standing in the doorway. "I'll take Trina's car next time I come pick you up."

"S'okay," I tell him, breath still coming in jagged gulps. "But you might have to help me down when I get home."

He smiles, then jogs around the front to get to the driver's side. I watch him with sick fascination, wondering if I'll ever have the strength to jog again.

"How are the kids?" I manage to ask, eyes drifting shut as we get on the road.

"They're great. Toby's so protective of Katie, and I have a feeling he'll be a good cousin for your little one too."

I smile, eyes still closed. "The baby will have lots of love, that's for sure." We drive in silence for a while. "Thanks for picking me up," I say. "I really appreciate it."

"You're family," he says simply, and I open my eyes. He slows the truck down as we turn into the busier center of Heart's Cove. His words sink down into me, diffusing into something warm and nice. *Family.* It's a much bigger word than I realized.

"So you gonna ask Trina to marry you or what?" I ask as he pulls up to my building. "Make this whole 'family' thing official?"

Mac grins, one hand on the steering wheel as he turns the truck off. "Has she asked you to drop hints or something?"

I let out a laugh that sounds more like a puff of breath. "No. She's still trying to convince herself that her last marriage ending in disaster means she never wants to do it again."

Mac tilts his head. "And you don't think that's true?"

"Trina would cream her panties to wear a wedding dress again. She probably has a secret savings account for it already."

Mac laughs, and his smile lingers as he slips out of the truck. The man lifts me right out of the passenger seat and lets me lean on him all the way to the elevators and into my apartment. By the time I lie down on my old sofa, I'm about ready to pass out.

"Thanks, Mac," I mumble, lids heavy.

"Anytime. Your mom will be over soon. She just texted me to say she's leaving Candice's place."

"Okay," I say, and fall asleep right after the door closes behind him.

A very small part of me wishes a man like Mac was staying and cuddling close to me while I lie on the couch feeling like garbage—and by "a man like Mac," clearly, I mean Rudy. But only a small part of me. The rest of me is still rational. I'm sure he's not thinking about nursing me back to health anymore. He's probably having margaritas with gorgeous, sexy, *healthy* women, grateful he dodged a bullet shaped like me. It's better for me to go through this alone.

WEEKS PASS, and I realize I was wrong. Even without the baby, there's no way I could have done this completely on my own.

I'm glad I moved to Heart's Cove, and as overbearing as my family is, I wouldn't trade them for anything.

I feel the baby kick for the first time at twenty-one weeks. It feels weird, like little fluttering in my stomach. It's happened before, I realize, delicate little flutters that I assumed were nausea or something chemotherapy related. Lord knows there have been enough odd and uncomfortable symptoms caused by my treatment. Shocked, I realize that for weeks, I've been feeling my baby flutter. This feels different. Stronger. It's not cancer related. It's something much more beautiful.

I happen to be outside when it happens, carrying a bag from the pharmacy with fancy moisturizer I bought myself as a treat. I lean against a brick building, hand on my stomach as tears well in my eyes. I can't help it. The joy I feel is indescribable because I know I'm doing it. Even with the surgery, and the chemotherapy, and all the damn brochures and questions and unknowns, there's a baby growing in my womb and it's *kicking*.

"Lily?" a voice calls out, right before I hear rapid footsteps approaching. "Is everything okay?" Rudy appears beside me, his face tight with concern. Bright eyes search my face, then shift down to the hand I'm clutching over my stomach. "What's wrong? Is it the baby?"

My throat is so tight I can't talk. Instead, I grab his hand and shove it against my stomach. "The baby's kicking," I whisper, my voice hoarse. "First time."

Rudy's features grow focused, and the baby stills for a moment. Would he be able to feel such small movements? Then the baby moves again, more vigorously this time, and Rudy's face melts into the most gorgeous, beautiful smile I've ever seen. He's as shocked and full of wonder as I am, and his other hand moves to my bump right beside my own. I look at the way his big, broad hands cover mine and span almost the full width of my little bump, and it feels so right to have him touching me like this that I could cry.

Well, I'm already crying, but I could cry some more.

"Holy shit," Rudy whispers, awe tingeing his words.

Then I remember what the hell I'm doing—who the hell it is that has his hands all over my stomach—and I stiffen. Rudy must feel it, because he reluctantly drops his hands and takes a step back. He rubs his neck and arches his brows at me. "I was worried when I saw you stop and grip the wall," he tells me. "I thought something was wrong."

Sniffling as I wipe tears from my cheeks and snot from my nose—sexy, I know—I shake my head at Rudy and try to compose myself. "It just surprised me, is all."

"I've never felt that before," he says, still slightly awed.

I snort-laugh. "Me neither. Except I just realized what I thought were chemo side effects might have been my baby all along."

Rudy smiles that brilliant, earth-shattering smile of his, and all I want to do is fall into his arms. I rack my brain, trying to remember why it was that things didn't work out between us. It was my fault, wasn't it? He kissed me and I got angry. But now my thoughts are all jumbled and I can't quite remember why.

"Can I walk you home?" Rudy asks.

My building is half a block away, so I shrug. "Sure. No margarita dates this afternoon?"

His lips twist. "Lily, that wasn't what it looked like. We're just friends."

"I thought you were business associates." My voice sounds bitter, and I mentally kick myself. Why am I being such a jerk? Why do I care? Why can't I just be a gracious, elegant woman who floats along the street beside him and makes him realize everything he's missing?

Instead, I'm a pregnant, frazzled mess who's acting like a jealous girlfriend. As if. *I'm* the one who broke up with *him*.

We get to my apartment, and when I open the door, Rudy sniffs. He frowns, glancing at the lobby.

My cheeks burn. "It's an old building. Smells musty, I know. You get used to it."

"You should be staying somewhere better," he says. "A house. Somewhere with room for you and the baby."

"Yeah, well, when the House Fairy drops one off for me, I'll move."

I get lost in his eyes for a moment, loving the way his lips curl at my dumb joke. Without a word, he hands me the bag with my fancy moisturizer, and I hadn't even realized I'd dropped it—or that he'd picked it up and carried it for me.

"Thanks," I say sheepishly. "And I'm sorry for being so rude. You can have margarita dates with whoever you want."

His lips quirk. "Glad I have your blessing."

My stupid, traitorous cheeks start burning even more. "That's not what I meant. I just... I'm..." I take a step into the lobby and grip the door like it's a lifeline. "I'll see you around." Then I force myself to close the door and walk to the elevators without looking back.

We broke up because I'm going through the hardest time of my life, I remind myself. I remember now. Between cancer and surgery and chemo and childbirth, it's too much for a fledgling relationship like ours. I have my family, and that's enough.

It has to be.

THIRTY-NINE
RUDY

FOR ONCE, I appreciate that Heart's Cove is a small town. Not only have I seen Lily at least once every week around town, but I've overheard my grandmother getting regular updates about her condition. I know her asshole of an ex hasn't been back since that day at the coffee shop.

The baby is due in mid-January, and being at the beginning of December now, that means she's about thirty-two or thirty-three weeks along. Not that I'm keeping track or anything. Ever since I felt the baby kick back in September, my mind just keeps track of these things without me having any control over it.

Lily finished all her courses of chemo and by all accounts, is doing okay. Of course she is—she's strong.

The days have passed in a haze of work and renovations and petty distractions, but I still feel like a chasm has opened up inside me. Weeks go by in the blink of an eye, only punctuated by the moments I see Lily.

It's pathetic, really. I should be over her by now, but there's still an ache in my chest that I can't seem to shake.

The only place I feel any kind of peace is my grandmother's bookstore. Today, as a chill settles in the air outside, I inhale the scent of paper and ink and glue and wait for another day to pass me by. Maybe after Lily's baby is born, I'll be able to move on. When I know she's safe and healthy.

I shelve a few new books we've received as Dorothy leans against the counter, chatting to my grandmother as if they're the best of friends.

I've noticed a change in the two of them. They'll say nasty things to each other, but there's less venom behind the words. They'll visit with each other and have perfectly civil conversations, when a few years ago there'd be projectiles flying whenever the two of them were in the same room.

I don't know if it's the fact that Dorothy has her own man in Eli now, or just that our community has grown in size and in love. But I'm happy for my grandmother. She doesn't make friends easily.

Kind of like me.

"Poor girl is just skin and bones now," Dorothy says as she straightens a stack of books on the counter. "To think she has to go through labor in just a few weeks too."

"She's strong," my grandmother replies, and I hear a hint of respect in her tone. "If she can get through everything she has so far, she can deliver a baby."

I could have told her that. From the moment I met Lily, I knew there was steel in her spine. Then she told me about the breast cancer, and everything made sense.

The book I'm holding is upside down—a fact I only notice after I've shelved it. I sigh, pulling it out, and slide it back in right side up. I've been distracted for weeks. Working helps, of course. The business is booming, and my grandmother's bookstore is ticking along just as it always does. The renovations I've done on my home are almost complete.

But it's all so meaningless. From a distance, I watch Lily fighting for her life and her baby's, and I spend my evenings ripping up old carpet and painting walls. Why? Why does any of it matter? The things that used to matter seem so empty now. It took all my effort over the past decade or so to establish myself in the world of real estate—for who? For what?

This buzzing in my skin won't settle, even though I'm in my grandmother's sanctuary. I need to get out of here.

"I'm going out for lunch," I tell Grandma, and nod to Dorothy. The two of them fall silent as I walk past, something unreadable in their gazes. They probably want me to start dating Lily again. Maybe they think I'm a coward for not being with her while she's going through all this.

Maybe they're right.

I inhale the scent of winter, buttoning up my light jacket and burying my chin in my chest. This winter has been a wet, cold drizzle, a perfect complement to the state of my mood.

Poor girl is just skin and bones now.

Dorothy's words echo in my mind, and I pause on the sidewalk. Maybe I should bring Lily some food, make sure she's okay. I shake the thought away as soon as it pops up. No matter how hung up I am on her, I'll have to admit sooner or later that we're not together. I don't have the right to take care of her. I can't call her mine.

My shoes scuff on the sidewalk as I make my way down the street, not even sure where I'm heading. There's a new Italian restaurant that just opened up, and they have a good lunch special. I could do Mexican or stop in for a sandwich at Four Cups.

Wherever I go, though, I'll be alone. That never used to bother me. I'd eat in restaurants by myself or with a date, and the experience felt the same either way. No real connection, only distraction. Now, I feel Lily's absence down to my bones.

The sky is a mass of dull, heavy clouds when I look up through the naked tree branches lining Cove Boulevard, and I know I need to get out of here. Our community is too intertwined, and I've heard Candice insisting that she's hosting Christmas this year. I managed to avoid Thanksgiving at Trina's house, thank God, but I had to reject six invitations to do it. I'm not going through that again at the end of the month.

Maybe it's time for me to pack up and move away. After a vacation over the holidays, I can take a page out of Lily's book and take off for a while. One of my employees could be promoted and my business could run itself. I could take a few months off. Disappear. Try to forget the way Lily's lips felt against mine.

Somehow, I end up at the community garden. There are new benches here now, and the naked remnants of new plants and trees that will burst with life in the spring. The empty lot behind the garden is vacant, and I've heard there's a petition going around to either incorporate it into the garden or turn it into a park and playground for kids.

Maybe Lily's child will get to enjoy it.

When I take a few steps closer, I see her. She's on that same bench where she sat when she told me it was over between us. Her head is tilted up to the sky, as if she's soaking up any rays of sun that pierce through the gray clouds.

And I can't help it. I change my trajectory and move closer.

Lily's eyes open when she sees me, and a sad kind of smile tugs at her lips. "Hey, Rudy. Happy belated Thanksgiving."

"Same to you." I sit down exactly where I sat last time. So close to her, but with a chasm between us.

"Any plans for Christmas?" she asks, and I wonder if I'm imagining the hopeful tone in her voice.

"Thinking of going down south," I say. "San Diego, maybe. Mexico. Never been to South America. I might see if there are any cheap flights anywhere."

She's quiet for a moment, then nods. "That sounds nice. You should go to Machu Picchu. It's worth braving the hordes of tourists."

I study her face, and realize Dorothy was right. Lily's lost weight. A lot of it. It's not that cold today, with just a bit of bite in the air, but Lily's bundled up like she's in Alaska. Her skin is pale, and she looks like she's drowning in her jacket. A few strands of dark hair stick out of the fluffy pink hat pulled low over her ears.

"How are you doing?" I ask. "I heard you finished your chemo."

She nods. "Waiting on the last blood test results to come back. Hoping everything's clear because I'm ready to move on." Her hand slides over her bump, and I wish I had the right to touch her. To put my arm around her and pull her into my warmth, to tell her that I'm right here and I'll make everything okay.

But that's not what she wants.

My eyes trace the curve of her cheeks, the sharp blade of her jaw. Her cheeks are too hollow. Would she go to lunch with me, if only so I could make sure she eats something?

"I heard you're moving out of your place," Lily says, eyes tilting back up to the sky.

I huff a laugh. "Those old ladies love to talk, don't they?"

Lily turns a smile on me, and it stops my heart dead. She shakes her head. "It's out of control." She pauses. "So you're really getting rid of that house?"

I shrug. "I'm in real estate. The market's up, and I just finished fixing it up. Makes sense to sell."

She nods. "It's a good little house."

"I knocked down a few of the walls on the ground floor," I tell her. "It's more open plan now. I put in a powder room downstairs too, but I kept that office as-is." The office where we worked alongside each other, where I felt at home in that house for the first time. "New kitchen too," I add, and it comes out as a hoarse whisper.

A touch of color stains her cheeks, and I wonder if she's thinking of the time I crowded her against the counter and kissed her like she belonged to me. She looks anywhere but at me, and it makes me want to haul her onto my lap and crush my lips to hers.

I'm not over her. Not even close. I haven't even thought of any other women since she walked into the bookstore and asked me for recommendations last summer. The only face I think of when I've got my hand wrapped around my cock is hers—but it's more than just sex. I want to be beside her. I want to be the one she leans on, the one she asks for help. I want to wake up next to her every morning and see that sweet, sleepy smile on her face.

I want *her*.

Lily groans, shuffling forward on the bench before bracing herself. "Standing up is getting more difficult every day," she says with a rueful grin. "Can you believe I had to ask my mother to tie my shoes yesterday? And I have seven weeks left of this crap."

I laugh, catching her arm to help her stand.

Then her brows tug, and she puts a hand to her stomach.

"Lily?"

"I—" She leans forward, gasping.

White-hot fear arcs through me, cutting a sharp line of pain through my chest. "Lily, talk to me." There's an edge to my voice, because I can see the pain twisting her features. She's clutching her stomach and taking short, sharp gasps. "Lily, what's going on? Talk to me, baby. I'm here." I put a hand on her back, my other hand wrapped around her arm to support her.

"Something's wrong," she squeezes out between breaths. "Something's wrong with the baby." A stain appears between her legs. She's wearing dark-gray maternity leggings under her jacket, but I can still tell the stain is red.

Pure, ice-cold panic jets through my veins, and then I'm moving. As gently as I can, I haul Lily into my arms. My heart hammers as I carry her out of the garden and onto the street.

I pause at the entrance to the garden as Lily lets out a whimper that spears me right through the chest. She's hurting. My woman is hurting and I need to get her help *now*.

Hospital. I need to get her to the hospital.

My mind whirls. Taxi? Or do I call 911 right away and wait for an ambulance?

Lily's nails dig into my neck and she lets out a pained cry that cuts me like a knife.

I'll drive, I decide, because there aren't any taxis in view and my car is only four blocks away, parked outside my office building.

Four blocks. I can carry her for four blocks—but will she be okay? Trying not to jostle her, I take a step, then see my cousin Jared exiting one of the shops on Cove Boulevard. His eyes widen as he takes me and Lily in, then waves me forward, clicking a fob that lights up a car on my side of the street.

"Put her in there," he calls out, waiting for a car to pass before jogging across the street toward us.

I put Lily down as gently as I can, too tense to reply to anything my cousin says. She leans against the side of the vehicle as I move the passenger seat as far as it will go and lean the seat back until it's almost fully reclined. Then I help her in, clicking the seatbelt over her bump.

Jared appears at my side. "You going to the hospital?"

I nod, then wrap my fingers around the keys he's extending toward me. I don't have time to feel surprised that the cousin who's always hated me is giving me free use of his car without question. "Thanks," I say, voice harsh.

"I'll go to the café and find her sister."

"Good." I'm already sliding behind the wheel and putting the key in the ignition. Jared is hustling toward Four Cups when I glance over at Lily.

With a fresh wave of terror, I notice the stain has spread. She's bleeding and in pain and I'm going to lose my fucking mind if anything happens to her or the baby.

I thought I was going on vacation? I thought I was going to *leave?*

Never in a million years.

Using the car's Bluetooth, I call 911 as I put the car in gear and speed down the street, hands gripping the steering wheel so tight I can't feel my fingers.

"Nine-one-one, what's your emergency?"

"I'm in the car with my—" I only hesitate for a second, because I know what Lily is to me. I've always known. "I'm in the car with my woman. She's pregnant, but there's blood and she's having severe abdominal pain." Distantly, I notice my voice is steady.

Lily reaches over and sinks her nails into my thigh so hard I know it'll leave marks, even through my jeans. It doesn't matter. Nothing matters except getting Lily some help and making sure I'm right here by her side.

Where I belong.

As I talk to the emergency responder, a sense of clarity

washes over me. It doesn't matter what Lily says, or how many times she pushes me away. It doesn't matter how long it takes or how many times I need to try to convince her. She's mine. She's been mine since the day she walked into the bookstore, and she'll be mine until the day I die. I'm claiming that baby inside her too.

My woman and my child are in trouble, but I'll be damned if I lose either one of them.

FORTY

LILY

THE LAST THING I remember is passing out when a pack of nurses and hospital staff haul me out of the car. I remember Rudy's face through it all, tight with tension but firm with resolve.

Then, nothing.

I open my eyes and realize I'm in a hospital bed. There's a blurry shape in the chair next to me, and for the second time in only a matter of months, I croak the first name that comes to my lips. "Rudy?"

He jumps up from where he was slouched, as if my voice woke him up. He comes into focus as he leans over the bed, his hands smoothing over my forehead and cheeks. "I'm here, baby. I'm right here. You're okay. The baby's in the NICU, but they think he's going to be okay."

A drop of water hits my nose, and I realize it came from Rudy.

"Why are you crying?" I ask, my voice sounding oddly distant. I try to lift my arm to wipe the wetness off his cheeks, because a man like Rudy shouldn't be crying. He should be dating someone young and carefree and unburdened.

But even as the thought crosses my mind, I know I don't want that. I want him to stay right here beside me forever and ever and ever.

"I'm crying because you scared the shit out of me, Lily," he says with a soft laugh. He presses his lips to my forehead, and it feels like he's doing it to reassure himself that I'm really here. "I'm glad you're awake."

"I want to see my baby." Everything feels fuzzy, but I find Rudy's hand and squeeze. "Take me to my baby, Rudy. I want to meet..." I blink, some of the blurriness clearing. "You said 'him.' It's a boy?" My voice trembles, and Rudy's face splits into a smile.

"A beautiful baby boy, Lily. He's perfect, just like his mama."

"I want to see him," I repeat in a hoarse whisper.

"You will," he assures me. "Let me just call the nurse, okay? You had to have an emergency C-section and you're not supposed to move."

I THINK I fall asleep for a while, because when I wake up, the room is full of people. My mother, my sisters, a couple of nurses...and Rudy. He's holding my hand, standing right where he was when I passed out as if he hasn't left my side.

I like the thought of that—Rudy being by my side. The

thought stays with me as my mother bustles on the other side of me. Pushing myself up, I pause when I feel lightheaded. I'm getting real sick of feeling like my body is giving out on me. The blanket covering me falls to my waist, and I touch my stomach, feeling bandages beneath the hospital gown.

More scars. A breath slides through my lips, but I also feel oddly proud. I've been sliced open and poked and prodded for months now, feeling like death was on my doorstep, but I'm still here. I'll have marks on my breast and stomach for the rest of my life, but I've made it over another hurdle.

I'm still breathing.

And I'm going to meet my baby today, no matter what the nurse or doctor or anyone says.

My mother and sisters are talking, telling me a million things that I don't have the energy to listen to right now. My mother squeezes my hand and I give her a smile, then turn to look at Rudy on the other side of me.

"Take me to see him," I tell Rudy, and he gives me the most beautiful smile I've ever seen.

He really is a gorgeous man. Too gorgeous. Makes me feel all weak and wobbly inside.

But he's strong, too, and he doesn't shy away from the tubes and equipment and bandages over me. He doesn't protest like my mother does about me moving, he just brings a wheelchair over and helps me into it, then smooths my hair back and puts a strong hand on my shoulder. I reach up and cover his hand with mine, letting out a long sigh.

Then Rudy wheels me to the NICU, and I go and meet my baby.

"I'm sad I didn't get to experience birth," I say quietly. After everything I've been through over the past few months, I wanted that moment when I got to push, when I got to feel my baby's skin against my chest.

One of the wheels of my wheelchair gives a squeaky whine with each turn. Rudy rumbles softly at my back, pushing me steadily down the bright hallway. "I experienced it for the both of us," he says grimly. "You're lucky you were asleep for it. I don't think I've ever been so scared."

We turn a corner and I see signs pointing to the NICU. "Your mom died when you were born," I say, remembering one of our first conversations, realization dawning. "You thought I was going to die too."

He huffs, and I wish I could see his face. Instead, we head down the hallway and turn into the ward.

My baby is in an incubator wearing a diaper that looks too big. He has a shock of black hair on his head and the most perfect fingers and toes I've ever seen. I suck in a breath, leaning forward in my chair until the stitches in my stomach protest. Rudy engages the brakes on my wheelchair and moves to the other side of the incubator.

Dragging my gaze away from my son, I look at Rudy. He meets my eyes over the baby and smiles gently. "He's perfect, Iliana."

Moisture gathers in my eyes as I look down again, slowly threading my arm through the hole to touch my baby's soft, soft skin. "He is," I whisper. "He's finally here."

Rudy hesitates on the other side of the incubator, then

clears his throat. "May I?" he asks, hands near the holes on the other side.

I nod, unable to speak. With infinite care, he runs one of his long, masculine fingers over my son's ear and down his arm. My baby immediately wraps his fingers around Rudy's index, and we both let out a surprised laugh.

"He likes you," I say. "I'm trying not to be jealous."

"I came here and read him some fairy tales earlier," Rudy says, redness rising on his cheeks. "I didn't know if you'd want me to touch him so I didn't, but I thought he might like some company in the first few hours of his life. He probably recognized my voice."

A hard, painful fist grips my heart. This beautiful, caring man dropped everything today to be here, and even made sure that my baby wasn't alone. We stay there for a while, until I shift in the wheelchair and Rudy notices me wince. Then, we're rolling that squeaky wheel all the way back to my room. I fall asleep with a smile on my face and my fingers intertwined with Rudy's.

THOSE FIRST FEW weeks are hard to keep track of. I learn that I had a placenta abruption, where the placenta pulled away from my uterine wall. I could have lost the baby if Rudy hadn't gotten me to the hospital so quickly. My son, Liam, was born at thirty-three weeks, three weeks shy of full-term. They'll have to keep him in the NICU for a while, but the doctors tell me he's doing great, and they don't think he'll have any long-term health problems.

I keep waiting for Rudy to tell me he's busy, that he has to leave. I keep waiting for his eyes to dim as he tells me that this is too much for him, and that he didn't sign up for a woman in remission from breast cancer with a preemie baby.

But every day, Rudy's here beside me. It doesn't matter what the weather is, what day of the week it is, or what's going on with his business. He always comes back, and I've started relying on his presence. I wonder if all the weeks I spent alone have been for naught, because I've just gone ahead and asked him to save me anyway.

One day, a week after I give birth, Rudy enters my room as he slides his phone into his pocket. He'd stepped out to talk to one of his employees, and he comes right back to take a seat beside my bed.

"So when's your flight?" I ask, voice carefully casual.

Rudy frowns. "My flight?"

"You said you were leaving for the holidays." I pause, holding my breath, because suddenly I feel awfully nervous about facing days or weeks without him by my side.

But Rudy just laughs. "Lily, you're going to have to try a lot harder than that to get rid of me. I'm spending the holidays right here. And if you get out in time, I'm spending the holidays at my house." A twinge of disappointment passes through me, until Rudy slides his broad hand over my jaw to cup my cheek. "And so are you."

I blink. "What?"

"Your apartment is tiny, and it's too small for the three of us. You'll move in with me."

My brows lower. There are a lot of things in those two

sentences that I have to question, because it sounds like he's ordering me around. A lot of assumptions Rudy seems to be making, including the fact that he seems to think I'm moving in with him, and he's using words like "the three of us." I'm ignoring the fact that I kind of love the way those words sound.

"Do I get a choice in the matter?" I snip, arching a brow. "Or are you going all caveman on me again."

"I'm going all caveman on you," Rudy informs me, dead serious. "If you don't want to move into my place, fine. I'll deal with your apartment, even if it does smell musty and moldy as hell. But I don't care, because I'm staying with you, Lily. We've wasted enough time dancing around each other. I've watched you bear these burdens on your own for the past six months, and I'm sick of standing aside. You made your point, babe, you're strong and brave and you kick ass. And now you're mine."

My heart just...melts.

But still! He's being such a damn *man* about this. "You do realize it's the twenty-first century, right?" I give him my best, sassiest eyebrow arch. "I don't belong to anyone but myself." My words are hard, but something ignites in the middle of my chest, and it feels a lot like hope. Rudy has been beside me from the moment I stood up in that garden until now. Maybe even before that. Wasn't he the one who took my cancer diagnosis in stride? Who still treated me like a beautiful, sexual woman? Who didn't even hesitate to ask me if I needed a ride to the hospital?

I pushed him away because I didn't think he could handle all the complications of being with me, but he's been at the hospital every day for over a week now, practically living in my room. I'm pretty sure I bled all over his cousin's car—which was another surprise, that Jared would so willingly hand his keys over, but I guess everyone is more complicated than they seem at first glance. He met my baby, and the awed look in his eyes matched the one he gave me when he felt my son kick. He looked like a proud father.

I think I might have misjudged Rudy. He'll be able to handle all these complications after all.

Rudy leans forward, resting his forehead against mine. His hand is still wrapped around the back of my neck, and he holds me in place long enough that I can take in his scent. It makes me a little dizzy because he smells so good.

"You're wrong," he tells me. "You belong to me, and I belong to you. We're moving in together, and I'm going to be the best father that kid could ever ask for, and the best man you could ever dream of."

"Now you just sound arrogant," I answer, but the fight is gone from my words.

Rudy pulls back an inch, and he must see the smile twitching at my lips because pure male triumph flashes in his eyes. "So," he says. "My place or yours?"

"Yours," I whisper. "Mine smells musty and it's too small for the three of us, anyway."

I grin at the flash in his eyes, then tilt my head up to catch his lips in a kiss. It lights me up all the way down to my toes, and I can't help curling both arms around his neck, burrowing my fingers into his hair. He smells like man and strength and safety, and he's all mine.

EPILOGUE

LILY

RUDY DID an incredible job renovating his house.

Our house.

The whole place gleams with new wood floors and fresh paint, and after I agreed to move in, he tells me he even set up a nursery in the closest bedroom to the master.

That first evening we have together, I end up leaning against the kitchen counter more or less in the same place I stood when Agnes interrupted our hanky-panky session all those months ago.

Rudy puts his hands on the counter on either side of my hips, his face the picture of male contentment. "You're here," he says, running his nose up my neck and placing a kiss just under my jaw. "Finally."

Curling my hands into his golden hair, I let out a shuddering breath. "I'm here."

Later, when we move to the bedroom, I open the door and

start laughing. Rudy's arm curls around my shoulders and I feel his smile in the warmth of his touch.

"I like what you did with the place," I say, eyes on all my throw pillows neatly arranged on Rudy's much bigger bed.

"I'm nesting," he replies, an echo of my words all those months ago. And when I turn in his arms to lay a kiss on his lips, the look in his eyes tells me it's true.

IF I EVER HAD ANY doubts about Rudy, he obliterates them in the weeks after I give birth. It's not a sexy time for me, I can say that much with absolute honesty. There's bloody wounds and budding scars to add to my ever-growing collection. I'm exhausted, sleep deprived, and nowhere near the glamorous woman who kissed Rudy in the yacht club bathroom.

Rudy doesn't seem to mind. Every night, he curls his arms around me and tucks me into his chest, and it feels like home.

Despite being born prematurely, we discover that Liam's lungs are fine, because there's no shortage of screaming and crying at all hours of the night. Caring for a newborn is just as difficult as everyone says, and I can hardly believe my luck at having Rudy by my side.

I'm sad I didn't get to give birth, and I'm sad I don't get to breastfeed, but those are disappointments I can bear, because the truth is, I'm a fighter. Both my baby and I survived the past few months together, and the only thing that matters is that we're here.

One morning I wake up and realize that Rudy let me sleep in, because I find him in Trina's old gliding rocking chair, feeding Liam a bottle. Leaning against the door jamb, I watch the two of them until Rudy glances up. He gives me a soft smile. "How'd you sleep?"

"I think I actually got six hours straight. I feel almost human."

"You have an appointment with Dr. Gardner today, right?" His eyes move back to the baby, and he shifts his hold so Liam is tucked into the crook of his elbow. Rudy strokes the baby's toes with infinite, tender care while holding the bottle to Liam's mouth.

My heart clenches, but I manage to make my voice work. "Yeah. Ten o'clock."

"I'll drive you," he says, and it's a useless statement because Rudy has insisted on driving me everywhere since I got out of the hospital. "I can take Liam for a walk while you talk to Dr. Gardner, and then we can grab some lunch. What do you think?"

"I think that sounds good," I whisper, emotion clogging my throat. I have a life here, and I don't feel the need to book a trip to a new country. I'll travel in the future, of course, but I hope I'll do it with Rudy and Liam by my side.

"Your mom called me too," he says, eyes still on the baby. "She chewed me out for not having her over at the house yet, but I think she was mostly kidding. Maybe. He's a few weeks old now and we have a routine down, so maybe we can have your mom and sisters over? My grandma's been asking about the baby too."

I laugh. "I'll tell my mom she can come over tomorrow. She's been blowing up my phone too. We'll see how that visit goes, then invite everyone else over after. Does that work for you?"

Rudy nods, flicking his eyes up to mine. "Yeah." He smiles, returning his gaze to the baby in his arms.

What is it about attractive men holding babies? It's got to be the hottest thing in the universe, which is saying something because right now, sex is the furthest thing from my mind—but the sight of Rudy feeding my child with love in his eyes makes my body freeze, emotion rooting my feet to the ground.

How could I get so lucky? How did I manage to find a man who can treat this child like his own, then look at me like I'm the best thing that ever happened to him?

"I don't deserve you," I blurt.

Rudy stops rocking, puts the now-empty bottle aside, then shifts Liam to his shoulder. He walks toward me while gently patting the baby's back, his hand spanning almost the entire width of Liam's tiny body.

Rudy moves toward me until he's standing just inches from me. His eyes hold mine for a beat, then he shakes his head. "Lily, out of the two of us, the lucky one is me."

"You really believe that," I whisper.

His eyes crinkle as those beautiful, masculine lips curl into a smile. "Of course I do. I love you, Lily. And I love Liam too." Still holding the baby against his shoulder, he reaches over to tuck a strand of hair behind my ear. "You want coffee?"

I blink, unable to process the question because Rudy just said he loves me, and it sounded like he really meant it. Gaping at him, I stand rooted to the spot until my man lets out a little chuckle. He ducks his head and kisses me softly, then moves down the hall, all while burping my baby.

Our baby.

Jaw hanging open, I listen to his retreating footsteps until I hear a kitchen cupboard closing and a mug being placed on the counter. Then I follow behind him and accept a steaming mug of coffee from the man of my dreams.

Staring into the brown liquid, I wait until the baby is burped and settled in his cot before moving to intercept Rudy when he makes his way back to the coffeemaker. I put my hands on his chest and lift my eyes up to meet his.

"I love you too, Rudy," I whisper, the words rough in my throat.

He takes one hand in his and lifts it up to kiss my fingers. "Good," he says. "Because I'm not letting you go."

"Right back at you," I say, a smile blooming over my lips. "So if you ever get sick of seeing this body that's been sliced open and stitched back up, well, too bad. There's no trading me in for a younger version."

Rudy's shoulders soften as he runs his hands up my sides to rest on my rib cage. He pulls me close, resting his forehead against mine. "Your scars don't scare me, Lily. They never will. They make you who you are, and that's the woman I've fallen in love with."

A last hard knot unwinds in the pit of my stomach, and I find myself melting into his arms. My life hasn't been a fairy tale, but I'm starting to think I might get my happily-ever-after.

· · ·

A FEW WEEKS LATER, when my family and friends have all met the baby and elbowed their way back into my life, I realize that I'm well and truly settled. Being with Rudy every day no longer terrifies me, nor does it feel stifling to have my family around to rely on. I'm not a burden to them; I never was. Therapy helps, of course, especially while my postpartum hormones wreak havoc on my body and mind. I'll get through that too, though, because for the first time since I was a teenager, I have a home.

As that reality really sinks in, I sit back on the sofa watching the early spring sun pierce through the clouds outside, and I find myself on the phone with my sister Trina.

"So your salon appointment is at three o'clock, and we're heading to the Cedar Grove around six."

Chewing my lip, I let out a sigh. My eyes move to the baby sleeping next to me, and I find myself stroking his tiny, soft hands. "I don't know, Trina. Girls' Night doesn't really seem important right now."

There's shuffling on the phone, and Simone's voice comes through the line. "Girls' Night is sacred," she intones. "And you haven't had more than an hour off since Liam was born. So from six to eight, you'll be with us drinking bad wine and singing Mariah Carey songs at top volume. Got it?"

The front door opens and Rudy enters, wearing suit pants and a shirt with the top two buttons undone. He crosses the distance to me in mere steps, placing a kiss on the top of my head before bending down to do the same to Liam. "Is that your sister? I've been told I'm on baby duty from six to eight tonight."

My lips twitch. "You guys set me up," I tell Simone in my best, hardest accusatory tone. "You got Rudy in on it too."

"Good. We'll see you at six." She moves the phone away and I hear her tell Trina to cancel my salon appointment. Moving the phone back to talk to me, she says, "There. I cleared your schedule. Six o'clock. Got that, Lily?"

The smile tugging at my lips grows to the full breadth of my face. "Got it."

As soon as I'm off the phone, Rudy hauls me into his arms and kisses me hungrily, his hands sinking into the flesh on my hips. He smooths his hands over me, humming against my lips. "Still as hot as ever."

A spark ignites between my legs. "It's been long enough." A hoarse whisper. "My OB cleared me for sex."

Rudy pulls back, searching my gaze, then his eyes take on a hot, predatory gleam. "The baby's sleeping," he notes conversationally.

"Be gentle," I say, shivering at the way his hands shape my curves.

Rudy kisses the tip of my nose, then gives me a soft squeeze. "Always."

NORA

THE CEDAR GROVE'S parking lot is jammed.

Girls' Night.

Mostly, my friends take a taxi or have a designated driver for their evenings here, but I've been told that Girls' Nights have started attracting other patrons, too. It seems they've taken on a sort of mythical reputation in and around Heart's Cove—hence the multitude of cars in the parking lot. If people aren't here to participate, they seem to like coming for the atmosphere.

And by "atmosphere," I mean a bunch of crazy forty-some-things letting their hair down.

Tonight is the first time I've been officially invited. Trina even booked a blowout at the salon for me earlier, only to click her tongue when I told her I wasn't in town and would be driving back from Reno this afternoon. She told me Lily's having her first evening away from her baby, and we're making an event out of it. Hamish even agreed to let us put up a sign inside the bar.

Lily only promised to show up for an hour or two, so I'm under strict instructions to arrive on time.

I sped all the way here and left Reno in the dust.

Thankfully, it's the final time I have to make that drive. I put in my two weeks' notice exactly two weeks ago, and today was my last day. I'm officially a full-time resident of Heart's Cove, with nothing holding me back in Reno. It feels like a weight has been lifted off my shoulders.

Except...

As I pay my taxi driver and turn toward the entrance, my stomach shrinks into a hot, hard ball. A line of gleaming motorcycles is backed into a neat line at the front of the bar, each one shining black and chrome under the parking lot lights.

I hadn't realized how much I missed seeing those bikes during the winter months, when rain and even a bit of snow coated our area. It seems the weather has warmed up enough for riding.

The motorcycle on the end of the row is navy, and I recognize the distinctive smoky swirls painted on the body. My stomach unwinds, sending heat spearing lower in my gut.

Even his bike is sexy.

The last time I saw Lee Blair was at Candice's housewarming party. When his eyes met mine across the room, I decided I couldn't do it. The girls had just pulled gossip out of me like it was their job, only to descend on Lily like hyenas.

As someone who hates being the center of attention, having

a pack of bloodthirsty gossipmongers asking me the size of Lee's penis is *not* something I want to put up with.

It's probably very big, my brain helpfully interjects, and I scowl at myself.

I'm not here to ogle the sexy, motorcycle-riding man who turns my insides to jelly. I'm here for my inaugural Girls' Night. I'm going to drink too much, dance like a buffoon, and make an absolute fool of myself surrounded by all my new friends.

My feet disagree, because they carry me closer to his motorcycle. I bet it would feel positively sexual to have that big machine vibrating between my legs, to have Lee's big, hard body pressed up against my chest.

The leather of his seat is blue too, I notice. A blue-black that gleams under the artificial lights of the parking lot. Glancing around to make sure I'm alone, I run a palm over the buttery-soft leather of the seat and feel a shiver dance in the very feminine core of me.

This isn't like me. My ex-husband worked in tech. His favorite word was "optimization." Bad boys riding motorcycles are not the type of men I've ever been attracted to. Not then, not now, not ever.

But I remember the way Lee's eyes tracked me around Candice's house, how he almost cornered me on the patio before I ducked away and ran to the kitchen to help Jen. When I finally went home after Candice and Blake's party, it felt like I'd run a marathon.

Palm still running over the soft leather of the motorcycle's seat, I fall into something of a trance. Maybe I'll talk to Lee again. Maybe I'll even do more than talk. Girls' Nights are for bad decisions, right?

He'd be rough, I decide. He'd grip those broad hands over my hips and pull me close, until all I could see was him. Maybe he'd sit me right here on the back of his motorcycle, spread my legs, and—

A loud, crashing noise jerks me out of my stupor. It sounds like a thousand bottles falling and shattering in the alley beside the Grove, echoing against all the brick and concrete. I stumble at the noise, still panting from my too-vivid imagination, and catch myself on the nearest object.

Lee's motorcycle.

In slow-motion, the two-wheeled machine starts tipping away from me. Inch by inch, it lifts off the kickstand beside me, hovers in a near-vertical position for a heart-stopping moment, then starts falling in the other direction.

"No, no, no," I hiss, scrabbling to grab the seat to pull the bike back over toward me, onto its kickstand. I *need* to stop this thing from falling.

But it's *heavy*, and I haven't been to the gym in far too long. That soft, luxurious leather I'd just been admiring slips from my grasp, and the bike tips all the way over...and into the next one.

Horror ices my veins as I watch the line of bikes crash over like a hellish line of dominos. One, two, three...they just keep falling over one after the other. I stand at the end of the line, wincing at each sound of metal on metal, metal on asphalt, metal on concrete.

My breath comes in short, staggered gasps as my shoulders squeeze up to my ears, the awful spectacle in front of me lasting an eternity, until the very last bike in the line trembles, and finally crashes over onto its side.

The silence is even worse. It presses down on me as I watch the line of tumbled motorcycles stretching out in front of me, wondering if I should just turn on my heels and run all the way back to Heart's Cove. I can call Trina and tell her I was held up in Reno. I'll come up with an alibi. I was never here.

Then—footsteps.

Frozen, I gulp down a hard gasp when Lee steps out of the shadows, his eyes sweeping over the trail of destruction caused by my clumsiness, finally landing on me.

There's nothing friendly in his gaze. He stares at me for an interminable moment, until I can't take it anymore.

"Oopsie daisy," I squeak.

The silence presses in, and Lee tilts his head a few degrees to the side. "Oopsie," he growls, taking two steps to close the distance between us, "daisy?"

Oops! Nora just knocked over a bunch of motorcycles like a horrible game of dominoes. But what happens when Mac proposes an arrangement so she can pay for the damage?

Check out Book Seven: DIRTY LITTLE MIDLIFE DILEMMA!

BONUS EPILOGUE

LILY

"'AMMA!" Liam screeches, his chubby little two-year-old arms thrust in the air. Taking off at a sprint, my son darts around my legs and makes his way to the front door, where my mother is standing ready to catch him.

Her arms wrap around him and she hauls him into her chest, covering his cheeks and neck with kisses and raspberries. Liam giggles and screeches, wiggling in his grandma's arms until she puts him down.

"We're going to have fun, aren't we, Liam?"

"Seeper," Liam says, pointing to the bag I packed earlier.

"Yes, we're having a sleepover," my mother says, running her hands through his hair. The shock of dark, dark-brown hair he was born with fell out to reveal light, nearly white-blond hair. It surprised us all, except for my mother. She took great delight in pulling out old photos of us to show that the same thing happened when we were born, before our hair darkened with age to the natural mousy-brown my sisters and I all choose to dye regularly.

"Bye!" Liam yells at me, squeezing his hand into a fist in that way toddlers have of waving goodbye.

I laugh, hauling him up over my shoulder. "Not yet, monkey. Your grandma is going to have a cup of coffee with me first." Liam giggles, going soft in my arms. It still surprises me when I can lift him so easily. I've been working out and getting stronger, and I'm so grateful for all the things my body can do. Even a year ago, I didn't know if I'd ever feel like myself again.

Putting Liam back down, the three of us head to the kitchen. I pour my mom and myself a cup of coffee each before giving Liam a sippy cup of apple juice.

My mother smiles at him, then shifts her gaze to me. "Blood test come back all good?"

I nod. "Still in remission."

Her shoulders soften a fraction of an inch. "Good."

I shift my gaze to Liam. "He had a bit of a sniffle yesterday, but it looks like he's all better. Just keep an eye on him, yeah? He might need an extra nap or something."

Age-softened hands slide over my cheeks as my mother tilts my head back to face her. "We'll be fine, Lily. You enjoy your weekend with Rudy."

I huff. "You're right. I just... It's hard to be apart from him."

"I know, honey," my mother says. "But you'll survive."

The front door opens, and Rudy calls out from the entrance. "Hello! Lottie?"

"In the kitchen," my mother yells back. She pats her pixie cut and straightens her shirt, and I hide my grin behind my mug.

Rudy has that effect on women, I've noticed. It's impossible not to feel the power of his masculinity.

"Lottie," Rudy says, that charming smile deployed to full effect. He wraps my mother in a hug. "Looking gorgeous as usual."

"Oh, stop it." She swats at his arm. "You're going to spoil Lily now, aren't you?"

"Always," he replies, eyes darting to mine.

"We're only going to Edgeville, so if anything happens with Liam, just call and we'll be right back," I say, trying to keep the worry from my voice.

My mother just rolls her eyes, not even deigning to tell me that she'll be fine.

"What have you got planned for your weekend?" my mother asks, picking up the sippy cup Liam threw across the room with a stern look at my son.

"Booked a whale-watching tour for tomorrow," Rudy says. "It's a three-hour thing, and it's the right time of year to see orcas."

"How exciting," my mother says before kneeling in front of Liam. "Now, no throwing your drink, Liam, otherwise you won't get to finish it."

Liam ducks his chin in a cowed nod. He takes the cup from his grandmother, then lifts it above his head with a mischievous gleam in his eyes, apparently ready to launch it across the room again. But all it takes is for my mother to arch a single eyebrow before he drops the cup to his lips and drinks from it instead.

Yeah, they'll be fine without me.

After a bit of bustling and double-checking bags, I strap

Liam into his car seat and watch him drive away with my mother.

Rudy's hands slide over my hips as he presses his chest to my back, his chin hooked over my shoulder. "You okay?"

"We've never spent the night away from him," I say. "I feel... nervous."

"Just nervous?"

Turning in his arms, I tilt my head from side to side. "Maybe a little excited."

Rudy smiles and drops his lips to mine. "Good. Follow me." He tugs me up to the bedroom, where he reaches into the closet to pull out a garment bag. "Trina helped me," he explains, unzipping the bag to reveal a gorgeous, diaphanous gown in rich, royal blue.

I gasp, touching the fabric. "What's this for?"

"We're having a nice dinner tonight," he informs me. "But first..." He spins me around, sliding his palm up under the hem of my shirt to rest on my lower back. "First, I'm taking advantage of the empty house."

Curling my hands around his shoulders, I arch a brow. "Works for me."

That's all it takes for Rudy to tear my shirt off over my head, his hands running up my sides to cup my breasts. Even now, a bit of tension steals over me.

Over a year ago, I had the final operation to swap my breast expander for a permanent implant. The scars crisscrossing my breast are clear evidence of my operations, though, not to mention the scar below my navel from my caesarian. Rudy runs his fingers over the soft material of my bra, backing me up until

I'm up against the wall. He starts with my natural breast, shaping it with his hands and tugging the cup of my bra down before taking it in his mouth.

I gasp, fingers burrowing into the golden silk of his hair, arching into his touch. His free hand cups my other breast, exposing it to the air and cupping it with a broad, male palm. I lost my nipple and most of the feeling in that breast, but having his hands on me still makes me feel quintessentially female. It helps that he laves his tongue over my surviving nipple, scraping his teeth over the swollen peak, loving every inch of me with his hands and mouth.

This is me. This is my body, scars and all.

Clawing at his shoulders, I shudder and gasp when he drops a hand between my legs. Then he's tearing my jeans off, unclipping my bra, and tossing me unceremoniously across the bed. Tugging me roughly to the edge, Rudy kneels on the floor and drapes my legs over his shoulders. He gives me a wicked, wicked grin.

"You're still dressed," I manage to gasp. "That's not fair."

"Quiet," he says, spreading my thighs as he licks his lips. "I'm busy."

And when his mouth touches all my most sensitive places, I find I don't care that he's still clothed. Not one bit.

A LONG WHILE LATER, after we've trailed lazy fingers over each other's bodies and let our breath and heartbeats return to normal, Rudy gives my bare bottom a squeeze. "Time for a shower. We need to get to dinner."

Mock-grumbling, I peel myself off the bed and make my way to the bathroom. But when I hear the door open behind me and watch Rudy's beautiful naked body join me in the shower stall, washing is the last thing on my mind. All it takes is for me to drop to my knees in front of him, and Rudy lets out a low groan that tells me he's more than happy to put off the practical parts of the shower for a few minutes.

Finally, we both manage to clean up and get dressed, and I feel flushed and sated as I brush on some subtle makeup. Looking at myself in the mirror, I once again appreciate the fact that Trina is a genius at what she does. She has an eye for fashion, and she understands how to clothe a body. I run my hands over my breasts, where the gauzy fabric drapes and cinches to show everything off.

I feel womanly and beautiful and whole.

"You look hot," Rudy says, meeting my eyes in the mirror.

"Stop right there, mister," I say, giving him a hard stare. "Hands off, otherwise we'll never make it to dinner."

Laughter in his eyes, he throws his hands up in surrender. We do, finally, make it to the car, our overnight bags safely placed in the back seat, and I relax as he takes us out of town and over to Edgeville.

When he takes the turn toward the yacht club, I make a surprised noise. "That's where we're going for dinner?"

"Yep," he says, refusing to elaborate, no matter how many questions I pose.

When we finally pull up outside and the valet takes the keys, I give Rudy a funny stare. "This isn't what I was expecting."

He just winks, then extends his elbow toward me. Huffing, I slip my hand into the crook of his arm, doing my best to hide the twitch in my lips. He's spoiling me in every possible way, and I can't help but feel special.

What follows is a beautiful, romantic dinner on the balcony of the yacht club. Expensive boats bob in the bay in front of us while fairy lights and stars twinkle above. We're alone in our section of the restaurant, with intimate candles and a delicate arrangement of flowers separating us on the table.

After the main course, Rudy lets out a sigh, his eyes growing serious. "Lily, you know I love you."

I smile. I can't help it—those words always make my lips curl. "I love you too, babe."

Suddenly, Rudy looks nervous. He wipes his hands on his thighs, glances out at the water, and finally turns his gaze to me. "These past two years have been the best of my life. You and Liam have brought me so much joy that I sometimes feel like I don't deserve it."

Heart thumping, I swallow past a lump in my throat. "What are you saying, Rudy?"

Sucking in a hard breath, he reaches into his pocket and pulls out a little velvet box. Rudy slips out of his chair and kneels beside the table as my eyes immediately fill with tears.

The box proves to be difficult for a moment, as Rudy fumbles to flip it open. Finally managing it, he turns it to reveal a delicate white-gold band topped with a bright blue sapphire ringed with sparkling diamonds. I inhale sharply, my hand flying to the pendant that I now wear every single day.

"I had it designed to match the necklace," he says, voice thick. Then, after another breath: "Marry me, Iliana."

A distant, irreverent part of my brain wants me to protest at the command. Instead, I blink and let tears fall down my face, then nod like an idiot while a sob wracks my chest. "Yes," I croak. "I'll marry you."

He slides the ring onto the third finger of my left hand, then pulls me into his arms and kisses me like the world is ending.

And that's when I hear the cheers. Over Rudy's shoulder, I see my mother with Liam in her arms, my sisters with tears in their eyes, and every single friend and acquaintance from Heart's Cove crowding behind them. I see Jared and his new girlfriend, looking genuinely happy for us, as well as Rudy's grandmother and great aunt and uncle.

"Rudy..." My eyes widen as he laughs, hooking an arm around my waist.

"Let's go celebrate," he whispers in my ear, his breath making a curl of heat tighten between my thighs.

"You planned this." It sounds like an accusation, because it is.

Rudy just catches my hand and kisses it gently. "Yep. I even organized a champagne tower."

I blink, following his gaze to the windows, through which I see two staff members wheeling a large platform carrying a tower of champagne coupes into a position of prominence in the main room of the restaurant.

"Jared promised to behave," he adds, and I can't help it. I laugh, then turn to wrap my arms around his neck, pulling him in for a hard kiss.

Cheers sound behind us as Rudy dips me so far I have to cling onto him to stop myself from falling. We straighten up, and with flushed cheeks and joy in my heart, I turn to the gathered crowd and let a smile split my face.

Then, we celebrate.

Finally, when Liam is cranky and everyone is worn out, I let Rudy take me to the hotel, and we love each other until we're flushed and sated, drowsy in each other's arms.

"Love you," I mumble against his chest, inhaling the scent of his skin as he responds by squeezing me close—exactly where I belong.

ABOUT THE AUTHOR

Lilian Monroe adores writing swoonworthy heroes and the women who bring them to their knees. She loves making people laugh and is eternally grateful to have found people who share her sense of humor.

When she's not writing, she's reading (or rereading) a book, walking, lifting weights, or attempting to play the guitar with very limited success.

She grew up in Canada but now lives in Australia with her Irish husband. He frequently asks to be used as a cover model for her books, and she's not quite sure whether or not he's joking.

ALSO BY LILIAN MONROE

For all books, visit:

www.lilianmonroe.com

The Four Groomsmen of the Wedpocalypse

Conquest

Craving

Combat

Calamity

Manhattan Billionaires

Big Bossy Mistake

Big Bossy Trouble

Big Bossy Problem

Big Bossy Surprise

Later in Life Romance

Dirty Little Midlife Crisis

Dirty Little Midlife Mess

Dirty Little Midlife Mistake

Dirty Little Midlife Disaster

Dirty Little Midlife Debacle

Dirty Little Midlife Secret

Dirty Little Midlife Dilemma

Dirty Little Midlife Drama

Dirty Little Midlife (fake) Date

<u>Brother's Best Friend Romance</u>

Shouldn't Want You

Can't Have You

Don't Need You

Won't Miss You

<u>Protector Romance</u>

His Vow

His Oath

His Word

<u>Enemies to Lovers/Workplace Romance</u>

Hate at First Sight

Loathe at First Sight

Despise at First Sight

<u>Secret Baby/Accidental Pregnancy Romance</u>

Knocked Up by the CEO

Knocked Up by the Single Dad

Knocked Up...Again!

Knocked Up by the Billionaire's Son

Yours for Christmas

Bad Prince

Heartless Prince

Cruel Prince

Broken Prince

Wicked Prince

Wrong Prince

Lone Prince

Ice Queen

Rogue Prince

Fake Engagement Romance

Engaged to Mr. Right

Engaged to Mr. Wrong

Engaged to Mr. Perfect

Mountain Man Romance

Lie to Me

Swear to Me

Run to Me

Doctor's Orders

Doctor O

Doctor D

Doctor L